W9-BAH-735

The ART of RUNNING in HEELS

Center Point
Large Print

Also by Rachel Gibson and available from
Center Point Large Print:

Rescue Me
Run to You
What I Love About You
Just Kiss Me

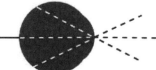

The ART *of* RUNNING *in* HEELS

RACHEL GIBSON

CENTER POINT LARGE PRINT
THORNDIKE, MAINE

This Center Point Large Print edition
is published in the year 2018 by arrangement with
Avon Books, an imprint of HarperCollins Publishers.

The text of this Large Print edition is unabridged.
In other aspects, this book may vary
from the original edition.
Printed in the United States of America
on permanent paper.
Set in 16-point Times New Roman type.

ISBN: 978-1-68324-804-0

Library of Congress Cataloging-in-Publication Data

Names: Gibson, Rachel, author.
Title: The art of running in heels / Rachel Gibson.
Description: Center Point Large print edition. | Thorndike, Maine :
    Center Point Large Print, 2018.
Identifiers: LCCN 2018009630 | ISBN 9781683248040
    (hardcover : alk. paper)
Subjects: LCSH: Large type books. | GSAFD: Love stories.
Classification: LCC PS3557.I2216 A89 2018 | DDC 813/.54—dc23
LC record available at https://lccn.loc.gov/2018009630

Mary Reed.
Okay cook. Iffy seamstress.
Wonderful mother.

The ART of
RUNNING
in HEELS

Prologue

• your love is simply irresistible

O OOOH, THAT'S GONNA leave a mark." John Kowalsky sucked a breath between his teeth and winced. Across the bedroom, a whistle blew from the sound bar beneath his fifty-five-inch television. "Georgie honey, have you seen the remote?"

Without lifting her gaze from the magazine in her lap, Georgeanne Kowalsky stretched a hand toward the bedside table. Her fingers slid across the smooth oak, skimming a Kleenex box, cell phone, jar of rocks, and finally the remote control. "Here you go," she said as she handed it to the man in bed beside her.

"Thanks." A whistle blew once more, followed by the slap of hockey sticks and grunts of colliding bodies that filled the bedroom of their home on the southern tip of Mercer Island.

"Kelly skates like his ass is a pylon."

Georgeanne's gaze skimmed a biscuit recipe from *Southern Living* as her husband indulged in his nightly ritual, insulting hockey players and channel surfing.

This was Georgeanne's favorite time of day,

when she could escape her daily routine. When John was beside her and not on the road. When she could breathe easy in the knowledge that her husband and each of her three children were safe and sound and where they were supposed to be. When she could relax, lulled into a comfortable routine, curled up beside her sweetheart, best friend, and lover.

"For shit's sake. Hit that son of a bitch. What's wrong with these young guys?" He pointed the remote across the room and answered his own question. "They're more concerned with their flow than putting points on the board."

Georgeanne chuckled. John had lived in the United States for thirty of his fifty-six years. He talked and walked like a natural-born citizen and often teased her about her Texas accent that clung to her like plastic wrap, but when riled, John sounded like a Canadian with his "oats" and "aboats." Occasionally, he even threw in a few "ehs."

"All that hair product has shrunk their balls and now they shoot like girls."

Georgeanne raised her gaze from the magazine and watched John cross his big arms over his bare chest. She'd heard this particular rant for years. The first time had been in 1996 when he'd gone on about Jaromir Jagr and the "girly curls" flowing from his helmet.

"God, what a sissy."

She glanced at the television screen as a New York Ranger slammed the sissy in question against the boards. His black "flow," wet from exertion, curled like big commas from beneath his helmet. "Didn't y'all offer Pittsburgh twelve million for Knox?"

"Not me. *I* didn't." John pointed the remote at his chest. "I hate the guy."

Until Georgeanne had met John "The Wall" Kowalsky, she'd known very little about hockey. Over the past twenty-one years, she'd learned a thing or two. Like she knew that "snipe" and "snap" were two totally different things. She'd learned the difference between a restricted and unrestricted free agent, and she knew that the beginning of each regular season signaled wild talks of trades and wilder rumors of trades. It was November and no different from any other year, as far as she could tell. "Has Pittsburgh matched the offer?"

"Not yet but they will." John lowered his hand to his right thigh. "He finished last season with eighty-nine points."

She also knew that her husband missed being out on the ice, playing the game he loved. She licked her thumb and turned a page in her magazine. He missed shit-talking in a face-off as he waited for the puck to drop.

They'd become predictable, she and John. An old married couple in their fifties, with two

11

children gone from home. Their oldest daughter, Lexie, was on a buying trip in Stockholm, visiting some of the best textile showrooms in the world. It seemed crazy, but her dog apparel business was thriving. Their second was in her sophomore year at Villanova, studying political science. Their son, Jon Jon, was asleep in his bed down the hall.

Predictable. There was something to be said for the comfort and ease of predictability. The luxurious warmth of loving a man so much and for so long that you couldn't recall a time when you didn't love him. A man who knew you inside and out and loved you without limit. A man who was your rock, and you were his soft place to land.

"Did you see that?"

"No," she answered without looking up from a perfectly staged picnic scene. The lifestyle program that Georgeanne had started in 1996, on a small Seattle cable station, had gone into syndication and was seen across the country. She was no Martha Stewart, but *Life With Georgeanne* had a respectable—

"He can't take a hit worth a shit," John scoffed, then finally remembered to apologize for his language. "Sorry," he said, although she doubted he was sorry at all. He pointed the remote at the television. "I can't watch this. Knox is such a girly man."

A smile curved a corner of Georgeanne's lips as she flipped another page. John was many different things to different people. To hockey fans, he was John "The Wall" Kowalsky, Stanley Cup champion and one of the greatest NHL players of all time. To the people of Seattle, he was head coach of the Chinooks. To his friends, he was the guy you wanted in your corner. To his children, he was the best dad in the world, and to her, he was John. Protective and loyal to those he loved. Dismissive and rude to those he did not. By turns exasperating and calm, but always predictable. Or perhaps she just knew him. Knew his heart and soul and his nightly routine. He watched hockey just long enough to call the players sissies, or worse. Then he'd surf channels until he found something educational. Something to "fill his dome" like PBS or National Geographic, or, like tonight, Nova.

"Future astronomers will not be able to tell that our universe was born in a big bang . . ." The remote paused long enough to learn a nugget or two. ". . . Dark energy itself will destroy dark energy . . ." When he'd had enough of Public Television, he surfed stations until he hit on his guilty pleasure: reality television. The guilty pleasure he could shit-talk to his heart's content.

"Tonight on this season's first episode of

Gettin' Hitched, twenty beautiful young women from across the country are here at the Hitchin' House. All gussied up and just busting at the seams to meet the current bachelor . . . Peter Dalton!"

"Where do they get these people?" He settled back against the pillows and dropped the remote on the bed beside him as the contestants began to introduce themselves.

"I'm Mandy Crumb from Wooster, Ohio. I love chili cook-offs and the Cleveland Indians!"

"Look at Mandy, all dressed up like a slutty hillbilly," John scoffed.

"I'm Cindy Lee Melton from Clearwater, Florida."

"Those shorts are so tight, they look painful, Cindy Lee."

"I love hot summer nights and jazz."

Georgeanne glanced at the television long enough to take in a young woman dressed in tiny cutoff shorts with the tails of her red gingham shirt tied between her breasts climbing down from a big tractor. It was a good thing the woman had small breasts or she'd fall out of the little shirt. Georgeanne never would have been able to wear a shirt like that. Not since she'd been twelve, anyway.

"I'm Davina Gerardo from Scottsdale, Arizona."

"I bet your daddy's real proud, Davina Gerardo

14

from Arizona." John shook his head in gleeful disgust.

"I love eighteen holes and the smell of fresh cut grass at We-Ko-Pa."

Georgeanne returned her attention to the biscuit recipe and answered John's first question. "I think they get these girls from strip clubs."

"I'm Jenny Douglas from Salem, Oregon. I love rain puddles and karaoke."

"Strippers aren't that desperate." He punched a pillow behind his back and settled in. "Not that I'd know," he added.

"Of course not."

"I can't believe they put this kind of shit on TV," he complained, but he didn't change the channel, and Georgeanne smiled.

"I'm Summer Williams from Bell Buckle, Tennessee. I love Muddy Waters and traveling back roads."

"Too easy. I like a challenge, Summer," John drawled, imitating her accent. "You shot that one right to me but I'm not taking your garbage goal."

"I'm Whitney Sue Allen from Paducah, Kentucky."

"You're so pale, you look inbred."

"John . . ." Georgeanne sighed.

"I love yoga and Daddy's peach wine."

"Of course you do. Your daddy is your own granddaddy."

"Not nice, John. Don't forget that I'm a Texan. Just because she's from the South doesn't make her inbred."

"It would explain this show." He paused as if in deep contemplation. "Inbred as hell and fed lead paint from toxic baby bottles."

Georgeanne looked at the television and the barefoot girl climbing down from the tractor before joining the others. "More likely they just weren't raised right." She turned her attention to her husband, and his dark blue gaze fixed on the reality show. "Bless their hearts."

"Their mothers should be whacked with an idiot stick." Without taking his attention from the TV, he leaned to his left and grabbed a bottle of water from the nightstand. "And their fathers should have their nuts snipped off." He chuckled at his own joke. There wasn't anyone on the planet who thought he was as funny as he did himself. "Jesus." He sat up as if the pillows had ejected him forward, and the bottle launched across the room.

"John—"

"I'm Lexie Kowalsky from Seattle, Washington." Georgeanne felt her brows rocket to her hairline as her head whipped around. "I love Chinooks hockey and my dog, Yum Yum."

Georgeanne blinked several times at the impossible sight of her oldest daughter climbing down from a tractor, her butt cheeks showing beneath her shorts, her large breasts threatening to bounce out of her top, all captured in ultrahigh definition.

Lexie straightened, tossed her blond hair, and gave the camera a big white smile that had once cost her parents thousands in orthodontia.

Georgeanne choked and couldn't get words out. She turned to her husband and pointed at their daughter, who was supposed to be in Stockholm.

John's stunned gaze met hers, but he had no problem getting his words out. "What the fuck?"

Chapter 1

• love is a hurricane

BENEATH THE OMBRÉ sky, an orange sun hung just above the Seattle skyscrapers, bathing the Emerald City in splashes of gold and pink, coalescing into smears of deep purple.

An early January breeze rippled across the surface of Lake Union and slid beneath the collar of Sean Knox's black coat. Pinwheels of white light danced across the silver frames of his aviator sunglasses and, behind the mirrored lenses, his gaze had turned lazy from the relaxing glow of Grey Goose. The vodka dulled the sharp edges around him and calmed the turmoil in the pit of his stomach. Before the night was through, he planned to get a whole lot lazier. Sean wasn't a big drinker, especially during the season. In order to get the best performance out of his body, he didn't fill it with junk, and he never poisoned himself with booze. Except tonight.

He raised a clear plastic cup to his lips and breathed in the smell of lake water and old wood. Below his lowered lids, he watched luxury yachts and commercial trawlers slice through the orange trail that led to the dock rocking beneath

Sean's leather shoes. He sucked an ice cube into his mouth and dropped his hand to his side. A few feet away, the *Sea Hopper* rode gold-tipped waves like a frog on a shimmering lily pad.

Sean shoved the ice cube into his cheek and asked over his shoulder, "How much longer?"

The owner of the seaplane, Jimmy Pagnotta, answered, "Ten minutes," without raising his gaze from the worn checklist in his hands. Sean had hired Jimmy a few times now. The guy always wore a World War II helmet and goggles to cover his man bun, and his Will Forte beard made him look like a cross between Charles Lindbergh and the Last Man on Earth. "Seven-forty-five at the latest," he added.

A black titanium watch circled Sean's left wrist, and he glanced at it as he crunched his ice. They were already fifteen minutes past the scheduled seven-fifteen takeoff. Sean hated waiting around, especially for people who couldn't seem to get their shit together, and who didn't give a thought to the chaos they caused everyone around them.

"Who did you say we're waiting for?"

"I didn't." Jimmy opened the cockpit door and shoved the checklist into a side pocket.

The owner of the seaplane didn't elaborate, and Sean turned his attention to the kayakers all bundled up in Patagonia and paddling past the *Sea Hopper*, toward the neighborhood of houseboats moored farther up the eastern shore.

Painted bright green, the amphibious aircraft had big red eyes above the cockpit and orange webbed feet on the sides. In warmer weather, the four-passenger floatplane was usually filled with tourists making a twenty-minute loop around the city. Half past every hour, people on the ground could look up and glimpse a flying tree frog gliding past the Space Needle or buzzing Bill Gates's mansion in Medina. The billionaire's property was a big draw for sightseers and a moneymaker for the tourism industry. Most people were impressed by the massive estate and beautiful grounds. Most people were awed by the obvious magnitude of wealth. Most people were fascinated by all the technology and toys that came with it.

Sean Knox was not most people. He wasn't impressed or awed by much. Not by a brilliant sunset or a sixty-six-thousand-square-foot mansion. He'd been poor and now he was rich. He preferred being rich but he wasn't awestruck by wealth. He was seldom careless with money. Some might call him a tightwad, but he saw himself as practical. He'd paid the pilot of the *Sea Hopper* three times the price of a commercial flight because it made sense. The chartered floatplane cut eleven hours off the traditional route to the small town where he'd lived the first ten years of his life. Sandspit, British Columbia, wasn't exactly a hub of activity, and he couldn't imagine why anyone else in Seattle was in a rush to get there this time of year.

This was the second time he'd chartered the seaplane since signing with Seattle last month. He hadn't planned on making the trip again so soon and he wasn't about to let the chaos that awaited suck him into staying longer than the two days he planned. He'd packed only a small duffel, a bottle of Grey Goose, and a six-pack of Schweppes tonic water.

"It's been ten minutes." He drained the cup and turned toward Jimmy. "Maybe your passenger isn't going to show up."

"It's been less than five." The pilot pulled a cell phone from the pocket of his bomber jacket and glanced at it for several seconds. "I wouldn't have agreed to a second passenger if it wasn't an emergency." He turned his attention toward shore as if he waited for some sort of signal.

Emergency or not, Sean hoped like hell the person they were waiting on wasn't trying to drive from anywhere within a twenty-mile radius of downtown Seattle. If that was the case, the other passenger was probably stuck in chaotic traffic due to that shitty show, *Gettin' Hitched*, and the mob surrounding the Fairmont Hotel, fighting for a glimpse of the latest reality show couple and cheering like the Seahawks had won the Super Bowl again. NBC had even set up jumbotrons downtown so fans could capture the happy couple exchanging their vows on live television with the rest of the country.

Sean had never watched the television program, but he couldn't escape it. *Gettin' Hitched* fever had spread across America faster than a virus in flu season, and it seemed everyone but him had become infected. Even the guys in the Chinooks locker room had talked about each episode like they were getting paid for their own personal recap and review. They'd discussed the scheming and backstabbings and had placed bets on which girl would be sent home each week. Of course, their interest had a lot to do with Lexie Kowalsky. Some of the guys knew Lexie, and her ability to back-check and deke the other bachelorettes off the show made them proud. It was probably no coincidence that the daughter of John Kowalsky had the grit and determination to cut each girl off at the knees and had won the privilege of gettin' hitched on live television.

Sean had never met Lexie. She'd been three weeks into a ten-episode season when he'd signed with the Chinooks. He'd seen her, though, on commercials and magazine covers and on mobile billboards driving around Seattle, every pixel photo-shopped, bright white teeth, brighter blue eyes, perfection from the top of her blond head to the tips of her pink toenails. She looked bigger than life, sitting on a tractor and towing a man all trussed up in baling twine. The guy had a

23 *Putnam County Library*

stupid smile on his face that made him look like a real pussy. No way on earth Sean would ever agree to something like that. He didn't care if he was being judgmental. Those two had signed up to be judged. His verdict: The bride was probably dumb as the billboards, the groom was likely a pussy, and both were as fake as their shitty show.

Sean felt the vodka kick up his comfy glow a few more notches. Lexie Kowalsky probably wasn't as pretty in real life as in pictures, and those boobs that practically fell out of her shirt in every photo were likely bought and paid for with her daddy's money. If Coach Kowalsky wasn't such an asshole, Sean might actually feel sorry for the guy.

It had been no secret that Kowalsky hadn't wanted to trade Kessel and Stamkos for Sean, and the thought of John "The Wall" dressed up in a tuxedo and forced to perform in the *Gettin' Hitched* chaos brought a smile to Sean's lips.

Sean turned his attention from the parking lot to Jimmy. "What kind of dire emergency can there possibly be that someone has to get to Sandspit in a hurry?" He took off his sunglasses and shoved them in the pocket of his jacket. "A local jam or jelly heist?"

"What?" Jimmy glanced at Sean, then returned his attention to the shore. "Not necessarily dire, but I . . ." Jimmy's voice faded to a whisper. "Holy shit. We're a go."

24

Sean's gaze followed Jimmy's as a silver MINI Cooper screeched to a stop in the parking lot. The door flew open and a white pouf erupted from the car like an old-school pan of Jiffy Pop. The pouf struggled for several seconds, expanding and growing, then it practically fell from the car, getting poufier. The whole scene was so unreal, Sean half expected clowns to start jumping out, one after another, honking party horns, and acting like fools. Yeah, Sean was a little drunk. Maybe more than a little, but he wasn't stupid drunk. He wasn't hallucinating drunk. Just to make sure, he said, "Tell me you're seeing what I'm seeing."

"Yep." The driver stuck a hand out the window and waved as if signaling something. Jimmy waved back, and the MINI Cooper sped away, leaving behind all that pouf. The setting sun reflected within the pouf like twinkly lights, and the cold breeze caught the ends of a veil and whipped it about a woman's head. At least Sean assumed it was a woman as he watched her swat at the veil like she was being attacked by bees. In all that over-the-top froth and twinkles, it could be a drag queen, he supposed. All at once, it spun right then left, bent forward, grabbed an armful of dress, and sprinted toward them.

"Get in. We're taking off."

"What?" Satin and gauzy veil swirled around and behind her as she raced across the parking lot and stepped onto the long dock. Sean raised a hand to shield his eyes from the pinpoint reflections in that horrible dress. "We've been waiting for that?"

Without answering, Jimmy scrambled into the *Sea Hopper*'s cockpit and fired the engine. The steady *tap-tap-tap* of the woman's heels on the wavering dock was drowned out as the three-blade propeller began to slowly spin.

"Get in!" Jimmy repeated himself as he jumped onto the dock again. He held a pair of headphones and shoved one at Sean. "We're out of here," he said, his voice as urgent as a drug smuggler's with the federales on his ass.

Sean took the headphones but couldn't take his eyes off those long legs and glittering pumps. The dock swayed on the waves, and Sean expected those high heels to wobble, snap an ankle, and pitch the woman into the lake.

"Get in," Jimmy repeated himself. With one last look at the woman, Sean stepped onto the struts and entered the small cabin. Jimmy had removed the first row of seats for comfort, but the plane was still fairly cramped. At least it was for a six-foot-two man who weighed in at two-twenty. He took the starboard seat and slid the Bluetooth headphones around the back of his neck. They reminded him of the Monster Beats he wore when he worked out, only these were more high-tech and had a slim microphone that sat at the corner of his mouth. He ducked his head to look out the double windows as he hooked the earphones over the backs of his ears. Sean had seen some crazy shit in his life, but this ranked right up there with singing dogs, talking fish, and elephants playing basketball.

Several moments passed before all that white appeared in the windows. The sound of the propeller grew louder, the blades lashing the water and whipping that veil around the woman's face. Jimmy fought all that gauzy froth, then she disappeared. Sean wondered how she was going to get herself and all that pouf into the *Sea Hopper*. He fit the headphones' small gel cups in his ears and adjusted the microphone at the left corner of his mouth. A few moments passed, and then all that gauze got shoved headfirst through the door. Through the headset, a female voice ordered, "Push, Jimmy!"

Sean might have offered to help if he knew where to grab. All he could see was the top of a rhinestone crown, a mass of blond hair, and yards of veil. He didn't think he should pull her in by her hair. He was a nice guy that way.

"Push how?" Jimmy asked.

"I don't know. Just push!" One hand reached for the metal frame of the pilot's seat, then like a champagne cork, the pouf exploded into the cabin with a breathless "oof."

Sean stared at the white explosion. The dress covered his feet and was even uglier close up.

The whole scene was getting crazier by the minute. Maybe he should slow down on the Grey Goose.

Jimmy untethered the *Sea Hopper* and climbed into the cockpit. He wore his headset over the top of his helmet and he shut the door behind him. He pushed buttons and flipped switches and pulled away from the dock. "Belt yourselves in," he said through his microphone as the seaplane taxied to the red buoy in the center of the lake. The small craft rocked, and the woman at Sean's feet struggled to her knees within all that dress. He heard a "Dang!" and then a total collapse. She lay facedown for several heartbeats before she managed to turn onto her back. The *Sea Hopper* shifted right, then picked up speed.

The woman's eyes were closed and a tiny microphone sat at one corner of her full red lips. A red mouth that was in stark contrast to all that white. Her lips moved and he thought he heard her whisper, "I'm in deep, deep trouble." As the seaplane hurtled across Lake Union, she kind of moaned and whimpered at the same time. The top of her dress hadn't exactly rolled with her, and her right breast looked like it just might pop free. One big, perfect breast pushing against all those rhinestones sewn onto the satin. Maybe he should help her fix that dress and adjust her boobs for her. He was good at adjusting boobs. He was real helpful that way.

She pushed the veil from her face and spit a piece of hair from her mouth. Her dark blue eyes opened, a little wild and crazy, and she had long black lashes. Not that Sean usually noticed a woman's eyelashes, but hers were hard to miss. Her cheeks were almost as white as her dress. She pulled air deep into her lungs, and her chest rose and fell. Her breasts strained the fabric to the point of bursting all those rhinestones. The seaplane lifted, and this time he definitely heard her say, "I can't believe I just did that. Everyone is going to kill me."

Sean chuckled and snapped the seatbelt in his lap. His chuckles turned into soul-deep laughter, drowned out by the three-hundred-horsepower engine. He guessed someone wasn't gettin' hitched after all.

Chapter 2

• love wholeheartedly,
but always have an escape plan

A LEXIS MAE KOWALSKY placed a hand on her stomach and closed her eyes. Through the earphones Jimmy had managed to get around the back of her head, she heard someone laugh. It wasn't Jimmy, but at the moment she didn't care. The floor beneath her rocked and rolled, and it wasn't the *Sea Hopper* that made her stomach jump around. "I'm going to be sick," she whispered. It was the thought of her father, waiting for her in the hall at the Fairmont, ready to walk her down the aisle, that made her stomach hurt. Her parents had been against her marriage to Peter Dalton. Her mother thought she should wait. Her father thought Pete was a sissy boy. They both couldn't believe she was getting married to someone she'd met on a reality TV show. They'd been right about everything, but Lexie had been too caught up in *Gettin' Hitched* fever to listen.

She'd really done it this time.

There had been moments, though, when her saner side had popped up and forced her to stop and think. In those few moments of sanity, her rational brain reminded her of the good and valid reasons to call off the wedding. The most important of all:

1. She didn't love Pete.
   a. Not one bit.

In those few moments of rational thought, she knew that marrying him was insane. Anxiety gripped her stomach and choked her throat, and she'd felt like screaming at the top of her lungs, "I can't marry Pete!" Just as suddenly, denial soothed her like a warm bath filled with rose petals and she embraced it. Denial whispered comforting lies in her head and told her exactly what she wanted to hear:

1. Pete seemed like a nice guy.
   a. He had good manners and opened doors.
2. She could grow to love him.
   a. He was handsome and he'd chosen her out of twenty women.
3. She didn't have the best of luck choosing men on her own.
   a. She was cursed with being a bad picker as evident in her pick of former boyfriends:
   (1) Tim.

    (2) Rocky.
    (3) Dave.
4. Millions of people thought she and Pete made a good couple.
    a. The whole country expected a big wedding.

Lexie had a big capacity for denial, but she could not always ignore the second reason for rushing into marriage with Pete:

1. She hadn't known how to get out of it.

The more she'd let it go on, the bigger it got. It was like a big boulder chasing her downhill and she'd felt powerless to stop it.

The only person she'd confided in was her best friend, Marie. She'd known Marie most of her life, and Marie had been the single witness to her panic attack in the housekeeping room at the Fairmont.

Fifteen minutes before she'd been set to walk down the aisle, her anxiety had grabbed her by the throat and made it hard to breathe. It grew more powerful than her capacity for denial and she'd blurted out to her best friend, "I can't do this."

The director of *Gettin' Hitched* had stashed the two of them inside the small housekeeping room while the crew set up to get a shot of her father seeing her for the first time. The thought of involving her dad in the charade made her add, "This is wrong!" She raised a shaky hand to her mouth to keep her true feelings behind her lips, but they shot out anyway. "I have to, but I can't! He has bad toes, Marie. Really gross!"

"And a mullet," her best friend added.

"Our kids will have bad toes and mullets!" She moaned. "But I have to marry him."

Marie had placed her hands on Lexie's shoulders and looked into her eyes. "Do you love Pete?"

"No, but I have to go through with this! My face is on the billboards and in magazines. *Gettin' Hitched Honeymoon* starts filming the day after tomorrow, and we film the reunion show in a few weeks! All the girls will be there. I have to be there. Married." Her cheeks got hot and she felt dizzy. "There's no getting out of it now!"

Someone knocked on the door, and Lexie about jumped out of her stupid dress. "Fifteen minutes."

"You have to tell them."

That was the right thing to do, but facing the director and producer and telling them that she couldn't go through with the wedding they'd spent big money to bankroll—all because she'd said yes at the final barn-burning ceremony— made her vision go black around the edges. "I can't."

Then her best friend held out her hand. "Let's get out of here."

"How?" Of the two of them, Marie had always been quicker on her feet. Lexie was the planner. She'd learned years ago that acting on impulse usually backfired. Sometimes with dangerous consequences.

"I'll tell them you need to go to the bathroom." Marie paused, and Lexie could almost see the scheme coming together in her brain. "You'll need money. All I have is twenty bucks."

Lexie patted her left breast. On the rare occasion when she couldn't carry a purse, her DDD bra came in handy. "I got a Visa."

"What else?"

"Driver's license and spearmint Tic Tacs."

"My car is right by the elevator in the parking garage."

"You have a MINI Cooper!"

"No one will suspect it for the getaway car." Marie found a piece of paper and pen on a housekeeping cart and handed them to Lexie. "All we have to do is get to it without raising suspicion."

"Then what?"

Without missing a beat, the master schemer said, "I'll call Jimmy. Let's hope like hell he isn't buzzing tourists around the Space Needle and can fly you out of here ASAP."

It was crazy, but so was marrying a man she'd known for ten weeks, spent maybe a combined

35

total of twelve hours with, and didn't love. It was impulsive. She didn't like to act on impulse, but it seemed like the only way out. She grabbed the pen before she changed her mind and wrote a quick note to her parents and an apology to Pete. "This is probably the worst mess either of us have been in."

Marie grinned like when they'd been fifteen and running from the greenskeeper at Broadmoor. "If you're a bird, I'm a bird."

The production crew kept such a tight watch over everything, Lexie was almost certain the plan would fail, but luckily they'd made it to the elevator without being seen. Her luck held as Marie called Jimmy, who was about to take flight from the Lake Union dock.

"Where's he headed?" Lexie asked.

"Canada." Marie dropped her phone in a cup holder. "He didn't say where. I imagine some-where in Vancouver. Probably one of those swanky lodges or a lake with waterfront cabins."

Again, luck was on Lexie's side. Her father was Canadian and she had dual citizenship. She had an enhanced driver's license, and a swanky little cabin sounded like heaven.

The most difficult part had been fitting into Marie's MINI Cooper. She owed her friend big-time. Jimmy, too.

The seaplane lifted from Lake Union, and Lexie didn't even try to get up. She stared at the dome light above her head, aware that she wasn't alone. Besides Jimmy, there was someone else onboard. Someone who wore big leather loafers without socks. She didn't bother to even turn to look up past the man's shoes; she was too busy trying not to get sick. "I can't believe I just did that." She pulled her hand from within the three-tier, chapel-length veil and placed it on her forehead. Everything about *Gettin' Hitched* had been planned and organized and controlled. Everything from the number of phone calls she could make from the pig-shaped phone in the Hitchin' House, to her *My Big Fat Gypsy Wedding*-style dress. The producers had wanted everything to be tacky. If Lexie hadn't been so fixated on winning, she would have seen the stereotypical portrayal of farmers, and if she hadn't let her competitive side give her tunnel vision, she would have done something to get kicked off by the third episode.

If there was one thing Lexie avoided, it was tacky. She'd been raised to turn in horror and shield her eyes from tackiness. In her mother's world, tacky was right up there with tying a bandanna around her face and not shaving her armpits. Or worse, wearing white shoes before Easter. It just wasn't done.

The plane leveled off, and her stomach settled. She struggled to sit up and had to roll one way, then the other, like a beetle trapped on its back.

"Are you okay, Lex?" Jimmy asked through the earphones.

"I've been better." She managed to scoot herself up and rest against the fuselage. The boning in her dress poked her ribs and pushed her breasts together. Her Louboutin satin-and-crystal stilettos hurt her feet. She was lucky that she hadn't twisted an ankle as she'd sprinted toward the *Sea Hopper*. She was an expert at running in five-inch heels and considered it an art form. For several years now, she'd run the Heels for Meals, a one-mile race to benefit local animal shelters, and she'd run after a pickpocket in Italy, but she'd never run on a swaying dock.

The damn crown on her head pulled her hair and hurt her scalp as the full ramifications of what she'd just done rushed at her. Tears stung the backs of her eyes. Her family would have discovered her gone by now. She'd run away from the mess she'd made and implicated Marie in her escape. She'd left her family to deal with it.

1. Because she was a coward.

"Need a drink?"

Lexie turned her head to the left and finally looked at the owner of the big shoes. Tears blurred Lexie's vision, but she didn't need to see perfectly to recognize a handsome man. The kind of handsome that made a woman glad she'd recently had her dark roots dyed to match her blond hair, and her eyelash extensions touched up. At the moment, she was immune to men. Even handsome men with dark skin and stunning green eyes.

"What do you have?" She brushed the tears from her eyes. The guy had dark brown hair that touched the collar of his jacket. The five o'clock shadow covering his square chin and jaws made his skin even darker. And he was big. The kind of big that came from genetics and workouts. Beneath that black jacket he wore, he was probably all hard abs, sculpted chest, and big pecs. The kind she'd sworn off after her last relationship. Well, the last relationship before Pete. Testosterone rolled off the guy like carbon monoxide. Invisible and deadly.

"Grey Goose and tonic." He pulled a fifth of vodka from a YETI cooler between the seats.

"Any lemon?" He was the kind of big that might intimidate some women, but not Lexie. She was five-ten and liked the way she fit against a big man's chest.

He chuckled, and fine lines creased the corners of his green eyes. "No, princess."

"I'm not a princess." Lexie was more of a wine drinker, but needs must, and a shot of vodka or two would calm her agitated nerves.

He pointed the bottle at her head. "You have a crown on your head."

"Yeah." She raised her hands and pulled the first of many bobby pins from her hair. Lexie had been raised around hockey players. Powerful men with big muscles and chests. At a young age, she'd been exposed to toxic levels of testosterone. She was immune to all three: powerful men, big muscles, toxic testosterone.

"Is that a 'yeah' you have a crown? Or 'yeah' you want a drink?"

"Both." Her fingers pulled more pins until she was able to pry the veil off her head. "More tonic than vodka." As a kid, she'd loved hanging out with her dad and the Seattle Chinooks. For the past few years, though, she'd paid less and less attention to the ice arena. She'd never admit it to her dad, but she hadn't seen a game this season. She'd focused most of her time on expanding her company, adding new sections and subsections to her business plan, which now included opening her first brick-and-mortar store.

"Hey, Lex." Jimmy looked over his shoulder at her, and green light from the instrument panel washed across his profile. "That was epic. Reminds me of the time I had to save you and Marie from Tony Bruno's houseboat."

That had been one of the few times she'd acted on impulse, and it served as a reminder that impulsive behavior had consequences, but high school shenanigans paled in comparison to today's spectacle. "Thanks for helping me out." Jimmy was steady and reliable and, more importantly, headed for Canada.

"Been a while since I had to rescue you two."

Lexie was ashamed to admit it, but other than two real occasions, she and Marie had only pretended that they needed rescuing. Ninety-nine percent of the time, they'd called Jimmy because he'd had a car, parents who were never home, and they'd needed a ride somewhere. They'd justified their behavior by telling themselves that it was okay because they were getting nerdy Jimmy out of his house. As an adult, she felt guilty about that and she'd been secretly trying to make up for it whenever possible by sending business Jimmy's way—no matter his latest scheme.

"I think the last time was when someone stole Marie's wallet and you two didn't have cab fare home from the mall."

While Lexie hadn't been drawn to crazy impulses, she had been a *huge* liar, but she was a mature woman with her own business now. She was responsible for a dozen employees. She had an image to protect. She might lie by omission to spare someone's feelings:

1. Marie's combat boot.
2. Jimmy and his aviator cap.

She prided herself on telling the truth. She hadn't concocted lying schemes in seven or eight years now, and she never gave in to crazy impulses.

Until today. Or rather the day she'd tried out for *Gettin' Hitched*. That one crazy impulse had ultimately landed her in the *Sea Hopper* wearing a dress that looked like a meringue kiss.

"I got a new business you might want to invest in."

Jimmy always had a new business. In tenth grade, it had been selling the pot he'd grown in his parents' greenhouse in Medina. In the twelfth grade, he'd been a bookie. Jimmy's businesses always thrived until the cops showed up. Even though she owed Jimmy for past lies and present peccadilloes, the last thing she wanted to do was listen to his latest scheme.

He told her anyway. "It's called Scooter Subs. I have three couriers who deliver sandwiches and chips on red Vespas retrofitted with metal coolers on the rack behind the seat. Food delivery is the future. You and Marie should get in on this one."

No thanks.

"Is Marie seeing anyone special?"

In middle school, Jimmy had developed a deep and abiding crush on her best friend. Too bad for him, Marie had never returned his feelings. Not then, not now. "Not at the moment."

He smiled, and she was afraid she'd given him false hope. "How long is the flight?" she asked to change the subject.

"Three and a half hours." He returned his attention to the controls in front of him.

Three and a half hours? It didn't take three and a half hours to fly anywhere in Vancouver. "Where are we going?"

"Moresby Island."

Lexie had never heard of Moresby Island, and she repeated herself, "Where?"

"Sandspit," the man with the big shoes and pecs answered.

Lexie glanced up at him as he dropped ice into a clear cup. "Sand what?"

"Exactly." He chuckled, but this time humor didn't crease the corners of his eyes, as if he found no pleasure in his destination. He opened a short bottle of tonic, and the water fizzed and bubbled over his fingers.

For a few seconds, she wondered who he was and why he'd hired Jimmy to fly somewhere he didn't seem happy about going, but she had her own problems. At the moment, Mr. Handsome's happiness wasn't one of them. She turned her attention to her lap and the veil her mother had helped pin in her hair. A fresh wave of anxiety rolled through her from the toes up. Her mother had hated the veil. Her mother had been right to hate it, but Lexie would rather have stabbed herself in the eye with a blunt stick than admit it. "I've done it this time," she whispered. A quiver in her heart worked its way to her chin.

She frowned at the pile of tulle in her lap and pushed it down with her hands. It sprang back up. "I made a fool of myself and my family on live television." She tucked and smashed and tried to roll it up like a sleeping bag. When she was finished, it looked like a big Pillsbury crescent roll. She punched the middle to flatten it more.

"It's dead, princess."

Lexie looked up into the green eyes looking back at her, watching as if he couldn't quite figure out *what* he was watching. Not that she blamed him. It probably wasn't every day a runaway bride boarded the guy's chartered flight.

He shoved the clear cup filled with ice and a healthy dose of vodka and tonic at her. His free hand motioned for her to hand him the veil. A chartered flight to somewhere called Sandspit. Lexie had never heard of Sandspit, and the way Mr. Handsome had said it, he'd made it sound like maybe Sandspit was next to Siberia. Lexie hoped their destination wasn't anything like Siberia. Siberia probably didn't take Visa, and she didn't have a coat. Plus the cold gave her dry skin and chapped lips.

"Thank you." She traded him the cup for the tulle crescent. It kind of burst open in his face.

"What the Christ?" He leaned behind him and wrestled the whole mess from the seats.

Lexie rested her head back and took a drink. It tasted like rubbing alcohol, but she didn't care.

She liked the way it burned a path across her tongue and down her throat. It burned away the quiver in her heart and the ache in her stomach. She took a few more sips to settle her chaotic nerves and kicked off her shoes. Alcohol wasn't a solution to her problems, but at the moment, it helped.

Now, if she could just move a little and get comfortable. The layers of net and crinoline petticoat beneath her dress were constraining and itchy, and she didn't want to sit on the floor for the next three hours. If it was possible to get out of the underskirt, she'd have to contend with a dozen or so yards of satin and lace and crystals that dug into her skin, but at least she'd be able to move and sit in the cozy leather seat.

Mr. Handsome, aka Mr. Unhappy Helper's attention returned to the YETI and he pulled out another cup. She watched his long fingers unscrew the little bottle of tonic, then she turned to look at the back of Jimmy's head and that ridiculous helmet he always insisted on wearing. He was a good friend but a tragic fashion victim. She wondered if the *Sea Hopper* had autopilot and if that meant Jimmy could leave the cockpit if it did. She thought of no one in control of the plane and got a little light-headed.

"Does the plane have autopilot, Jimmy?"

He laughed. "No. Just me."

The sound of ice cubes in a plastic cup made

her attention return to the guy with the green eyes and big shoulders. Beneath the dome light, his dark brown hair shone. The kind of shine that came from good products. A chunk of his hair escaped the comb job that looked like he'd done it with his fingers, and curved over his forehead as he looked down at the bottle in his hand. He had beautiful eyes, good hair, and nicely defined lips. The uni-brow practically crawling across his supraorbital ridges could use a pair of tweezers. He looked up as if he'd read her mind. He smiled and she thought, *Holy crap.*

She took a sip from her glass. She didn't know anything about him, other than he'd chartered the *Sea Hopper*, drank vodka, and had a smile that was pure trouble. He'd helped her out with the veil—even if he didn't look too happy about it. All she really knew was that he was a vodka-drinking unhappy helper. He could be a prison escapee on a cross-country killing spree, for all she knew, but needs must. She held out her hand toward him. "Lexie."

He shoved the vodka bottle back inside the cooler, then looked into her face. His gaze ran down her shoulder and bare arm to her hand. He hesitated for several heartbeats before he took it in his. "Sean."

She hadn't realized her fingers were cold until she felt the warmth of his skin. His palm was almost hot against her, and she had an urge to shove her hand beneath the sleeve of his jacket and steal heat from his wrist. Instead she pulled away and kicked her shoes from her feet. "Well, Sean, I need to ask you something," she said through a sigh as her toes were freed.

"What's that?"

"How much experience do you have undressing a girl?"

Chapter 3

• love needs time;
desire needs opportunity

TINY BUBBLES GOT caught in Sean's throat and he forced himself to swallow. "Come again?" He wasn't sure he'd heard right. He'd heard of beer goggles. Maybe he had vodka ears.

"Geez, Lex. What are you planning?" Jimmy asked.

Sean wanted to know the same.

"We need to unbutton the back of my dress so we can get to the zipper on this stupid petticoat. It's big and itchy and driving me crazy."

He wasn't sure if he'd ever seen a petticoat, but he was sure he shouldn't see one now. Not in a small seaplane, and not with Kowalsky's daughter. He and the Chinooks coach tolerated each other out of respect for the organization, but he knew he probably shouldn't undress John's baby girl. "Do you have a knife, Jimmy?" Maybe she could cut her way out without his help.

"Negative. I might have some toenail clippers in my duffel."

Toenail clippers? What the fuck? Three hours

49

wasn't all that long to sit on the floor in a big itchy dress. She might be uncomfortable but she wouldn't die. Sean set his glass on his knee and stared hard into Lexie's big blue eyes. He used the kind of hard stare that intimidated defensemen on the ice and sent little dogs scurrying from the room.

The corners of her red lips turned up like she didn't notice. Her smile looked kind of pouty, or maybe it was just her full lips. He'd been wrong about Lexie Kowalsky; she hadn't been photoshopped at all. At the moment, she wore too much makeup, probably due to her aborted television appearance, but it didn't matter. She was beautiful. She was real. She was sitting in front of him like she'd been dipped in whipping cream. Her father wasn't his biggest fan, and she was asking him to undress her.

"Thanks, Sean," she said as if he'd agreed.

Like she didn't have a clue who he was.

"You're a sweetheart."

He lifted his gaze from her mouth to her eyes again. Her *clueless* blue eyes. She didn't recognize him at all, and he smiled. Maybe if he'd had a clearer head, he would have told her right then and there. Maybe his smile wouldn't have turned into a silent chuckle if he hadn't felt a reprieve from the possible showdown with Coach Kowalsky.

She scooted herself until she was on her knees

50

and presented him her back. A mass of blond curls fell to the middle of her back, and she slid a hand behind her neck and pulled them to one side. "I appreciate your help."

The back of the headset rested against smooth skin, and she smelled like expensive perfume. Tiny buttons closed the back of the dress, starting between her shoulder blades and running down her spine to somewhere below her behind. Everything about her looked soft. From her hair and skin and eyelashes, to the smile she gave him over one shoulder.

"Sorry I don't have a buttonhook."

Sean couldn't remember a time he'd ever undressed a woman without taking her to bed. He shoved his cup in the cup holder between the seats and raised his hands to the first button. It slipped through his fingers, and his knuckles brushed her skin. He tried again with the same results, but the third time, he managed to pinch the little button through the loop.

She was beautiful and soft. She was chaos and madness. She was a real pain in the ass. The second button was more difficult than the first, and he swore beneath his breath as he pinched hard.

"I know I'm a pain in the ass," she said; apparently his aggravation had been picked up by the mic at the side of his mouth. "Sometimes."

Through the earphones, Jimmy chuckled as

51

if he agreed. "How'd you end up on *Gettin'*
Hitched, Lex?" the pilot asked. "I was surprised
to see you on that show. I just never figured you
for a woman desperate to get married."

"I'm not."

Sean's fingers were too big and he fumbled
with the third button. He looked down the long
row of all those slippery buttons and tiny loops
and wondered if he should just rip the dress down
the back.

"I tried out for the show because I thought it
would be great free publicity for my business. It
seemed like a good idea at the time." She shook
her head, and a curl escaped her hand and fell
down her back. "I needed to do something big.
Something to increase my brand and get greater
exposure." Sean picked up the lock of her blond
hair to move it out of the way. "Yum Yum's
Closet is online retail only," Lexie continued,
"and can't compete with big retail chains. I plan
to open my first retail store in Bellevue near the
mall and I needed to get the word out."

Sean stilled as her soft hair fell across the back
of his hand once more. Yum Yum's Closet?
Sounded like a sex shop to him. Like Naughty by
Nature or Frisky Business or Cox in a Box.

"Did it work?" the pilot wanted to know.

"Ten minutes after the first episode aired, my
Web site got sixty hits per thirty seconds and
crashed. Online sales are up fifty-eight percent in

just three months. Most of my Fabulous FiFi line is sold out."

Fabulous FiFi?

"I never knew pet stores were so dog-eat-dog." Jimmy laughed at his own pun.

For reasons unknown to Sean, disappointment lowered his brows as he pushed her hair aside once more. "You own a pet store?"

She looked over her shoulder and her blue eyes gazed up into his. "I manufacture and sell animal couture."

"You sell dog clothes." It was more a statement of disbelief than anything. Sean had an aversion to yappy dogs. Especially yappy dogs in leather jackets and biker hats.

"Yes, but I've expanded the business to include toys and beds and safety items." She shrugged one bare shoulder, and the lock of hair fell down her back again. "Most anything an animal might need."

"Animals don't need clothes," he pointed out, and brushed the curl aside again. It got stuck on some rhinestones or crystals or whatever and stayed there.

"They don't need special parks and condos, either, but I never hear anyone badmouthing dog parks and cat condos."

"Don't get Lexie started about dogs," Jimmy warned.

Sean tugged and pinched and managed to get

53

the fourth and fifth buttons through the little loops. The silk fabric parted and a red imprint from the tight dress creased her flesh. He brushed his thumb across the welt on her perfect skin. He'd probably been a real tool for thinking she should stay in an uncomfortable dress that pinched her skin for the next three hours.

"I love all animals." Her cheeks flushed a soft pink and she ducked her face. "And I have a talent for animal couture. My mother said I come by it naturally, inherited from my great-grandmother, who had a fondness for making clothes for her chickens. Although why she wasted her talent on chicken clothes is a mystery. Chickens are messy and end up on a rotisserie."

What the hell? Someone in her family made chicken clothes? Was she crazy?

"When I was young, I made clothes for all my stuffed animals and even my Chia Pets. Then my daddy bought me my first dog, when I was seven. I've made all my dogs' haute couture ever since. After Pongo, I had Lady and Tramp. Now I just have Yum Yum. She's a Chinese crested and very yummy."

"Geeez-us." All her bizarre rambling about dogs and clothes and chickens was just crazy. A whole lot of crazy wrapped up in a beautiful package. A beautiful package with smooth skin that invited a man's kiss. On the side of her neck where she smelled so good.

"A few months ago, I made a Superman cape for an iguana. It was a special order, of course."

Despite being crazy, his body responded to her. A hot yank in the pit of his stomach that spread to his groin. A totally natural response, given that he was undressing a beautiful woman. He didn't fight it, but that didn't mean he was enjoying himself. He didn't enjoy getting hard-ons for crazy women bound to create chaos.

"This isn't working," he said. "My fingers are too big and those buttons are too small." She looked up at him, and he added, "I'll have to rip it down the back."

"Oh." She stared into his eyes for several heartbeats. "I don't know. The producers might want it back."

Sean grabbed the open sides of the dress and gathered as much silk as possible in each fist. Several buttons whizzed past Sean's head and peppered the fuselage as the sound of ripping cloth filled the cabin. One final yank and the dress lay open, exposing smooth skin, more ugly red welts, and a white corset. Sean lowered his gaze down the lacing, to the indent of her spine at the bottom of her corset. Without being asked, he reached inside the dress, pushed aside the itchy net stuff, and pulled a metal zipper down as far as possible. Then he raised his hands like a calf roper and sat back in his seat.

"Oh my God, that feels wonderful." She

reached behind her and scratched a red mark in the small of her back. "I can almost breathe." She wiggled back and forth and tried to stand. With her hands at her breasts, holding up the dress, it took her several suspenseful minutes before she was able to stand as much as possible.

Sean took a drink and watched her over the bottom of his glass. If she removed her hands, her breasts would fall out of her dress. He waited in anticipation, but wasn't the least bit surprised when exasperation pulled her brows together, and she asked for his help once more.

"I need you to reach up under the dress and pull my slip down. The darn thing practically stands up on its own. I'd do it myself but . . ." She paused to look down at her hands.

He smiled and returned his drink to the cup holder. He had a better solution than rolling around beneath her dress and looking up her long legs. He reached behind him and dragged his duffel into his lap. He pulled out his old plaid shirt and tossed it at her. The brown-and-gold fabric hit her shoulder and she grabbed ahold of it. Her plump breasts and deep cleavage strained her dress even more.

"Thanks."

"You're welcome." That was his favorite shirt, but the sacrifice was worth it. He returned his duffel, kicked back with his Grey Goose, and watched the show.

She threaded one arm then the other through the sleeves, then buttoned it. She wiggled some more as she wrestled her way out of the dress. She turned this way and that, pulled and pushed and shimmied, and her head disappeared in the pouf.

"Are you okay, Lex?"

"Yeah." Then she stepped from the pool of white, all long legs and smooth thighs. The shirt hit her several inches above her knees, and she tossed her hair to one side as she stooped to pick up the dress. The dome light shone in her hair, touched the side of her face, and caught in her sparkly shoes next to her pink toes. She tucked and folded and rolled the pouf as she had the veil. Instead of handing it to him, this time she knelt on the passenger seat and stuffed it behind. She bent across the back and pushed. Then she pushed some more, and for several brief seconds, soft brown flannel rode up the backs of her legs, and Sean caught sight of white panties, rounded bottom, and smooth thighs. He supposed he should offer his help, but he didn't want his hand anywhere near her perfect butt.

"That was a workout." She sounded even more winded and kind of breathy as she turned around and sat. She modestly pulled the end of the shirt to cover her thighs, as if he hadn't already gotten an eyeful. "I'm pooped." She grabbed her drink and took a sip. "How much longer, Jimmy?"

"A little over two hours."

She swallowed and wrinkled her nose. "Are you flying back tonight?"

"No. Tomorrow morning."

"I ran out of the Fairmont without my purse. All I have is my Visa." She leaned her head back against the seat, her eyes wide, as if the full consequences of her actions suddenly hit her like a two-by-four to the forehead. "I don't have cash or my phone or clothes or makeup."

Makeup wouldn't be fourth on his list.

"There's probably an ATM at the Harbor Inn," Jimmy said.

"Do they offer massage?" She shrugged her shoulders and moved her head from side to side. "I could use a massage."

Sean laughed. "'Fraid not, princess. People go to Sandspit this time of year to fish for salmon," Sean added. "There's nothing fancy in town. No turn-down service anywhere on the island."

"Bummer. I do love a mint left on my pillow." She pulled her hair to one side and looked at Sean. "Are you going there to catch salmon?"

"I don't fish for chinook these days."

"That's a good one, Sean," Jimmy said through a laugh. Sean waited for the pilot to say more, to finally give Lexie a clue. Instead he pushed aside the small Bluetooth microphone and communicated with the ground below.

"What takes you to Sandspit?" Lexie asked.

58

"My mother lives in Sandspit." It was inevitable that she would learn who he was. He wasn't purposely keeping her in the dark—ok, maybe just a little—but he'd sleep easier tonight knowing he wasn't going to get a call from John in the morning. If that made him a coward, he could live with it. "My mother is ill." In fact, she was dying. Again.

"I'm sorry."

This time she said she had pancreatitis. "She'll pull through." For as long as he could remember, his mother had been sick. If she hadn't been sick with one ailment or another, she'd made him sick. His childhood had been filled with unnecessary doctor and hospital visits, and she'd shoved unnecessary medicine down him until the age of ten when his uncle Abe had intervened and they'd gone to live with him in Edmonton.

"What time are we leaving in the morning, Jimmy?" Lexie asked.

"I want to be in the air by nine."

"I don't know if I can face everything that early." She moaned. "I'll need a pot of coffee."

"If you want to hide out, I'm flying back to pick up Sean in a few days." Jimmy glanced back at her. "You might consider laying low until things settle down."

"No. I have to get back." She yawned. "By the time we land tomorrow, I'm sure everything will have blown over."

Chapter 4

• love hides in strange places

W HERE IN THE world is the *Gettin' Hitched* bride?"

Lexie sat cross-legged in the middle of her bed at the Harbor Inn. She stared in horror at the *Today* show and co-anchor Savannah Guthrie. "Lexie Kowalsky left a stunned Peter Dalton at the altar last night," she added, "leaving a sour taste in the mouths of millions of fans."

"Millions?" Lexie uttered.

"Cynics speculate it's part of the storyline, that it was planned from the beginning, but Pete says he's truly heartbroken."

Savannah Guthrie? It was a big enough story that the co-anchor was reporting on it? In the first hour? So much for things blowing over.

"No one seems to know what has become of the Seattle native who competed with twenty women to become this season's *Gettin' Hitched* bride." Savannah continued as NBC cut away to footage of a bewildered-looking Pete standing at the altar, surrounded by white roses and lilies. "The producers of the reality show insist this came as a complete surprise. Telepictures, a division of

Warner Bros. Television, released a statement that reads in part, 'We at Telepictures want to assure fans of *Gettin' Hitched* that this was in no way part of the show. Lexie Kowalsky had given us no clue that she wasn't one-hundred-percent happy with the show and committed to Pete.'" Footage of a director holding the note Lexie had written in the housekeeping room cut to footage of her dad's black Land Rover. "The would-be bride's parents, Seattle Chinooks coach John Kowalsky and his wife, Georgeanne, had no comment."

Most major networks had camped outside the Fairmont, waiting to get videotape of the hitchin' bride and groom. Instead, they got footage of a KIRO 7 reporter jumping out of the way seconds before getting hit by an SUV speeding away from the Fairmont. The cameraman did manage to get shots through the windshield of her father's scowl and her mother's hand over her face.

The reporter turned his microphone to people on the street. Several claimed to have seen her racing away from the scene in a MINI Cooper. Others said a Harley. The footage then cut to photographers camped out in front of her apartment in Belltown and the gates to her parents' house on Mercer Island.

"Stay tuned to our fourth hour," Savannah said as the camera came back to her. "Kathie Lee and Hoda will take calls from the thousands of fans who believe they've spotted Lexie Kowalsky, the woman that viewers are now calling the 'Not *Gettin' Hitched* bride.' "

"Thousands?" Lexie said weakly and got a little light-headed. "Kathie Lee and Hoda, too?" She kind of hoped that she'd pass out and put herself out of her misery. If only for a few moments. Not that it would matter. When she came to, nothing would have changed. She'd still be the runaway Not *Gettin' Hitched* bride.

There was a loud knock on the door, and she jumped like a parolee on the run. Her light head spun a little more and she almost fell on her face when she stood. Her feet moved across the beige carpet and she looked through the peephole. Jimmy stood on the other side, and she quickly let him in before leaning her back against the door. It had been Jimmy who'd seen the news and alerted her to the rapidly growing fiasco. She couldn't go home or even to her parents' house. She felt like a Whack-A-Mole, afraid to pop her head outside, and both she and Jimmy had agreed that she had two choices:

1. Stay out of sight.
2. Try and blend with the locals.

"Feeling any better?" he asked over his shoulder. This morning he wore some kind of gnarled-up sweater and worn corduroys. If her life wasn't such a mess, she might have suggested, in the kindest way possible, that he burn those clothes in order to save himself and those around him the horror. But her life was a mess, and she said, "No! People are going to call Hoda and Kathie Lee if they spot me." She swallowed hard. "Like that book, *Where's Waldo?*"

He shook his head and turned a plastic sack upside down. "Hunted down Pokémon-style."

A weird little choking sound came from her mouth and she raised a hand to her lips. It was worse than Waldo or Whack-A-Mole. "Pokémaniacs."

The contents of the bag spilled on her bed. "Well, Pikachu, if it makes you feel better, no one at the Sandspit Mart or the Waffle Hut is talking about anything but the four-hundred-pound halibut someone caught yesterday. I'm going to see if I can get a look at it before I take off."

"Waffle Hut? You had breakfast?" Lexie didn't think she could eat at the moment, but her stomach had growled all night due to the fact that she'd been too nervous to eat yesterday, too.

"I got you some Tastykakes and ginger ale."

Lexie groaned as she moved toward the bed. A bag of cinnamon doughnuts, two cans of Canada Dry, and a prepaid phone lay on the bed, along with shampoo, toothbrush and toothpaste, and some clothing.

"I've been thinking. It's more than possible that someone saw you board the *Sea Hopper* last night. The lake was busier than most week-days, with all the tourists in town to catch your wedding. It's probably only a matter of time before someone realizes that it wasn't a big marshmallow they saw getting crammed into a flying tree frog."

Jimmy had a point but her brain was too scrambled to think beyond the black sweatpants, red "Spirit of Sandspit" T-shirt, and pair of knockoff Uggs.

"What if someone asks about it?"

And a fish hat. "Don't tell the truth." Not just a regular fish hat, either.

"You want me to lie."

Lexie picked the cap up and turned it from side to side. "No, prevaricate."

"Same thing."

A red salmon head stuck out the front and its tail out the back. "What the heck, Jimmy? I thought we decided that I need to blend. I can't blend with a fish on my head."

He shrugged. "It's a cool hat." This from the guy who wore an old aviation helmet and goggles. He pulled out a wad of Canadian bills and handed it to her. Jimmy was like an undercover spy and had argued against her using a credit card that could be traced within minutes of use. Instead, he'd paid for the hotel in advance and had taken money from his own card. "Gotta go. I'll be back in two days to get you and Sean."

Lexie decided not to argue about his taste in hats. She was grateful for his help, and really, what had she expected from the man who'd always dressed as if he was engaged in a fashion grudge match? "Thank you. I'll pay you back. Promise. I don't know what I would have done without you." She hugged her friend, and he wrapped his comforting arms around her. "I owe you big." She stepped back and looked into his eyes on the same level as hers.

"I know," he said through a grin. "But what are old friends for?"

"Do you want your coat back?" She pointed to the leather jacket hanging in the small closet.

"No. I'll get it day after tomorrow."

"Thanks again." The pocket in the leather jacket was ripped out, but she was glad to have it.

He took a few steps toward the door and laughed as he opened it. "Don't get into any more trouble while I'm gone."

"God no." She shook her head. "I'm not leaving this room."

She locked the door behind him and returned to sit in the middle of the bed. A can of ginger ale rolled against her bare knee and she picked it up. She popped it open, then hit the mute button on the television remote control. She wore the flannel shirt she'd borrowed from Sean the night before. Had it really just been the night before that she'd run out on her wedding, hopped into Jimmy's plane, and ended up in Sandspit, BC? Had it been less than twelve hours ago when she'd looked up into eyes the color of jade and the five o'clock shadow of a man who looked like he'd jumped off the cover of *Men's Health* magazine? Had it been less than twelve hours ago that he'd given her his shirt? So much had happened that it felt more like forty-eight hours had passed.

Once they'd landed in Sandspit, they'd all piled into a green Subaru. The keys had been in the ignition, and Lexie had wondered if she was now involved in grand theft or if the car had been left at the docks for Sean. She'd figured the latter, but by that point, she'd been exhausted and freezing and hadn't cared. He'd dropped her and Jimmy off at the Harbor Inn without even saying good-bye. She wouldn't have been surprised if he'd left the smell of burnt rubber in the air.

He didn't owe her anything. He'd helped her with her dress, given her a drink and his shirt to wear, but . . . it might have been nice if he'd waited until Jimmy checked in before he'd sped away like he was driving a getaway car, leaving her to hide outside in her Louboutins, his flannel shirt, and Jimmy's bomber jacket.

She took a drink of ginger ale and made a face. Ginger ale always reminded her of being sick as a kid. Not only had she looked like a tacky hooker, she'd felt like a prison escapee hiding in the bushes, but she couldn't exactly walk into the hotel lobby and request a room.

Instead, she'd waited around one side of the building while Jimmy had rented two rooms. The doors to each faced the parking lot. She didn't think anyone had seen her enter number seven; at least she hoped not. Especially now that Hoda and Kathie Lee were getting into the hunt for her.

Next to the fish hat lay a pay-as-you-go phone that already had the minutes loaded for her. She stared at it with anxiety and dread, but she couldn't put off the inevitable and picked it up. Her heart pounded as she dialed, and with every ring it grew louder in her head.

"Hello."

The corners of her lips trembled and her voice broke. "Hi, Dad."

"Lexie? Where are you?"

"Sandspit, British Columbia."

"Where?"

She almost smiled. "It's a tiny town in the Hecate Strait."

There was a pause on the line before he said, "That's damn near Alaska. How in the hell did you get all the way up there?"

"Jimmy Pagnotta and the *Sea Hopper*."

"The flying tree frog?"

"Yeah." Tears fell from her eyes. "I couldn't marry Pete."

"Well, you picked a hell of a way to get out of it." The tone of his voice got deeper with anger. "I imagine Marie helped you with this ridiculous stunt."

"Yes, but it's not her fault."

"It would have been a hell of a lot easier if you'd told me or your mother that you couldn't marry that pansy ass instead of leaving your whole family to twist in the wind." She could hear his anger building, and she knew the inevitable was about happen. "There are reporters camped outside the gates and two idiots jumped out from behind cars in the parking lot at the Key Arena! Your mother and I waited up all night to hear from you! We didn't know if you were in Seattle or Mexico or actually made it to Sweden this time."

"Sorry," she said just above a whisper, and waited.

"You ran away instead of nutting up and dealing with the colossal fuckup you created!"

"I don't have nuts, Dad."

"Jesus Christ, Alexis!" he managed just before the inevitable hit and his words turned into a long stream of mostly incomprehensible swearing. She could practically hear the steam blowing out of his ears.

She hated to make her parents angry. They had

such perfect lives. She tried to make hers perfect, too, but she always seemed to fail. Especially when she acted without a thorough plan. "I'm sorry." Tears stung her eyes and a sob came from deep in her chest next to her heart. "Everything got so-o big so fa-ast. I fe-elt trapped."

"Don't cry," he said, which made her cry even harder. "You didn't kill anybody." He paused, then added, "Right?" as if that was a possibility.

"No-o." She pulled her knees up to her chest. "I should ha-ave nutted u-up."

"Honey, you don't have nuts." Her dad's blowups were inevitable when he was pushed too far. Her latest "colossal fuckup" was definitely in the pushed-him-too-far category. Way too far, but her dad's blowups always blew over quickly.

"Ho-ow's Mom?"

"Worried. Scared. Mad, but it isn't like she's never run away from a wedding." She heard a silent little laugh in his voice and relaxed a bit. "She hated that dress."

"Me too."

"When are you coming back?"

She let out a hiccupped breath. "Day after tomorrow. Hop-pefully no one will see me flying back in. And the gates to your neighborhood and the front of my apartment will be reporter fr-ree."

"Your mother will be waiting for you here, but I'll be in Pittsburgh."

She breathed deep and let it out slowly. "I'm

sure you'll whoop some Penguin ass," she managed without a break in her voice.

"I'm not so sure. I'm down a defenseman and my newest hotshot sniper won't be on the roster. He said he has a family emergency, but he probably took time off to deep condition his flow."

Lexie laughed for the first time in days. She knew how her dad felt about players concerned with their hair. She also knew that her dad hated showoffs. Apparently, Mr. Hotshot was both and had earned a double dose of disdain.

"Goddamn nancy-pants. I'd love to rearrange his Chiclets and see how arrogant he is without his front teeth."

She could bring up that several of her father's teeth were implanted ceramic and titanium. Instead she wanted to know, "How's my Yum Yum?"

"You and little dogs." She knew him and knew he was shaking his head as he talked about her Chinese crested. He refused to say her dog's name and called her "naked nancy-pants" instead.

"You gave me my first little dog," she reminded him. "Remember Pongo?"

"Of course. He shook and was pathetic and got me into trouble with your mother."

Pongo had been her first teacup Chihuahua and had loved her dad. Despite her father's claim to the contrary, his dislike of "nancy-pants"

71

dogs was just a front to hide the soft spot in his heart.

"You should have named him Trouble," he said about the dog who'd followed him around like a groupie. Despite being called a nancy-pants and worse, Pongo had loved her dad, and the day Pongo died, she didn't know who had been more torn up, her or Dad. "In fact, you should have named all your dogs Trouble for all the chaos they cause." He paused, then added, "Look, Lexie, you're too nice. And you're impulsive and you have a big heart and that gets you into all sorts of hot water. You get that from your mother."

She wasn't impulsive anymore. "Where is Mom?" Well, except for lately.

"You know your mother, no reporter is going to make her hide. She's taken Jon Jon to school, where I'm sure he's going to get razzed like crazy. But he's tough; he can take it."

Her father had a big heart, too, she knew. He was just really good at hiding it. After several more moments, she ended the call. She needed to call her mother. She could get her on her cell phone, but she wanted a few moments of calm before she undertook another emotional conversation. Of her two parents, her mother would be harder on her. Never mind that she'd also run from her own wedding years earlier.

Lexie deserved it after what she'd just put

them through, but that didn't mean she looked forward to the disappointment that she was sure to hear in her mother's soft Southern voice. Not disappointment that she hadn't gotten married, but disappointment that she was in a big mess.

Lexie tossed the phone on the bed and thought about her current situation. Was her dad right? Was she too nice? Well, she did hate to hurt people and sometimes put others' feelings before her own.

She lay back on the bed and closed her eyes. She felt an urge to run even as she wanted to crawl beneath the covers and hide. She took a deep breath and slowly let it out. She needed to clear her head and calm her nerves, and she stared up at the ceiling. Her gaze focused on what looked like a jellyfish stamped in the texture. Next, she picked out a tailless shark, a cat's paw, and a deer with seven legs. Her nerves and mind settled enough for her to think about her current situation, what she'd done and how she'd ended up in a hotel room in Sandspit, British Columbia. She didn't have to think very hard. Most of the time it came down to the same thing.

Lexie Kowalsky was a people pleaser. She'd made bad decisions and stayed in bad relationships out of the fear of disappointing anyone. This time she hadn't wanted to disappoint the producers of a reality show or Peter Dalton or millions of *Gettin' Hitched* fans. Her fear often made her stuff down her own feelings. Marie called her an "emotional cutter."

Lexie didn't know if she'd go that far, but she did know that several contradictions fought within her.

1. Responsible.
   a. Flighty.
2. Loved an organized plan.
   a. Too impulsive.
3. Passive people pleaser.
   a. Extremely competitive.
4. Hated to lose.
   a. But loved a sportsmanship trophy.

Her competitive side had encouraged her to run faster, play harder, and hip-check the other *Gettin' Hitched* brides. Normally she would have felt horrible about "accidentally" bouncing a football off Whitney Sue's head during the pigskin challenge, but her sights had been set on winning a romantic date with Pete. A date that had been anything but romantic, not with a film crew inches from her face.

Pete. She didn't want to think about him, and her gaze searched the ceiling until she picked out what looked like an ant jumping off a rock. She hated to think that he'd actually loved her. The thought made her heart pound and her nerves jump, and she needed more than concentrating on random patterns in the texture to keep her brain occupied.

She sat up and grabbed the shampoo off the bed. Her hair was sticky and gross from last night and she moved to the small bathroom. Jimmy had forgotten conditioner, and for a split second she thought about running to the store. She needed good conditioner to keep her hair from going ashy, but the thought of being spotted shoved the thought from her head.

She turned on the shower and unbuttoned the shirt Sean had given her. The soft fabric smelled woodsy with a hint of musk, and slid down her bare shoulders and back to land at her feet. She stepped out of her white panties and took them in the shower with her, washing them with the thin bar of hotel soap before hanging them over the rod. As warm water spilled from the shower and ran through her hair, she thought of everything waiting for her at home, especially the love of her life, Yum Yum. No matter what, she could always count on the love in her little dog's eyes.

The first time she'd seen the Chinese crested had been two years ago when she'd dropped off food at the Emerald City Pet Rescue. It had been impossible not to notice the bald little dog with black skin and white dots. White hair stuck out of her ears, and her tail and paws were covered in long hair. She shook as if cold, and her black eyes had been filled with pain and sadness.

Lexie was not only a sucker for dogs, she was a complete sap for anything sick and helpless. Yum Yum was both.

The six-month-old puppy yelped when she walked, and rather than deal with her luxating patella, her owners had dropped her off at the shelter instead of paying the two grand to fix her congenital defect. Lexie had gladly scooped up the little dog and paid for the surgery. She helped rehabilitate the puppy and told her repeatedly that she was *yummy* to give her a much-needed dose of self-esteem. She'd made her clothes to keep her warm and built ramps that looked like fashion runways to help minimize the abuse to her knees.

From those simple beginnings, she'd started Yum Yum's Closet, her online specialty pet supply business that she operated out of her apartment. Two years later, her business had tripled and her designs were now manufactured by a small-batch company in Marysville. She'd chosen a space for a retail store and was in the process of picking out paint and wallpaper.

Lexie lathered her hair with shampoo and washed her body. It felt good to scrub away the last bit of makeup and mousse left over from the day before. After the shower, she wrapped herself in a towel and walked back into the room. The television continued without sound, water dripped from her hair, and her stomach rumbled, reminding her of how little she'd eaten in the past twenty-four hours. She wasn't one of those girls who picked at her salad but never really ate. Like her mother, she loved to cook and kept the pounds off her butt and thighs with routine exercise. A frown pulled at the corners of her lips as she looked at the Tastykakes and ginger ale on the bed. She was either going to pass out from hunger or go mental.

Perhaps both. Jimmy had said something about a waffle house, and the thought of blueberry waffles and maple syrup made her feel even more faint with hunger. Bacon and eggs and coffee. Real coffee. Not the weak stuff from the four-cup brewer in the hotel room.

She glanced from the Tastykakes to the television. Maybe while she'd been in the shower, the country had lost interest in her. Maybe she could sneak out of her room and gorge on waffles and bacon. Maybe she wasn't trapped inside room seven after all.

The intro to the fourth hour of the *Today* show played across the screen as the camera zoomed in for a tighter shot of Hoda and Kathie Lee sitting behind a glass table. Just below the hosts' names on the lower third, the ticker read: *Where in the world is the* Gettin' Hitched *bride?*

"Welcome, everyone," Kathie Lee began. "It's giveaway Friday, and we're giving viewers the opportunity to win a trip to Cancun."

"To enter," Hoda added, "call the number below and let us know if you've had a Lexie Kowalsky sighting."

Or maybe not.

Chapter 5

• love at first sight deserves a second look

I T'S NOT WORKING."
Lexie Kowalsky jumped like someone had stuck a pin in her. Beneath the bill of a ridiculous hat, she raised her deep blue gaze. "What?"

"If you're trying to blend in with the locals, it's not working." Not when her hair stuck out like straw from beneath a cap that made it look like she had a fish swimming through her head.

"What makes you think I'm trying to blend?" She raised a cup of coffee and blew into it.

And not when, despite the hair and the fish, she looked good enough to spread on the table and eat. "I talked to Jimmy before he left." Sean took the chair across from her at the Waffle Hut. "I hear people are taking a whole lot of interest in looking for you." He'd also seen the whole cast of *The View* talking about her at his mother's house just before he'd escaped her nonstop health complaints.

As a couple of tourists walked past in parkas and rubber fishing boots, Lexie ducked her face and reached up as if adjusting the bill of her cap. "There's a Cancun vacation from Hoda and Kathie Lee at stake." With her hand covering the side of her face, she asked, "Are you going to rat me out?"

"No."

"Thank you." She pushed her hair over her shoulders and sighed as if relieved by his answer.

"I've been to Cancun many times." He lowered his gaze as a lock of her hair slid back over her shoulder and rested against the fish on her T-shirt. The Spirit of Sandspit sculpture was the pride of the community and one of the first things tourists saw when they landed at the airport, but stretched across her big breasts, the salmon looked more like a whale. "It's not my favorite vacation destination."

A waitress approached, and Sean paused as she set down a plate of waffles and bacon and a little pitcher of syrup.

"Can I get ya anything, Sean?" she asked.

The woman wore a sleeveless fleece over a red turtleneck and looked at him through glasses sitting a little crooked on her face. He was sure she was a friend of his mother's, but he couldn't recall her name. It was past noon and he ordered a Molson to take the edge off the pounding in his head. His gaze slid to her badge. "Thank you, Louise."

"My pleasure." She glanced at the top of Lexie's fish cap. "Can I bring you anything else?"

"Coffee, please."

He continued their conversation as he watched Louise walk away. "Now, if someone offers a trip to Cozumel . . ." He returned his gaze to Lexie. "That's a whole different ball game. I'd have to turn you in for a chance at a Cozumel vacation."

"Seriously?"

No. "Yep. There's a little bar on the southern tip of the island that serves the coldest beer, cranks the best reggae, and encourages the women to go topless."

A disapproving frown pulled at the corners of her full kiss-me-baby lips as her long fingers with short, pale pink nails wrapped around the syrup. "Classy."

"This from the woman who chased pigs on national television."

"And won." She drizzled syrup into the deep waffle squares. "Without getting very muddy, I might add."

He sat back and folded his arms over his chest covered in a gray Henley. "I wouldn't know about the mud. I never watched the show."

She set the pitcher on the table and glanced at him. "Then how do you know about the pig?"

"I saw it on a commercial."

She placed a paper napkin on her lap, then picked up her fork and knife to slice off a piece of waffle. One bite and she sighed. Her eyes

81

closed and the corners of her lips lifted as if she was in heaven. "Mmmm. So good." Or having an orgasm. Damn.

She swallowed and her eyes opened. "You never watched the show?"

"No," he answered as the waitress set his beer on the table.

"How's your mama doin' with that leaky pancreas?" the waitress asked.

Sean just smiled like he always did and looked up into the woman's face, probably aged beyond her years by the harsh, salty air. "Better."

"She must be in a world of pain."

"I believe she'll make a complete recovery." *Like always.*

"Last time I saw her, it was . . ." Louise paused in momentary thought. "Geez, it was probably at the trade show this past October. She mentioned she might be moving to the States with you."

Which was why he was in Sandspit. To make sure she didn't.

"She just can't take the winters. Poor thing." Louise's eyes pinched at the corners like she was trying to figure out why the woman eating like a lumberjack seemed familiar.

"She sure is proud of you."

Sean watched Louise watch Lexie. The top half of Lexie's face was hidden from Louise's view beneath the bill of a fish hat. "I'll tell Mother you asked about her."

"Okay." Louise's brows lowered and she turned to leave. "Enjoy."

Sean glanced over his shoulder as she walked away. "I'm sure she didn't recognize you." He turned back to Lexie, her head still ducked.

He watched her mouth as she asked, "How sure?"

"Fairly."

"That's not very reassuring." Slowly she lifted her face, the brim sliding up her cheeks and nose to her deep blue eyes. "What's a leaky pancreas?"

Fiction. "She doesn't have a leaky pancreas. Louise is mistaken." He reached for his beer and took a drink.

"What's wrong with her?"

Sean shrugged and lowered the glass. "We were talking about you and that idiotic show," he said to change the subject away from his mother's pretend illness.

"I never should have gone on that stupid show." She dabbed her mouth with the paper napkin and reached for her coffee. "I should have figured out some other way to get national exposure for Yum Yum's Closet." She sliced off a bite of waffle and put it in her mouth.

That's right. Through the blur of a pouf and gauze, he recalled her mentioning something about a dog clothes business last night. "Sounds more like you never should have won."

She lifted one shoulder in agreement and placed

83

a napkin in her lap. "I'm supercompetitive." She took a bite of waffle and chewed. A drop of syrup rested on her bottom lip.

That's what he'd heard about her. He watched the drop for several seconds before the tip of her tongue licked it away.

"I come by it naturally, on my dad's side. He used to play hockey for the Seattle Chinooks and had a reputation for scoring goals and fighting."

He knew that, and it was part of the reason he'd sought her out.

"His name is John Kowalsky. If you live in Seattle, you might have heard of him."

"Most people have heard of John." He'd had his first ass-chewing from the coach the very same week he'd moved to Seattle and put on his Chinooks jersey. He'd scored a hat trick against the Sharks, and the coach had pulled him into his office to bitch at him. "Goddamn it, Knox," he'd said with his finger in Sean's face. "This is a team sport. Your cocky showboating is disrespectful as fuck!" Sean had heard it before, but he had the skill to back it up, and the fans loved it when he rode his stick after scoring a goal. Just three nights ago, Kowalsky had chewed his ass again. He'd scored the winning goal in the last five seconds of the game, and had ridden his stick from one end of the ice to the other.

"A lot of people look up to my dad." Lexie took another bite and swallowed.

"He's a hockey great." Sean would give him that.

"Yeah. He's a great guy, too."

He probably wouldn't go that far.

"His heart is just a big marshmallow."

He definitely wouldn't go that far.

"Unless you get on his bad side." She stabbed another piece of waffle. "He'll come at you hard if you get on his bad side." She paused in thought as she chewed. "But that rarely happens. A person has to do something really offensive, like steal from poor people." She reached for her coffee. "When I was ten, he actually caught a guy trying to steal from a Salvation Army bucket. So he put him in a headlock and fed him his lunch." She raised the cup and added as she blew into the coffee, "He hates cocky showboating about as much as I hate dog beaters." She set her cup on the table and looked across at him. "You never did mention what you do for a living."

He was on the same level as a *dog* beater? "Nothing as exciting as chasing pigs and running away from weddings." He took a drink of his beer and sucked the foam from his top lip. Last night, her cluelessness about him had seemed kind of funny. Like an inside joke. Not to mention a few extra hours before he had a conversation with John about a certain wedding dress and flying buttons. In the light of day, not so funny. He'd sought her out today to tell her that he was a

Chinook. It wasn't a secret and she was bound to find out. He'd looked for her today to tell her and because there were parts of last night she might not want her dad to know about. He would be willing to help her out because he was a nice guy, but now she'd called him a thieving, dog-beating showboat, and he didn't feel like helping her or telling her shit. "What do your folks think of you being the runaway *Gettin' Hitched* bride?"

"Not happy. Mortified. Worried." She looked away and took a bite. "Once my dad got over his initial blowup, he was okay. But my mom . . ." She shrugged a shoulder. "She's happy that I didn't marry Pete, but she's hurt that I didn't come to her instead of running away."

Sounded reasonable to Sean. "What did your folks think about you being on the show? Chasing pigs and competing for that Pete guy?"

"I didn't talk to them while we were taping, but of course I could guess." She put her fork down and reached for her coffee.

"You couldn't contact them?"

"Yes, but we could only make one call a week on the phone in the Hitchin' House, and those were recorded. I didn't want a recording of my mom crying and my dad swearing over the pig phone."

"Pig phone?"

"It was a landline phone shaped like a pig." She

86

took a sip from her cup. "It was pink and grunted instead of ringing."

Of course it did. "What did your parents think about your groom?"

"Dad thinks Pete's a pansy ass."

"Is he?"

"I don't know." She shrugged one shoulder. "My mother couldn't quit crying and thought I shouldn't marry a man I didn't know. She was right. I'd had two solo dates with him, but we weren't really alone. The whole film crew was there."

"Are you shitting?"

"No. Some of the other girls met him alone in his private Pig Pen." A separate bungalow on the property which housed his euphemistically titled bedroom, Hog Heaven. "I never went to his Pig Pen."

"Again." He leaned forward. "Are you shitting?"

"No. I didn't want to humiliate my parents or embarrass myself."

That wasn't what shocked him. "You were going to marry a man you didn't know and hadn't spent any time alone with?"

"I know it sounds crazy." From beneath the fish head on her hat, she lifted her gaze to the picture of the *Pesuta* shipwreck on the wall behind him as if to gather her thoughts. "But the show was crazy." Her brows lowered. "We got caught up in it. At least I did."

He held up one finger. "Your parents didn't want you to marry him." A second finger. "You didn't want to marry him." Then a third. "So why in the hell were you getting ready to marry him?"

She returned her gaze to his and said as if it made perfect sense, "Our pictures were on the tea towels, as the saying goes."

What saying? And what the hell was a tea towel?

"We did manage to have a few moments alone when the camera crew packed up for the day. Like after the surf challenge." She took another drink and shook her head. "He did seem really moody that day. Like someone forgot to put sprinkles on his birthday cake." Her nose wrinkled. "We were still on the beach and I was busy trying not to stare at his disturbingly long toenail."

"What?"

"That should have been my first clue that I couldn't marry him." She set her cup on the table. "Then he said he doesn't like little dogs—which normally qualifies as a deal breaker."

His toenails and dislike of dogs were probably the least of the problems between them. "A lot of people don't like little dogs."

One brow winged up her forehead. "In my experience, men who don't like little dogs are compensating for something."

He leaned back and reached for his glass. "Like

what?" He knew what she meant; he just wanted to hear her say it.

Beneath the brim of her cap, her eyes moved back and forth as if she was a perp in a room filled with cops. Her cheeks turned pink and she lowered her voice like she was going to say something shockingly vulgar. "Small penis."

That was it? Penis? Sean hated the word "penis." It sounded small. "Not all men who don't like little dogs are hung like babies."

"How many men do you know who don't like little dogs?"

Just him, and he didn't have a problem in the hung department. He took a long pull of beer, then asked, "Explain it to me again. Why in the hell were you about to marry a moody guy with bad toenails and small junk?"

"Well, if you love someone—"

"Don't tell me you loved the guy," he interrupted. "It doesn't happen that way."

Her big eyes rounded. "How many times have you been in love?"

"Enough to consider marriage?"

"Yes."

"Never."

"Then you don't qualify as an expert."

"Not saying I'm an expert. Just curious how a girl like you ends up engaged to a man she doesn't even know."

"A girl like me?"

Mindful of the trap women set to snap off a man's leg, he answered carefully, "Not ugly."

"Pressure." She sat back in her chair. "And convincing myself that it was love at first sight."

He scoffed.

"You don't believe in love at first sight?"

"No." He chuckled and shook his head. "I believe in lust at first sight." He was looking at it square in the face. Staring into lust. Lust and chaos. A dangerous combination for him.

She sighed and gave up the pretense of maybe, sort of, could have been in love. "I told myself that I was probably wrong about his moodiness, and I figured he could get pedicures." She set her knife and fork on her plate and pushed the remains of her waffle away. "Everyone can't help but fall in love with Yum Yum and . . . and we could compensate."

He shook his head. "Princess, there's no compensating for a small dick."

"I once dated a guy and . . ." Her voice trailed off and she didn't finish.

"Exactly." He looked at her, sitting there in her ridiculous fish hat, looking absolutely beautiful. Sean Knox had sat across from a lot of beautiful women. Some were a punch in the gut and a feast for the eyes. Others piqued his curiosity and left him wanting more. Lexie was both: a double dose of seduction and cut with some grade A drama.

That made her a trifecta of trouble. The kind he didn't need.

He raised one hip and pulled a wallet from his worn Levi's. Last night, he got a real good glimpse of her corset. He imagined it had been designed for her wedding night, and the thought of some man peeling her out of it had made him peel out of the Harbor Inn parking lot, once he'd dropped her and Jimmy off.

He'd needed to put some distance between him and Lexie Kowalsky, but here he was. Back again, thinking about her underwear and soft skin. "I got your waffles covered." Sean pulled out a green queen and tossed it on the table. He'd checked up on his coach's daughter. It was the right thing to do and bound to make him look like a hero in the eyes of his teammates.

"Are you leaving?"

He glanced up from the twenty and into her blue eyes. "Yeah."

"Where are you going?"

He'd done his duty.

"To your mom's?"

"Maybe." He shoved the wallet back into his pocket and stood.

"I'd love to meet her."

"Why?" She rose also. He couldn't imagine why anyone would willingly subject themselves to Geraldine Brown.

"Well . . . she's sick with a leaky pancreas. That

sounds . . . debilitating. I could help out and . . . make some soup."

Soup wasn't going to cure his mother's hypochondria.

"I am an excellent nurse and I have people skills."

"No. Thank you."

She grabbed his forearm and dropped the pretense of a soup-making nurse with people skills. "I'm bored to death, but I can't exactly walk around town. I might get recognized." He ran his gaze from the top of her head, down the fish hat and shirt, to the baggy sweats tucked into a pair of ugly boots. Sean wasn't an expert in women's fashion, but he hated baggy sweats and fucking Uggs. "If I have to spend all my time cooped up in my room, I'll go crazy."

He didn't owe her anything. Hell, he'd already given her his shirt and paid for her breakfast. The thought of her chatting it up with his mother made his brows pinch together.

Her eyes widened and her grasp on him tightened. "I'll go all Bates Motel."

For a few seconds, he gave it some thought as he lowered his gaze to her hand wrapped around his forearm. She was fresh meat for his mother's deathbed stories, the ones she told repeatedly to anyone within hearing or shouting distance of her. If he threw Lexie to his mother, she'd refocus her attention away from him.

When he didn't answer right away, Lexie took that for a yes, and a big smile curved her lips and lit up her eyes. She released him and grabbed a worn bomber jacket that had to belong to Jimmy. She shoved her arms through the sleeves, then followed him out of the waffle house. Fresh snow crunched beneath their boots, and puffs of their breath hung in the air as they walked to his mother's Subaru. Sean opened the passenger door as Lexie shoved a hand down the front of her shirt. His breath caught in his lungs, leaving only her little puffs to hang between them.

"Chap Stick," she said, as if that explained anything. Her hand fished around between her breasts before she pulled out a tube of Burt's Bees. "I don't have a purse or pockets in my sweats. This jacket has huge holes instead of pockets." She coated her lips with honey-scented balm.

"What else do you have in there?" He was tempted to look for himself.

"The phone Jimmy bought for me." She shoved the yellow tube back down her shirt. "Don't freak out if you hear 'Crazy Train' coming from my bra. That's my ringtone. It seemed appropriate." She got into the car and said, "Thanks for letting me tag along. I won't cause problems. I promise."

She broke that promise before he drove from the parking lot. "Can we stop somewhere so I can get some bottles of water?"

"I thought you weren't going to cause problems." They stopped at a drugstore, where she hung a blue plastic basket from her elbow. She filled it with two bottles of water, a bag of pretzels, breath mints, mascara, and a "zit stick."

"Thanks, Sean." She grinned as they pulled away from the store. "I won't cause you any trouble *now*."

He doubted it. From the top of her fish hat to the bottoms of her ugly boots, Lexie Kowalsky was all kinds of trouble. The kind that—*All aboard!* Ozzy Osbourne yelled from Lexie's boobs. Sean accidentally jerked the wheel and nearly drove off the road. Ozzy laughed like a lunatic as she dug into her shirt. *I, I, I, I . . .*

Lexie pulled out a TracFone and glanced at it before answering. "Hi, Marie. Oh yeah? Did Jimmy give you this number?" She listened for several moments, then said, "Sandspit, British Columbia." There was a brief pause, then she said slowly, "Sandspit . . . British Columbia . . . No. Sand—spit." She spelled it out, then laughed. "I know, right?"

Sean drove up the two-lane road and gathered from the one-sided conversation that the driver of the silver clown car was on the other end of the line. Lexie scratched her head beneath the fish hat.

"I'll be home day after tomorrow," she said as he turned up a gravel drive. "Come over and we'll open a bottle of wine and order takeout . . . Okay. Love you, too." She ended the call, and the phone went back down her shirt. Then she placed her hands on the outside of her T-shirt, cupping the undersides of her breasts, and adjusted herself.

"Are you okay?"

"Yeah." She pushed one side and then the other.

Sean forced his gaze from her shirt as he drove around a weathered A-frame house that had once been the main lodge at a KOA. He pulled to a stop and glanced at Lexie adjusting herself one last time. "Do you need help?"

She looked across at him, blinked as if she'd forgotten she wasn't alone, then said, "I got it."

"What you got down there beside a phone and Chap Stick?" And big breasts.

"A couple of toonies, some sawbucks, and a Borden." She dropped her hands. "My driver's license and hotel key."

Money and a hotel key. "You have a lamp in there like Mary Poppins?"

"I *wish* I had a magic carpetbag, right about now." She didn't wait for him to walk to her side to open her door. "I'd pull out my makeup bag, good shampoo, and black cloche."

Sean had no idea what a cloche was, and didn't think he wanted to find out.

"And underwear."

Underwear was something he *did* know about, especially the lacy stuff worn by Victoria's Secret models. The sound of her boots on snow and gravel seemed unusually loud as she followed behind him toward the back door. He wondered if he should warn her about his mother. Give her a quick heads-up, but how could he explain Geraldine Brown? He'd tried in the past, but people tended not to believe him when he told them that his mother's illnesses were all an act. That she was at death's door at least twice a year. It sounded crazy because it was crazy. If he talked about it, people tended to think he was crazy, too. Either that or a coldhearted asshole of a son who didn't care about his dying mother.

The back door squeaked as Sean opened it, and Lexie followed him inside. Instantly he was reminded of exactly why he'd stopped bringing his friends home at the age of twelve. Pill bottles and every kind of over-the-counter medicine took up most of the counter space. And just like when he'd been a kid, a rush of heat rose up his neck and face.

"Sean?"

He paused in the middle of the small kitchen as the old familiar heat scalded his esophagus. As a kid, he'd always had the most embarrassing mother on the block, or at his school, or sitting in the bleachers.

"Is that you? Are you back?"

This latest illness had been inspired at the medical clinic when a nurse suggested she get a glucose tolerance test for pancreatitis. "Were you expecting someone else?" Six months ago, she'd gone to the doctor for a scratchy eye, but she'd left his office at death's door. Again. That time angina had come knocking and, of course, she'd answered.

He stepped into the living room and was somewhat relieved to see his mother lying in her recliner, covered by one of the multicolored afghans she was always crocheting. An Elasto-Gel Cranial Cap covered her head, secured with Velcro around her throat. He'd bought her the cooling cap when she'd had "meningitis." What it had to do with her pancreas was a mystery. One he didn't care to solve.

"I brought a guest," he said, and glanced back at the woman close behind him. "Mom, this is Lexie Kowalsky." He didn't know which hat was stupider, the fish hat or the cranial cap. "Lexie, this is my mother, Geraldine Brown."

Lexie stepped around him and moved to the recliner. "It's such a pleasure to meet you, Mrs. Brown." She actually took his mother's hand and patted it.

Geraldine turned her head and studied Lexie. "You're not a local girl."

"No. I live in Seattle."

"Well, Sean." She looked from Lexie's face to

97

his. "You didn't tell me that you'd brought . . . a special friend?"

Lexie wasn't a special anything. "Surprise."

"I'll say."

Lexie dropped his mother's hand and Sean was almost certain she recognized the *Gettin' Hitched* bride. Geraldine Brown watched nonstop television, and Lexie was big news. His mother didn't mention anything about the show, and Sean grew suspicious.

"How long have the two of you known each other?"

Lexie looked over her shoulder at him and they answered at the same time.

"For a while" collided in midair with "Not long."

Lexie's eyes widened. "For a while, but sometimes it seems as if we just met," she said, then turned her attention back toward his mother. "Has that ever happened to you?"

"Just once. Sean's father was the love of my life. I felt like I'd known him forever, yet never long enough." She sighed for dramatic effect. "We were soul mates, but he died when Sean was two."

Theodore Knox had been his mother's second husband. She'd gone on to marry once more.

"I'm sorry for your loss."

Geraldine managed a chin quiver. "Thank you."

For God's sake. It had been twenty-five years.

"It's past noon. Are you hungry, Mother?" he asked before she went into her long-winded story of how she'd tried desperately to nurse the love of her life back to good health after a fall from a roof in Prince Rupert. His uncle Abe had always said that his mother had become addicted to the attention she received while caring for her dying husband and had turned into an attention-seeking hypochondriac afterward.

"I'm too nauseous to eat." She reached up and adjusted the Velcro strap beneath her chin. "What do you have in mind?"

"I bought chicken, pasta, apples, bananas, and green vegetables." His mother didn't believe in fresh fruit and vegetables, but Sean was more mindful of what he put in his body. During the season, he consumed five thousand calories a day. He ate a prescribed diet of healthy carbs, lean protein, and fresh fruit and vegetables. He drank two to four liters of water, and the occasional vodka tonic or beer.

"Bread?"

"Multigrain."

His mother's scowl told him exactly how she felt about multigrain anything. "You know multi-grains give me terrible gas and diarrhea."

The last thing he wanted was to discuss her bodily functions. It might be her favorite subject, but he'd rather take a hammer to his skull. "Or I can stick a frozen pizza in the oven for you."

"It has cheese. Cheese is good for me," she argued like a kid, but at least she wasn't studying Lexie's face like she was about to jump up, all excited about the *Gettin' Hitched* bride.

"Fake cheese."

"Hot dog."

"Lips and assholes."

"You know . . ." Lexie said, and put a finger to her chin. "I can probably come up with something better for you, Mrs. Brown. A woman suffering with delicate health, as you do, needs proper nutrition. Not pizza."

He'd been raised on hot dogs, Kraft macaroni and cheese, and frozen pizza. His mother didn't like him or anyone telling her she wasn't eating right. Although it was true, he half expected her to cross her arms over her chest and have a fit.

"I know you're right," she said.

What? It must have been the words "suffering with delicate health" that turned her so compliant. That or the Elasto-Gel had frozen her brain.

"I just ate, but I'd love to make you a good meal. I'm a really good cook," Lexie assured them. "I get it from my mother's side. Along with my talent for fashionable pet apparel." With a slight smile, she turned on the heels of her boots and walked from the room and into the kitchen. He watched her go, his gaze sliding down her back and her long hair, pausing for a moment to appreciate the curve of her waist before stopping

100

at her nice round butt. He didn't know who was crazier, the woman in the cranial cap or the one in the fish hat.

"Sean," his mother said just above a whisper.

He turned his attention to his mother and sat on the end of the sofa beside her chair. "What?"

"Do you know who she is?"

"Certainly."

"She's the *Gettin' Hitched* bride. I was all set to watch the ceremony last night, only she ran away." She pointed at him. "With you."

"Not exactly. We were on the same plane."

"You stole her from Pete!"

"No I didn't."

"You stole the *Gettin' Hitched* bride!"

That's why his mother hadn't mentioned it right away. She thought they were together. Like a couple. "You're wrong. It's not what you're imagining. We met on the plane last night."

She placed a hand on her chest like she was about to have a heart attack. "Hand me the phone. I need to call Hoda and Kathie Lee."

"You don't want to go to Cancun. You don't even have a passport."

"I could get one. Quick, I need to call NBC."

The thought of the world finding out that Lexie was with him, in his mother's house, was frightening. "You can't do that." The sound of pots and pans drew his attention to the kitchen, then back again. While his mother would love that chaos, he would not. "You can't call Hoda and Kathie Lee."

"You're right. Wendy Williams is offering a trip to Disney World in Orlando, Florida." She stuck a finger beneath her cap and scratched her head. "I'd get a passport to go to the Magic Kingdom. I'd love to see that Cinderella's Castle and maybe ride in a riverboat."

"Since when?"

"Since I'd get to talk to Wendy and get a free trip to boot."

He believed her. She'd jump from her chair and claw her way to the nearest airport for a chance to see Wendy and wreak havoc. He didn't want that to happen for several very good reasons. First, the discovery of the *Gettin' Hitched* bride would bring a mass of news crews and hordes of paparazzi to his mother's front door. He could see himself standing between his mother in her cranial cap and Lexie in her fish hat, news camera rolling and cameras flashing, trying to look like the sane one. Second, the thought of his mother sitting on Wendy's couch talking about her latest ailments gave him the same kind of red-faced anxiety as it had as a kid. He'd never known which mother would show up at the hockey games. The relatively normal mother or the one with the battery-powered heating pad, talking about her menstrual cramps. Or worse, the one exaggerating his own sickness, making chicken pox sound like MRSA. He'd been powerless to stop her then. He was an adult now. A hockey player who routinely took hard hits against the boards and returned the favor with a roundhouse punch to the face.

When Sean Knox stepped on the ice, he owned it. He was in control. Off the ice, he owned that, too. He was in control—except when it came to his mother. No one but his uncle Abe had possessed the ability to control his mother. He'd been the only person she'd even listened to, but he'd died two years ago and she was more out of control than ever.

"You can't tell anyone."

She stared hard in his eyes and jabbed a finger at him. "Why do you care? She's not your girlfriend. You said you didn't steal her from Pete." Her gaze narrowed as if she was looking for any reason to call BS. "You just met her last night."

He frowned and his eyeballs pinched. Again he thought of standing between both women wearing stupid hats, strobes flashing and cameras rolling. His entire brain squeezed as he forced himself to say, "Okay. You were right. I stole her from Pete."

"Ha. Wait till I tell Wanda about this!" His mother crowed as she actually rubbed her hands together. "This is so much better than her son marrying Miss Maple Leaf, 2012. She's been lording that over my head for five years now."

Fuck! He didn't know which hurt worse, the pain in his brain or in his eyeballs. God, somehow last night's little ha-ha joke had turned into a full-blown secret. "You can't call anyone. Not Hoda or Wendy or Wanda." His brain. His brain definitely hurt worse. "We can't have that kind of attention on us right now."

"Humph." She crossed her arms, clearly disappointed that she couldn't lord her news over Wanda's head. "What does your coach think about all this? One of his very own hockey players stealing his daughter on national TV?"

How in the hell had this happened? "He doesn't know yet." He wasn't a liar. "Lexie doesn't know yet."

"Lexie doesn't know you stole her from Pete?" She looked at him like *he* was the crazy one in the room. "I'm confused."

She wasn't the only one. "Of course she knows that." He didn't like secrets as much as he didn't like lies. Mostly because he sucked at keeping them all straight, but here he was, smack in the middle of both. "Kowalsky doesn't know Lexie is with me, and Lexie doesn't know I play hockey for the Chinooks." It was always best to go with the truth, and those two things were the truth. "And you can't talk about it."

"Are you okay, son?" She put her hand on his knee. "Did you get hit in the head without your helmet?"

104

It felt like it. Like a butt hit to the forehead.

"You need some Xanax."

Great. His mother was prescribing medication.

"Or maybe I need the Xanax. I'm confused." She reached for a prescription bottle on the TV tray next to her. "How could she not know you play hockey for the Chinooks?"

"She's been out of town filming that stupid show since I was traded." He shrugged. "Maybe because I played for Pittsburgh and she doesn't pay attention to players from other teams. Maybe I look different without my helmet. I don't know for sure, but she doesn't even seem to recognize my name." But even the truth had this whole thing spiraling into chaos. "Kowalsky doesn't like me very much." His mother still looked doubtful, and he added, "Lexie isn't real bright. She has a lot of good qualities, but her attic's a little dusty."

"God compensates special people." His mother smiled like a sudden flush of romance made her all warm inside. "You must really love her."

Sean avoided chaos. He hated shit storms. He was responsible for both. He didn't know quite how it had happened or how to stop it.

"You kidnapped her from Pete and right from under her dad's nose, too."

Kidnap? Love her? From under her dad's nose?

Geraldine sighed. "She must be your soul mate."

Good Lord! *Soul mate?* He tried to speak but couldn't find the words. He didn't know her. He wasn't even sure he liked her. "Yeah. That's it," he lied.

"Then I won't call Wendy or say a word to Wanda." She lifted a pretend key and locked her lips. "For now," she said out of one corner of her mouth. "Even though I'm about to bust."

He wasn't sure she wouldn't bust the moment he turned his back. Not when a chance at the Wendy show and national attention dangled in front of her like a tantalizing illness. "Lexie probably needs help," he managed as he stood. He fought the urge to run. To get the hell out of his mother's crazy house. "Yell if you need anything," he said over his shoulder as he walked from the room. Only he couldn't run from the crazy he'd brought to the house with him.

Lexie stood at the kitchen sink, and if she hadn't looked up and smiled, he might have hopped the ferry to Prince Rupert. From there, he'd catch a flight to Seattle or Pittsburgh. The team was on the road and he'd much rather get a shot to the cup than be anywhere near Sandspit.

The bright sun bounced off the snow outside, cut a blinding trail through the window, and caught in Lexie's hair. The fish hat lay on the counter, and she turned her attention to meat she placed in a hot pan on the stove. "I'm making Asian pork tenderloin I found in the refrigerator.

It'll taste so good, Geraldine won't even know she's eating healthy," she said as she put a lid on the pan. "I'll make simple hoisin and a yummy cucumber salad."

Sean glanced over his shoulder at his mother and the sharp rise in her brow. Despite the invisible lock and key, she needed convincing. He took a cheese grater from Lexie's hand and tossed it on the counter.

"Why did you do that?" She turned toward him and lifted her gaze to his, confusion pulling at her brows.

"This is crazy."

"I know! I need that to shred the cucumber."

He slid his hand around her waist to the small of her back. "If you don't want my mother to call *The Wendy Williams Show* for a chance at her dream vacation, make this look good."

"What?"

"This." He pulled her against his chest and slowly lowered his face to hers. "Kiss me like you mean it, Lexie," he whispered against her mouth.

She sucked in a small breath. "Wendy, too?"

"Wendy, too." He brushed a soft kiss against her lips, teasing a reaction out of her. Her eyes rounded but she didn't push away. Her soft breasts rested against his chest, enflaming his body. He kissed her to save her from Wendy and himself from the chaos his mother always created. That was the only reason, he told himself. Her lush mouth parted, and the ache in the pit of his stomach slid between his legs. He struggled to keep the kiss easy even as he craved more. Even as desire smacked his chest and hit the pit of his stomach like a hot ball of lead. He was in control. In control of the chaotic pull making him hard, belying the soft touch of his mouth to hers. Then her hands slipped up his chest, across his shoulder, to the back of his neck. She combed her fingers through his hair, and a shudder worked through him, running down his spine from the back of his skull to his butt. He was tempted. So damn tempted to slide his tongue into her mouth and his hands to her behind, pull her against his hard dick.

All aboard! Lexie's breast vibrated against his chest. *I, I, I, I* . . .

Sean dropped his hands and took a deep, cleansing breath. Saved at the last second by Ozzy Osbourne.

Chapter 6

• love me tonight

IF YOU DON'T want my mother to call The Wendy Williams Show *for a chance at her dream vacation, make this look good.* That was the reason Sean had given her for the kiss. That was the reason she'd told herself not to push him away, but later in her hotel room that night, Lexie knew that wasn't completely true. She hadn't pushed him away because she'd liked the way his lips felt pressed to hers. Rock-hard lust, constrained with gossamer kisses.

Wearing a towel around her head and one covering her body, Lexie raised Sean's flannel shirt to her face. It smelled of Chanel perfume—left over from the wedding escapade—and woodsy musk, the scent she'd now come to associate with him. She buried her nose in the armpits and determined they didn't stink. She pulled on the panties she'd washed the day before and a new pair of black leggings Jimmy had provided.

When Sean had dropped her off last night, they'd agreed that he'd pick her up at eight A.M. because Geraldine Brown needed to be charmed one more day.

"She likes talking to you," he'd said. Lexie didn't know if that was true or if he wanted Lexie to talk to his mother so he didn't have to. She'd noticed tension in him when he was around Geraldine. A tightness in his jaw that hadn't been there earlier at the Waffle Hut. Either way, she was just happy for something to do other than obsessively watching TV and getting anxiety over the latest *Gettin' Hitched* bride news.

Lexie was a natural-born charmer—a talent she'd inherited from her mother's side—but it hadn't been difficult to schmooze Geraldine. She mostly just had to listen to the woman's many complaints and ailments and say "Bless you" at the appropriate times. As a kid, Lexie had been a hypochondriac and could easily spot one in a crowd. She hadn't had to use her natural ability with Geraldine. The ridiculous cap had been an easy giveaway.

She dried her hair, then lightly applied mascara to the tips of her eyelashes. She loved her mink extensions and felt more presentable after a few swipes of mascara. Just because she was on the run didn't mean she had to go completely tree hugger.

Once more she shoved her phone, folded cash, and Chap Stick in her corset. Minus a purse or pockets, her bra was the best place to stash necessities. At the age of fifteen, she got her first D bra and discovered that her cleavage could be useful. Now a triple D, the sides of her bras were higher and she could easily stash essentials without too much trouble. The corset she'd put on two days ago was more decorative than functional. The underwire dug into her flesh, but it did have a wide bridge that kept her phone from falling out.

At exactly eight, Sean pulled up in the Subaru and they headed to his mother's. He hadn't shaved, and the dark scruff covering the lower half of his face made him appear perfectly sinister. The kind of sinister that cheated death and seduced virgins.

Gloomy clouds hung just above the pine trees, matching the equally gloomy scowl creasing his forehead. Most of the way there, his big hands gripped the steering wheel as if it had done something offensive. He hardly spoke, leaving long lapses of silence that Lexie felt compelled to fill. She told him about Yum Yum and her problems with her knees and the humidity. She talked about the conversation she'd had with her dad earlier.

"The team's in Pittsburgh tonight," she said. "My dad hates the Penguins."

Sean finally spoke. "Why?" He'd managed to muster one word.

"He blames Jaromir Jagr for all the hair gel in the NHL." She looked across the car, into the gloomy shadows of his gloomy face. "He had to trade two Chinooks for one Penguin, and he told me he doesn't think the guy is worth his contract."

"Asshole."

Calling the Chinooks' newest sniper an asshole was extreme, but some fans *were* extreme. "Are you going to be grumpy all day?"

Without taking his eyes from the road, he said, "Probably."

Lexie gave up, and neither spoke the rest of the way.

Geraldine sat in the same spot as the day before. The cooling cap no longer covered her short dark hair, but the same eyesore afghan covered her. In Lexie's experience, women who crocheted that many unnatural colors together were generally crazy. That or blind.

Eggs and ham, spinach, and flaxseed bread waited for Lexie in the kitchen. She got to work making a healthy crustless quiche, and toasted the grainy bread. They all ate on faux-wood TV trays straight out of the sixties.

"I can't wait to see if anyone called in about that trip to Cancun," Geraldine said between bites. "Or if Wendy—"

"This is really good, Lexie," Sean interrupted. "We're grateful." He looked up and took a drink of coffee. "Isn't that right, Mother."

"Beats cornflakes."

Lexie didn't know if that was a compliment or not. "Thank you."

After breakfast, Sean pulled on jogging pants and a Nike sweatshirt before he ran out the door, leaving Lexie to entertain his mother. First up on Geraldine's list of morning programming:

1. The *Today* show.
   a. Hoda and Kathie Lee.
2. *Santa Diabla*.

"I don't speak much Spanish," Geraldine confessed, glued to the telenovela. "But Humberto is so handsome and romantic."

The show opened with a woman crying, the dramatic sound of a beating hcart in the background, and Lexie knew it was official now. She was being punished for:

1. Flunking Spanish class.
   a. Not a fan of *rajas poblanos*.
2. The misunderstanding with the Mexican *policía* in 2010.
   a. The dog had looked homeless. She hadn't tried to steal it.

Blessedly, the telenovela was only a half hour. Next up on Geraldine's watch list, *Wendy Williams*.

"How you doin'?" Wendy asked, wearing a tight white dress and fingertip veil. "Let's head on over to Hot Topics." She walked across the stage in white stilettos and arranged herself in a lavender velvet chair. "You know my staff loves a theme," she said through a deep chuckle and arranged the veil about her shoulders.

"I bet you're up first in Hot Topics," Geraldine said, the telephone just inches from her fingers.

"I appreciate you keeping me a secret for a few days." Out of the corners of her eyes, Lexie watched the older woman's hand.

"Let's get to it," Wendy said as Lexie's publicity picture from *Gettin' Hitched* appeared on the screen behind Wendy.

"I was right!" Geraldine crowed.

"It's been a day and a half since Lexie Kowalsky—you know, the *Gettin' Hitched* bride—ditched her wedding to poor Pete Dalton. I've been told by someone on the set"—she lowered her voice for effect—"they'd planned a big fancy reception at the Fairmont Hotel in Seattle. They were serving prime rib and roasted potatoes infused with rosemary." She laughed. "You know I love prime rib. Red in the middle with horseradish. Yum!" She went on to name the rest of the menu Lexie and Pete had picked out for their wedding dinner. "Now, I also heard she's probably hiding out in the UK at the Manchester Dog Show. You know how much she loves dogs. That's where I'd be. You know I love my Shaq." A picture of a dog replaced Lexie, and the audience gave a collective "ah." "If anyone sees the runaway *Gettin' Hitched* bride, call me." Wendy pointed to a pink phone on the table beside her as she went on to describe the all-inclusive trip to Disney World.

Lexie's stomach twisted into a knot, waiting—waiting for Wendy's phone to ring. Had she been spotted? Would someone call in? Did anyone know where she was hiding, beyond the woman in the recliner beside her?

"With all the people in the world looking for you, you're right here in my living room."

Lexie waited for Geraldine's hand to move. So much as a twitch and she was going to tackle the older woman. "I know how much you want that vacation. When this all blows over, I'll send you to Disney World."

"No, thank you. It's not the same as winnin' it." Geraldine turned and looked at Lexie. "I told Sean I'd keep your secret." She picked up an imaginary key and locked her lips. "I'm not telling a soul," she said from one corner of her mouth.

Halfway through *Wendy*, Lexie called her mother and learned that her agent was trying to get ahold of her. *People, Us Weekly, OK,* and *Star* magazines wanted exclusives, while TMZ and the *National Enquirer* had staff looking everywhere for her.

"Are you safe, honey?" her mother asked. Lexie looked across her shoulder at Geraldine and could not give her mother a reassuring answer. "That's all I care about right now."

The back door of the house opened, drawing Lexie's attention to the kitchen. She heard the creak of Sean's footsteps seconds before he walked through patches of deep shadow and bright sunlight toward her. "Yes," she told her mother without stopping to think about it. "I am." For some reason, she felt safe with a man she didn't even know. A man she was pretty sure didn't even like her very much. "I'll call you when I get home tomorrow," she said, and hung up the phone.

He stopped in the doorway and raised his hands up and behind him, grabbing fistfuls of his sweatshirt. As he pulled the sweatshirt over his head, a white T-shirt beneath rose up his hard stomach and ripped abs. The end of the T-shirt stopped at mid-chest, hovering for several drool-worthy seconds before sliding back down to the waistband of his jogging pants. He used the sweatshirt to dry his hair, wet from sweat and chilled dew hanging in the air. He looked from one woman to the next. "What's going on?"

"Ah." Lexie had to remove her tongue from the roof of her mouth. "Nothing."

"No one's called Wendy for that vacation."

"I'll be upstairs."

Doing what? Lexie wondered. Her answer came shortly with the unmistakable bump and clang of a weight machine.

"He must lift every day," Lexie said, more to herself than to anyone else in the room.

"He has to keep fit for his job."

"What job?" She removed her gaze from the doorway and looked at Geraldine. "He's never told me what he does for a living."

"Oh." Geraldine's eyes rounded. "Commercial fisherman."

That didn't sound right. "He said he doesn't fish?"

"Oh."

"What?" Lexie said through a laugh. "Is it a secret?"

"Yeah." Geraldine nodded. "So secret we can't talk about it."

Which of course made Lexie super curious. "Does he work for the government?"

"If I told ya, I'd have to kill ya." Geraldine laughed like she was real funny. Evidently Geraldine meant it, too. Above the sound of Wendy's last segment, Geraldine talked about everything but Sean. She recited a lifetime of her misery. With every "Bless you" or "I'm so sorry" Lexie uttered in commiseration, the older woman elaborated and exaggerated her suffering.

I'm being punished, Lexie thought. Punished for:

1. Running out on her wedding.
2. Cowardly hiding out.

3. Having bad thoughts.
   a. Masking tape.
4. Geraldine's mouth.

Finally, at noon, she left her spot on the couch and made lunch. She whipped up chicken salad sandwiches, complete with grapes, walnuts, and cranberries. She garnished the plates with radish roses. Geraldine loved the garnish, hated the multigrain bread, and ate it all despite that.

Lexie didn't wait around to chat with Geraldine. Instead she stuffed several paper napkins in the breast pocket of the shirt Sean had loaned her, loaded up a plate, and walked up the stairs next to the back door. The top floor was mostly one big room filled with exercise equipment and a hallway with several closed doors near the back. Lexie's footsteps faltered, and she almost dropped the plate as her eyes came to a skidding halt on a sweaty, half-naked Sean doing crunches on an exercise ball. An Edmonton Oilers hat covered his head, and he'd changed into a pair of red gym shorts and CrossFit shoes, but her eyeballs weren't stuck on his shoes. They were glued to his bare chest and the sweaty glow covering his bare skin. A bead of sweat dripped from the dark hair in the hollow of his armpits to the exercise ball. Normally, all that sweat would have grossed her out, but he wasn't a normal guy.

"I made lunch," she said, and made her way

across his line of vision to a workout bench.

She took a seat and placed the plate beside her. When she looked over at him, he was sitting on the ball, knees shoulder width apart, just looking back at her blankly. That's when she noticed he was wearing earbuds.

"I made lunch," she repeated herself. She tried not to stare as he rose and walked toward her, all hard muscles and sculpted abs. A bead of perspiration ran down the center of his chest to wet the happy trail circling his navel and disappearing beneath his waistband.

"Thanks." He grabbed a towel from a weight machine and dried his face and chest. "You can go back downstairs if you want."

For some reason, that sounded like he wanted to get rid of her, but she wasn't ready to leave. "I'm good." He stopped in front of her, and her eyes just naturally landed on his happy trail dipping south. She felt her cheeks warm as she lifted her gaze up his flat belly and the defined muscles of his chest. She looked past his square chin and into his deep green eyes looking right back at her. She felt like a perv, but where was she supposed to look? "I just need a few moments of sanity before I go back down," she said. "I need a short break from hearing the details of your mother's near-death experiences," she said.

One side of his mouth twisted upward in an uneven smile as he tossed the towel aside and sat on the other end of the bench. He picked up half a sandwich and took two huge bites.

"Hungry?"

He smiled as he chewed and pointed to the other sandwiches.

"No thank you." She'd snacked as she'd made lunch, but mostly she wasn't hungry after listening to Geraldine's bowel movement disorder. "The description of your mother's skin lesions and bloody stools made me lose my appetite."

His smile fell and he reached for a big bottle of BioSteel on the floor. His green eyes got a little squinty at the corners, like maybe she'd insulted his mother.

"Not that she isn't a lovely woman."

He swallowed almost the entire bottle before he lowered it. "She's a hypochondriac."

Even though several feet separated them, Lexie felt the heat of him rolling off in waves. It surrounded and pressed in on her. Overpowering her senses like a blowtorch to the face, and she liked it.

"Growing up, I was a hypochondriac," she said into the uncomfortable silence. She reached into her breast pocket and pulled out the paper napkins and put them next to the plate. "Band-Aids were my addiction, and I loved the pain relievers my mother kept on hand for me. It wasn't until I was about ten that I discovered the pain relievers were actually white Smarties." He grabbed another sandwich and a BioSteel from the pack on the floor by his foot. "I know you're probably thinking that I should have figured out that the medicinal Smarties where just like *all* Smarties, but I didn't figure it out until I was ten." She glanced up at the A-frame ceiling painted a bright white. "I don't know why it took me so long to figure it out."

He popped the top off his sports drink and sucked down half the bottle. "White Smarties taste like orange cream."

She lowered her gaze to his. "And yellow like pineapple." She looked into his green eyes. "Most people think all Smarties taste the same."

"I know my Smarties."

She raised a brow. "Did you line them up according to color?"

"Of course."

"We're Smarties connoisseurs." She laughed and shook her head. "In the same room."

He smiled and pulled his hat from his head. A lock of damp hair escaped and curled over his forehead, touching his brow like a big C. "What are the chances?" He combed it back with his fingers, taking his time adjusting his cap as if getting it just right on his head. "I ran into town earlier, and your picture is on a bunch of newspapers. I'm surprised no one has spotted you."

"I'm surprised your mother hasn't turned me in." She wanted to ask if he was a spy, or at least worked for the Canadian equivalent of the CIA. "This whole thing has gotten way out of control." She watched him reach for another sandwich and added, "It seems like it started out small, but every day it just snowballs bigger." He handed her a bottle of BioSteel. "Thanks." She took a sip of the sports drink that reminded her of Gatorade. "I don't know how I got here or what to do about it."

"I know the feeling." He swallowed, drawing her attention to the muscles stacked around the hollow of his throat. "Shit can go sideways real fast."

She wondered if that was a military term and fought the urge to look lower as the words "devil's playground" slid across her brain like a serpent's tongue. She purposely raised her gaze up his face to his sweaty hat. "Are you an Oilers fan?"

"We used to live in Edmonton." He glanced at her, then pointed at the plate. "Are you sure you don't want to eat?"

"I'm sure."

He reached for another sandwich. "Can't hardly live in Alberta without being an Oilers fan."

"My dad played for the Oilers. Of course, that was before I was born." She stood and moved away from the devil's playground to a cable weight machine in the middle of the room. The pins in the dual weight stacks were set at three hundred. "Hockey players get traded a lot, but my dad played in Seattle until he retired after ten seasons. My mother wishes he'd stop coaching and retire completely."

He took the napkin from the bench and wiped his mouth. "Why?"

"Hockey teams are on the road a lot." Wasn't there something about the devil's workshop, too?

"Yeah?"

"Yeah." She reached into her shirt and pulled out her Chap Stick to cover her suddenly dry lips. She hadn't been to First Baptist for a while, but she was pretty sure she'd been warned to stay away from both. "He gets cranky and jet-lagged, and Mom thinks he's getting too old to keep up such a hectic pace. She wants him to stay home and help hang wallpaper, but I doubt that will happen."

The one-sided smile she recognized tugged at the corner of his mouth and was followed by an unexpected chuckle.

"Every time he comes home from the road, he complains more and more about old injuries." She liked his laugh. It was deep and honest and slid down her spine. "But I'd much rather hear him complain about old injuries than grumble about some of the players." She took the top off the Chap Stick and smeared her lips. Hadn't there also been something about devil's tools? "Those rants can last a long time."

"What does he rant about?" He stood and moved toward her.

"Everything." He hooked an arm over the top of the weight machine and looked down into her eyes. He was close and half naked, and against her will, she responded to the phero-mones attacking her senses. She should move. Run away. "If he thinks a guy's taking a dive." The serpent's tongue whispered, *Maybe later.*

His hand rose from the machine and he pushed her hair from her temple. "What else?"

The slight touch scattered warm tingles down the side of her neck and across her chest. Earlier, he'd made her feel safe, and now he made her feel tingles. Maybe it was stress. Only she felt relaxed. Maybe it was the devil in her head. Only that voice sounded a lot like her own.

"What else?" His finger slid down the side of her face to her jaw.

Maybe it was Stockholm syndrome. Only she hadn't been kidnapped. "What?"

"What else does your dad get grouchy about?"

"Oh." She took a deep breath and let it out, hoping to clear her head, but not having much luck with his touch on the side of her face. "He gets really grouchy if he thinks some guy cares more about his hair than scoring goals."

He dropped his hand.

"He thinks a guy's hair shouldn't flow beneath his helmet," she explained, and took a step backward. "When I talked to him yesterday, he wasn't happy with the team's new sniper. I guess the guy needed some time off to deep-condition his flow." The little tingles began to dissipate and she said through a relieved laugh, "Dad said he's a nancy-pants."

"A what?" One dark brow rose up his forehead. "What's that?"

"Nancy-pants is a . . . a . . ." She tried to think of a word, other than the one the guys on the team used.

"Pussy?"

That was the word, all right.

"Your dad thinks this guy is a pussy?"

She probably wouldn't go that far.

A deep furrow creased his forehead, and he moved across the room to a hook with his white T-shirt on it. "Because of his hair?"

"There are probably other reasons." She was slightly relieved when he pulled the shirt over his head. "Maybe he's not worth his big salary? Or isn't a team player and gives the veterans on the team attitude. Dad says he's a showboat and rides his stick across the ice."

"Maybe your dad doesn't know what he's talking about."

That sounded oddly belligerent. "Are you a Chinooks fan?" But nothing she hadn't encountered before. Hockey fans could be fiercely loyal to their favorite players.

"The jury is still out on that." A deep scowl creased his forehead as he moved to the bench and reached for his sports drink.

"Are you mad at me?"

"You?" He shook his head and tossed a BioSteel at her. "Your father's wrong, though."

She caught it with one hand and moved toward him. "My dad's a good judge of character. The guy probably has other issues."

"Probably." His gaze swept across her face, and the corners of his mouth turned up into a slight smile. "Probably has issues, and one of those snowballs you were talking about is giving him a big problem."

"What problem?" His fingers touched her face, and she fought the urge to turn her cheek into his hand.

"This." He lowered his mouth to hers and said against her lips, "You."

Lexie had the feeling they weren't talking about a hockey player anymore. She slid her hands up his T-shirt and rose to the balls of her feet. Through the material, his skin felt hot beneath her palms, and his heart boomed in his chest. "I'm not your problem." She touched the tip of her tongue to his top lip, and his breath whooshed from his lungs.

He chuckled and slid his hand to the back of

her head, tangling his fingers in her hair before he said, "You're chaos." He tilted her face up, and her mouth parted even further. Then he softly sucked her bottom lip, and she felt it, too. The kiss a stark contradiction to the hot rush flowing across her chest, spreading fire and creating chaos. Lexie took a step back before she gave in to it. One of the last things she needed was added mayhem in her life. Not even if that mayhem had solid muscles and sexy green eyes.

SEAN PULLED THE Subaru to a stop at the Harbor Inn and walked Lexie to her room. They moved through pools of light as a chilly ocean breeze caught her hair and brushed it across her cheek.

"I guess I'll see you in the morning," she said, and for some reason felt a bit panicky. Which of course was silly. She'd known him for only two days. "Bright and early." She stopped in front of room seven and looked up into his face. She didn't know Sean. She probably would never see him again after tomorrow. "I'm looking forward to going home, but not to the *Gettin' Hitched* madness."

The light above the door shone down on them; his lashes cast a faint shadow as he returned her gaze. "You're tough. You survived my mother." The tips of his fingers brushed her neck as he pulled the ends of Jimmy's collar under

127

her throat. "I think she may have even liked you."

"What about you?"

"Do I like you?" One side of his mouth lifted, and the same breeze that tossed her hair about her head brought his scent to her nose, and she breathed him in. Funny that she'd known him for such a short time but she recognized the smell of his skin. Funnier still, it calmed her when she didn't know she was nervous.

"You're a pain in the ass." His silent laughter and obvious amusement creased the corners of his green eyes.

She leaned back against the door. He calmed her. Everything about him felt safe, stable in a world that had become so uncertain. "Well, you won't see me after tomorrow." He didn't correct her and she looked away, into the dark parking lot. "I won't be a big pain in your ass anymore." He placed his fingers on her cheek and turned her face to him.

"I didn't say you were a *big* pain in the ass." His fingers touched the side of her jaw and raised her face to his. "I guess you're okay."

"I'm glad you think I'm okay." She meant it to come out a little sarcastic; instead she sounded a little breathy.

"For a runaway bride."

"I guess you're okay for a guy who had me babysit his mother for two days."

He brushed his thumb across her bottom lip and smiled. "Did you have somewhere else you needed to be?"

She kissed his thumb, then put her hands on his big arms. "Acapulco." She swayed into him, and her breasts pressed into his chest. Her palms slid to his shoulders, and she rose onto the balls of her feet. "I'm supposed to be on my honeymoon in Acapulco."

As he had the day before, he dropped a soft kiss on her mouth. "With a guy you don't know."

She didn't know him, either. Only two short days, but after his mouth came back for a third kiss, she wasn't counting anymore.

His tongue touched hers and swept into her mouth, hot and intense and curling her toes into her boots. A deep, satisfied "uuh" came from his chest, and she combed her fingers into his hair. He liked it, and the "uuh" turned into a deep groan. The kiss caught fire and she clung to him, the only stable thing in a world gone out of control. She slid her hands down his sides and back until he captured her wrists. Without breaking the kiss, he pinned them to the door above her head, and something deep and primitive within her responded to the force of his restraint. She moaned deep in her throat as desire twisted and knotted her stomach.

"This is the time to tell me to leave."

"Do you want to leave?" She licked her lips.

"No."

She didn't want him to leave, either.

1. She didn't want to be alone with her own thoughts.
2. She felt safe with him.
3. She liked the way he kissed her.

"Do you want to come inside for a drink?" she asked.

"What do you have?"

"Ginger ale."

Silence stretched between them and she thought he might resist the temptation of ginger ale and her. They both knew if he went inside her room, they would end up naked. Which was a bad idea.

1. She didn't know him.
   a. He could be a killer.
2. It was impulsive, and following her impulses was bad.
   a. Standing in Sandspit with a man she didn't know.
3. Kind of promiscuous.
   a. She liked to have feelings for a man first.

"Where is the key card?" he asked.

"Next to my phone." Or ending up naked could be good:

1. She didn't know him.
   a. Would never see him again.
2. Impulsive.
   a. Would never see him again.
3. Promiscuous.
   a. Who cares!

"I'll just get that for you." The desire in his gaze turned even hotter. He wanted to be with her as badly as she wanted to be with him. It was crazy but felt perfectly sane.

"I'm a helpful guy." He held her wrists with one hand and lowered the other to dip inside the bomber jacket. Easily, he unbuttoned the shirt. He parted the fabric, and the cold breeze swept across her breasts and hardened her nipples. His lids lowered a sleepy fraction, and he pulled a breath deep into his lungs. "Where could it be," he asked, and brushed her skin along the edge of her corset.

"Do you want a hint?"

"No." He pulled the phone from her cleavage and stuck it in his back pocket. "I'll find it for you."

"Because you're a helpful guy?"

He shook his head and slid his fingers between her breasts. "Because I'm a guy who is dying to get you out of that bra." He pulled out the plastic card and let go of her wrists to unlock the door. "If you invite me in, that's what I'm going to do."

Now was the time to say no. To herself and to him. That would be the smart thing to do, but she didn't want to do the smart thing. She didn't want to go inside the small hotel room where nothing waited for her but her own thoughts of the past few days. "Do you have a condom?"

"Yes."

She pushed the door open and stepped inside. "Come in, Sean," she said, and he followed her inside. Except for the light from the parking lot slicing through a crack in the curtains, the room was completely dark.

"Come here, Lexie."

"I thought you wanted ginger ale."

"I hate ginger ale."

She took a step toward the sound of his voice as the bomber jacket fell from her arms. Within the blackness, he tangled his fingers in her hair and pulled her head back. He kissed her parted lips like a man who knew what he wanted and was going after it. His tongue slid inside and withdrew with hot, insistent strokes. He created a luscious suction, and his hand moved through her hair and down her back, drawing her close until the hard bulge of his erection pressed into her stomach and the tingling knots in her belly slid between her legs. She pushed her pelvis against the bulge, and within seconds his hands were everywhere, touching her all over. They pulled at each other's clothes until they were naked and Sean's hands were on her breasts, her hard nipples pressed into his palms.

"Ahh . . . baby," he said, his voice a low gravel before his mouth found hers once more.

It was crazy and hot, like nothing she'd ever experienced before. Two people giving in to a purely physical need. An overwhelming need for sex and nothing else. There was no need to talk about it. No need to define it.

His hand moved down her left thigh and he lifted her leg to his waist. The long, hard length of his erection slid against her, and when he spoke his voice hovered in the darkness. "You feel so good, Lexie."

Tiny slivers of pleasure tickled her nerve endings, mingled with the blood coursing through her veins. He thrust against her, both hands gripping her behind. He was right. It did feel good, but not as good as it could feel. She wrapped her arms around his neck and whispered, "Take me to bed." She lowered her leg from his waist.

Sean hit the switch on the wall. Blinding light jabbed Lexie's eyes and she buried her face in his neck.

"Sorry," he said as he walked her backward. "I didn't know where the bed was."

He pushed her down on the bed and followed. "And I want to see you." His gaze followed his hand to her waist and hip and back up to her breasts. He touched her nipple with the tips of his fingers, then lowered his face and sucked her into his mouth. His cheeks drew inward and he moved his hand down her stomach and between her thighs. She moaned and ran her fingers through his hair. The pleasure so delicious, the heat of his mouth so exquisite, her back arched against his wet mouth and hand. He kissed her breast, and his short breaths heated her already hot skin. Then he was on his knees between her thighs. Cool air brushed across her nipples. He reached into his back pants pocket and pulled a condom from his wallet.

There had been a time in Lexie's life when she'd thought that a man with a condom in his wallet was presumptuous. She was close to thirty, and was just awful glad he'd come prepared.

He stuck one edge of the black package between his teeth and ripped it open. Then his eyes sought hers as he wrapped one hand around his hard shaft and rolled the condom down his engorged flesh.

"You're a beautiful woman, Lexie." His eyes were sleepy with lust as he knelt between her knees and planted one hand next to her head. "Everything about you is sexy as hell." Then he thrust into her and she couldn't help her deep sigh of pleasure. He rested his weight on his forearm, and his other hand grabbed her thigh. She felt him everywhere, his body covering hers as he moved within her, touching and stroking the exact place where her pleasure was centered, in and out, driving her wild. Withdrawing slowly and plunging deep. And with each stroke, he pushed her toward climax. She slid her hands down the contours of his back to the hard cheeks of his behind. Beneath her palms, his muscles flexed with the motion of his slow, thrusting hips.

"Yes. Right there. Yeess," she whispered against his mouth, moving with him as he pumped harder, deeper, faster. Heat and desire, flushing her skin and tangling her nerves into hot, twisted knots. "Sean? Oh my God."

"Talk to me." His hot breath touched her face and she sucked him in like oxygen.

She opened her mouth but the words spinning around in her head were embarrassing, unlady-like, and best left unsaid.

"You feel so hot around me." Sean didn't seem to have trouble expressing himself as he drove into her, pushing her harder. "Tight and wet and good."

Orgasm gripped her insides with pleasure. It ripped through her, again and again, as Sean's climax tore a deep, primal groan from his chest. "Lexie," he said on a harsh exhale as her body pulsed around him. His deep, relentless thrusts pushed her to more intense pleasure. "Do you want more of this, Lexie?"

"Yes." She couldn't think past the second

orgasm setting her on fire. And then she did. She opened her mouth and swore like a hockey player. A natural ability she'd inherited from her father's side.

Chapter 7

• love & lust #neverconfusethetwo

S EAN RAISED A to-go cup and swallowed the last cold dregs of his Starbucks. He glanced at his watch, then tossed his duffel on one of two twin berths inside the private cabin of the *Northern Adventure*. Earlier, he'd scrambled to book passage aboard the ten-thousand-ton ferry and had to bust his ass to board before the boat left on its daily route across the Hecate Strait.

The last time he'd seen Lexie, she'd been wrapped up in hotel sheets with drowsy eyes and a satisfied smile. The last time he'd talked to her, he'd told her he'd pick her up in the morning on his way to the dock. Where Jimmy and the *Sea Hopper* would be waiting to take them home.

It was cold inside the cabin but not enough to see his breath. He set the cup on the nightstand between the beds, then pulled his Oilers ball cap from his head and tossed it next to the empty cup. Eight fucking hours. He had eight hours to kill until the ferry docked in Prince Rupert. If the ferry docked on time, and if everything went according to plan, he'd have enough time to catch his flight to Vancouver. In Vancouver, he had a four-hour delay before his final flight to Seattle.

Fourteen fucking hours. Instead of the three-hour trip aboard the *Sea Hopper*, it was going to take him all damn day to get home. He had Jimmy Pagnotta to thank for the abrupt change to his travel plans. The pilot had called him just before Sean had stepped into the shower at his mother's house. "I'm at the dock in Seattle. Just about to take off. The press is camped out in the office down here," he warned. "Just thought you should know."

Yeah, swarming press was something he wanted to know about. Especially when it involved a certain runaway bride with the last name Kowalsky. Jimmy hadn't come right out and admitted that he had something to do with tipping off the media, but only a few people knew where Lexie was hiding out and when she would return. One of those was the *Gettin' Hitched* bride herself. Of course her parents knew, but they would never leak information about their daughter. There was the crazy MINI Cooper driver, but he doubted someone who had gone to so much trouble to help Lexie would rat her out. He hadn't tipped off anyone, and while he could never completely vouch for his mother, he could almost guarantee that she wouldn't call anyone until he was off the island.

Sean threw his coat on the spare berth, then sat on the edge of the bed. He wore the same pullover and thermal sweats of the day before, and he bent over and tied his cross trainers. He didn't need the hassle of the world knowing he'd spent the last two days with the *Gettin' Hitched* bride. He'd always avoided that kind of gossipy attention, and he for damn sure didn't want questions fired at him like a line of pucks on the centerline. Especially fired at him from her father.

He and the coach tolerated each other. He respected John's legendary career, and Kowalsky respected Sean's legendary talent. Until Lexie had told him that John thought he was a nancy-pants with a girly flow, he'd thought they'd come to some mutual understanding. Found common ground and were . . . he didn't know. "Friends" would be stretching it.

Sean turned up the thermostat and crawled between the sheets wearing his clothes. He'd slept very little the past few days, and last night not at all. Being around his mother always brought back memories he wished like hell he could forget, but they rushed him at night when the rest of the world grew still. There was no turning them off, no stillness. Just his brain bouncing from one random memory to the next, bringing the same knot of anxiety he'd felt as a kid.

Until the age of ten when he and his mother had moved from Sandspit to live with Uncle

Abe, he hadn't known how other people lived. He'd had some idea, of course, that other kids' mothers weren't sick all the time. Once he'd started school and made a few friends, he'd noticed how different his life was, and that other mothers weren't living "on borrowed time," only to have miraculous recoveries. Geraldine had experienced so many miracles, Sean had lost count.

Until the age of ten, he'd lived in fear of waking up and finding his mother dead. He'd lain awake at night wondering what would happen to him and where he would live once she died, but that wasn't the worst of it. The worst were the times she was actually okay. When the crazy roller-coaster ride stopped. Those spaces in time when she'd cook meals, wash clothes, and take long walks with him. When they'd talk about his dad or his school or how many years it would take for him to walk to the moon. It was those times that he loved her so deeply his heart hurt with joy. It was those times that he felt safe and secure. It was those times that made him hate her for tricking him again. Those times gave him hope. This time, this time things would be different. Then she inevitably snatched the good times away, crushing his hopes and pulling him on her chaos roller coaster again.

That all changed when they moved to Edmonton and he could just be a kid. His uncle provided the stability that he'd never had, and he'd introduced him to hockey. The first time he'd strapped on a pair of his uncle's old skates, he'd been hooked. Like a lot of Canadian boys, he'd played shinny hockey in backyard rinks and frozen ponds. He'd played peewee and midget and, at the age of sixteen, been big enough and had the skills to play in the major junior league for three years before he'd been picked up by Calgary in the second round of the NHL drafts. He'd lived in Calgary, Detroit, Pittsburgh, and now Seattle. He'd spent most of the past nine years in hotel rooms and arenas. It was often hectic and high-energy but never chaotic.

That's the way he liked it. He kept thousands of miles between himself and chaos, thousands of miles between himself and drama.

Until now.

Sean rolled onto his back and stuffed one hand beneath his pillow. This time drama would arrive several hours ahead of him. Drama in the form of a tall blonde with a smoking smile and hot body. Lexie was a walking fantasy. A tall, thin fantasy with soft bouncy parts when she walked. Or ran. Or rode him like the queen of the Calgary Stampede.

His free hand slid beneath the quilt and he adjusted himself through his pants. Having sex with Lexie hadn't been part of his plan. Of

141

course, her jumping aboard the *Sea Hopper* hadn't been in the plan, either. A whirl of white satin, sparkly shoes, and chaos, it hadn't been in his plan to undress her and brush her soft skin with the tips of his fingers. Sean was used to changing it up on the fly. He could read a play seconds before it happened in front of him and make adjustments. He saw patterns and stayed one step ahead, anticipating his next move.

He never saw Lexie coming. He hadn't misread the fear and apprehension in her blue eyes. He saw the vulnerable quiver at the corner of her full mouth, but he'd failed to adjust or anticipate the touch of her hands or the taste of her lips. He hadn't stayed one step ahead of her drama, and his next move had been a mistake. A big mistake that had landed him in bed at the Harbor Inn. A bad mistake that had felt so good. So good, if he'd had more condoms, he would have repeated the mistake a few more times. He'd tried to draw out the pleasure for as long as possible, running his hands over the soft skin of her belly and between her thighs. She'd been so responsive he hadn't had to guess where to touch her to hear her moan, or where to put his mouth to make her arch her back and whisper his name in a lusty breath. He hadn't had to wonder what she'd felt as he'd slid into her hot body. She moaned and writhed and had so many orgasms he'd lost count. Drawing him in even more with each pulse and squeeze of her body. Just as he finally let himself join her, she'd yelled at him to keep hitting her sweet spot and he'd been all too happy to oblige. She'd told him he was good, great, wonderful, then she'd called him a cement head, of all things.

Sean frowned. He wasn't a cement head. He played smart hockey. Everyone knew that. He knew the right position at the right time, and he knew the right thing to do with a puck in any situation.

He wasn't a cement head, but it was like Lexie had hit him with a brick. While he'd like to blame her for last night, he wasn't that big an asshole. He'd walked into that hotel room last night knowing it wasn't right. Not in the least. He should have told her that he was the nancy-pants her dad bitched about before she got naked with him. She should have been informed before she'd made that decision.

He still wasn't quite sure how the secret—which was more of an omission—had snowballed into an avalanche. Each time he'd meant to tell her, the timing hadn't seemed right. Not the first night, the second, or the third. When he'd left her asleep in the hotel room this morning, he'd decided to tell her on the long plane ride back to Seattle.

Now here he was on a ferry in the Hecate Strait, and she was headed home by now on the *Sea Hopper*. He hadn't returned to the hotel this morning as he'd planned, and he didn't feel good about that. She'd deserved better, and once he was home, he'd find her and apologize. No excuses. No distractions. No putting it off until the right moment. She was a nice woman. Once he'd looked past the pretty face, big boobs, and *Gettin' Hitched* bride fiasco, she was a smart girl. Not just because she had an apparently successful *dog clothes* business, but because she had the ability to walk into a room, size up a woman under an afghan eyesore and stupid gel cap, and know exactly how to handle her. Lexie had said it was an inherited talent. Uncle Abe'd had that talent, too. If it was something that really was inherited, it clearly skipped a generation with Sean.

Sean thought about Lexie and Jimmy chatting via the headset. He wondered how long before the topic of him came up and she learned exactly who Sean was. He imagined she'd get real angry. She'd probably hate him. He didn't blame her.

He was a fucking asshole.

Sean stacked his hands behind his head and stared up at a water spot on the white ceiling. He wondered what John Kowalsky would think when he learned that Sean had spent time with Lexie in Sandspit. The coach would learn about it whether he or Lexie told him, and it wasn't like Sean had really kidnapped Lexie from her wedding. They just ended up on the same seaplane. John should probably thank him for helping his little girl. Sean just hoped like hell the coach never learned he helped her out of her clothes—twice.

John would have a lot to say when he found out Sean had stripped his little girl naked. If Sean had anything to say about it, John Kowalsky would never find out, but he didn't have anything to say about it. When and where and how the news got delivered was up to Lexie, and Sean hated that he had no control over the situation. All he could do was wait for the axe to fall.

Ten miles into the Hecate Strait, the gentle roll of the waves rocked him into a deep sleep and he awoke as the ferry docked in the port of Prince Rupert. Rain hit the starboard porthole as Sean shoved his feet into his shoes and laced them up. He grabbed his coat, duffel, and ball cap, and made his way down the hall to the exit. He'd been born in Prince Rupert but didn't recall living there. As a very young child, he and his mother had moved to Sandspit with Ed Brown. He didn't recall much of Ed Brown, either. Other than that after his mother divorced Ed, she'd immediately caught the bird flu.

Fat drops of rain hit Sean's face and he pulled the hood of his coat over his head. Vehicles drove from the open hull as he moved down the gangplank toward the terminal. Before he'd left Sandspit, he'd been given the number of a taxi service, and he pulled out his phone. Within fifteen minutes, he was on his way to the airport on Digby Island. Forty minutes later, he relaxed in a third-row seat on the double-prop airplane. Well, "relaxed" might be a stretch. There was no relaxing in the cramped seat, and he slid one of his long legs on the aisle side of the seat in front of him. "Loosening up" might be a better phrase. The more miles he put between him and his mother, the more he felt himself unwind. He could honestly say he loved his mother. He did, but he couldn't be around her for long before she drained him like a cheap flashlight. While his energy faded, she didn't seem to notice. Or if she did, it never bothered her. She'd never taken responsibility for anything, and the older Sean got, the colder his feelings got, too.

The stewardess set a little bottle of water and a tiny bag of peanuts on the tray in front of Sean. He was starving and figured that he'd plant his ass in a sports bar at YVR.

Past girlfriends had called him cold and distant—among other things. It was more than likely true. He was twenty-seven, and the closest he ever got to the warm and fuzzies for a woman was in bed. Out of bed, he didn't want to take on the responsibility of anyone else.

Just himself—and his mother. He made sure she had plenty of money. He'd had the house she'd wanted moved to the place she'd wanted it. He'd bought her the Subaru and had it shipped from Prince Albert. He visited her whenever she was at death's door. He did what he could for her, but they'd never been close.

Sean ripped open the bag of peanuts and dumped them in his mouth. He'd been close to only one person, and that had been his uncle. Abe had been his father figure and had changed his life. If not for his uncle, Sean didn't know where he'd be today. If not for hockey, he'd probably be in a mental institution somewhere banging his head against a wall to dull the pain.

He opened the water and drained the small bottle. Sean had good relationships with his friends. At least he thought he did, but those relationships weren't family. There'd been only one person in his life that he'd ever considered family. One person who'd looked out for him. One person he'd been able to talk to about anything, and when his uncle had died, Sean cried like a little girl. With the old man gone, the feeling of family was gone, too.

The twin-prop Air Canada circled the Vancouver airport several times before landing. The closer the airplane taxied to the gate, the more energy Sean felt flow through him. By the time he found Canucks Bar and Grill, it practically snapped from his fingertips. Electric posters of Henrik Sedin and Brandon Sutter greeted him as he moved to the hostess stand. The restaurant's motto was "We Are All Canucks," and he pulled his cap lower on his forehead. Not all of them were Canucks, and he felt a bit like a traitor. He took a seat at the bar and quickly ordered a rib eye, grilled vegetables, and water with a slice of lemon. The service was great and the food was better. Five televisions hung above the bar; two of them ran the Bruins versus the Jets in Winnipeg, and two showed the Giants/Packers NFC game. The fifth, CNN.

Even though the sound was off, Sean could practically hear the slap of sticks hitting the ice and the grunts as McQuid caught Ehlers in the corner and brutally checked him into the boards. In the third period, Marchand rocked a one-timer into Hellebuyck's five-hole and lit the lamp.

That, he thought as he cut into his steak, was something that made his heart thump. A laser shot in the five-hole filled him up with so much electricity, it always felt like his hair would singe. Putting points on the board had never felt like a responsibility to him. It was fun. He got off on it. He was one of the best shooters in the NHL. Putting the puck in the net was a challenge, one that he would gladly shoulder.

The bartender recognized him and gave him a beer on the house. Sean might not play for the Canucks, but he was a Canuck by birth and had played for Edmonton at one time. The two men shot the shit for a few minutes until the other man left to mix martinis.

148

On the two TVs, a Bud Light commercial interrupted the Bruins/Jets game, and Sean glanced at CNN as he shoved a big piece of meat into his mouth. The closed caption rolled down the screen as three commentators discussed plastic bottles floating up onto a California beach. One second the screen was filled with white plastic, and in the next, the news feed cut to a long dock. A familiar green seaplane bobbing at the end.

KING 5 is at the scene. While the captions rolled, the door to the seaplane opened and someone jumped out. Even if the woman wasn't wearing yoga sweats and his brown shirt, the fish hat was a dead giveaway. At first it didn't appear as if Lexie spotted the cameras and news crew. Her attention was directed at her phone, and she didn't notice the media crosshairs on her forehead. Then suddenly she looked up, and her eyes rounded like those of a deer caught in the headlights.

The morning sun sparkled in the pumps she'd worn the first night he'd met her. For a split second, Sean wondered what she'd done with her boots, but then all hell broke loose.

Lexie? Miss Kowalsky, can you tell us where you've been? the closed caption read.

Blond hair beneath her fish hat flew about her head as she blew past the reporters. Her long legs chewed up the dock, her breasts bounced like

149

soccer balls inside his shirt, and he thought for sure she'd fall and break an ankle.

Sean cut into his steak and thanked God he wasn't in the middle of the chaos. Like the closed caption on the television, two thoughts scrolled through his mind.

First, she shouldn't run like that. It looked painful and she could hurt herself.

Second, fourteen hours didn't seem all that bad. He shoved a bite of steak in his mouth and reached for his Stella. From where he sat, a four-hour layover in Vancouver seemed like he'd dodged a bullet.

Chapter 8

• all's fair in love and war

LEXIE'S LUCK RAN out the moment the *Sea Hopper* landed in Seattle. She'd asked Marie to pick her up at the Lake Union dock, but that had been just one more mistake added to the heap in her growing pile. Lexie didn't want to involve her friend more than necessary. These days Marie was an upright citizen who taught first grade at the respectable Waldorf School. The last thing she needed was to be seen on the five o'clock news driving a getaway car. She'd gotten away with it the first time. Twice was pushing her luck.

If Lexie's dad was in town, he would have met her with a couple of hockey players to run interference and body-check a few reporters into the drink. Someone had leaked the information that the runaway *Gettin' Hitched* bride had jumped aboard the flying tree frog, had hopped out of town, and was now hopping back in. Lexie suspected Jimmy. The fact that he hadn't mentioned the scene that waited for her during the flight to Seattle put him at the top of the list. Plus he had the most to gain by the free publicity and sudden

151

notoriety. Not that she could blame him—much. She'd done the same thing for her business. And she couldn't really yell at him for being a traitor since he'd helped her out big-time. If he was the one who'd talked, she figured they were even now.

Halfway up the dock, she noticed the media rushing toward her from the floating veranda next to the check-in office. Earlier, she'd stepped in a muddy hole in her boots and had to take off at a full sprint in her Louboutins. She barely made it to the parking lot and Marie's MINI Cooper before being swarmed. As they sped away, dodging reporters and paparazzi, Marie glanced at Lexie from the corners of her eyes. "What the heck are you wearing?" she asked as they darted into the noon rush on Fairview.

Lexie looked down at her sparkly Louboutins, yoga pants, and Sean's brown plaid shirt. Since he hadn't shown up to board the *Sea Hopper*, she supposed it belonged to her now. But Sean was the last person she wanted to discuss with Marie or anyone. "I stepped in a freezing cold puddle and my boots—"

"No," Marie interrupted. "That thing on your head."

"Oh." She pulled off her fish hat and set it in her lap. "Jimmy bought it so no one would recognize me."

"Jimmy? The king of bad taste?" Marie looked

in the rearview mirror and switched lanes. "I hate to point out the obvious, but nothing says *Look at me* like a woman with a fish stuck through her head."

Sean had pretty much said the same thing. Lexie put a hand on the dash to steady herself and ran her fingers through her tangled hair with the other. Outside of her family, only five people knew she'd been hiding out in Sandspit, British Columbia. Out of those five, she'd thought she only had to worry about Geraldine Brown. Obviously she'd overestimated Jimmy's loyalty. "I'm so tired," she said through a yawn.

"Being a fugitive from the hitchin' posse is exhausting," Marie said as she dodged in and out of traffic as if they were actual fugitives running from the law.

That and staying up late and having sex with a man she'd known for two days. She figured she'd had about four hours of sleep before the sun had sliced through a part in the curtains and cut across the empty pillow next to hers. She'd managed a few hours of sleep on the *Sea Hopper* but woke feeling even more exhausted.

She didn't know if Sean had:

1. Stayed behind at his mother's.
2. Slipped and fallen.
3. Been abducted by aliens.

All she knew for sure was that he'd kissed her hair and told her he'd pick her up and drive them to the wharf. He'd never shown, and the only thing Jimmy said was that Sean wouldn't be flying to Seattle with them. She hadn't asked Jimmy any questions, fearing Jimmy might ask *her* questions that she didn't want to answer. "I'm going to sleep until next week." In the end, Sean's reasons didn't matter:

1. He didn't owe her anything.
2. She didn't care.

Still . . . there was a little irrational part of her that would have liked to see him again. Maybe have dinner and show him she wasn't a crazy person. Maybe impress him with her real life. She could take him to a hockey game and to meet her dad afterward. She'd been under the impression that he didn't have a favorable view of her father, but every man she'd introduced to her dad had loved meeting John "The Wall" Kowalsky.

"I think you ran even faster than last time in those shoes. I thought the KIRO reporter and her cameraman were going to tackle you, for sure," Marie said.

Lexie thought so, too, and had practically felt their breath on the back of her neck. She turned and looked out the back window. "I don't see

154

anyone following us now. I think we lost them, Thelma."

"You're Thelma. I'm Louise."

For as long as they'd been friends, they'd had an ongoing argument over which character resembled them most in BFF movies. Everyone knew that Thelma got to do Brad Pitt in a dumpy hotel in Oklahoma. Wow. She really *was* Thelma today. She'd had sex with a man who was a virtual stranger. Sean had vanished like Brad Pitt, too. Of course, Sean hadn't stolen her money or anything else.

"You know I'm saving myself for Chris Pine," Marie said as she merged onto I–5.

Then Marie would have loved Sean Brown, Lexie thought as her friend sandwiched the MINI Cooper between an Amazon Prime semi and an ARCO tanker truck. "Your driving is giving me anxiety, Louise."

"Do you want me to let you out on the side of the interstate? I'm sure someone will pick you up sooner or later." Marie glanced at her, then back at the road. "Maybe not with that hair, though."

A scowl pulled at Lexie's brows and she folded her arms beneath her breasts. "Funny. Just take me to my apartment."

"You can't go back to your apartment. I'm sure it's surrounded by now." Then Marie said the dreaded inevitable. "You have to go to your parents'."

It made sense. Her parents lived in a gated neighborhood on Mercer Island. She had no choice, but she hated the idea of running home, and she wasn't looking forward to the interrogation that waited for her when she stepped foot inside.

LUCKY FOR HER, when she walked inside her parents' house, no human was there to greet her. "Where's my baby?" she called out. She heard yips from the vicinity of her parents' room, then Yum Yum rounded the corner wearing a cable knit hoodie from the Erin-Go-Aw sweater collection. As always when she saw her dog, her heart turned mushy. "There you are!" She kicked off her shoes, sank to her knees, and scooped up the hairless dog. "Mommy missed you." Yum Yum's body shook with excitement and her black tongue darted out and licked Lexie's face. "Have you been a good girl?" she asked as she rose to her feet and headed down the hall.

Lexie knew her dad was in Pittsburgh, and she figured her mother was at work at her television studio in Tacoma. Her younger brother, Jon Jon, was probably at school. Like a convict with a get-out-of-jail-free card, she felt a slight reprieve from the disappointment she would surely see in her mother's eyes. With her dog cradled in her arms, she walked into her old bedroom, now converted into a gift-wrap center filled with bright

156

paper and shiny ribbon. Beside the door, she found her purse and the suitcases she'd left at the Fairmont.

Just last week she'd packed for her honeymoon in Acapulco. With one hand, she opened the biggest suitcase and dug past her baby doll chemise inside. She pushed aside her Mrs. Dalton silk robe and pulled out a clean pair of panties and matching bra. "You need a mud bath." Her nose wrinkled and she set Yum Yum inside the open luggage. Like all hairless dogs, Yum Yum tended to smell like old corn chips if not given regular mud baths with mineral conditioners to clean and hydrate her skin.

In anticipation of her tropical honeymoon, she'd packed sundresses, bikinis, and shorts. She pulled out her blue dress and didn't want to think about where she'd be at that exact moment if she hadn't called off the wedding. She didn't want to think of the people she'd hurt, especially Pete. He didn't deserve the humiliation of getting left at the altar on national TV.

In the bottom of her purse, she found her phone. It still had half a charge, and she'd rather poke out an eye than make the call, but it was the right thing to do because she needed to:

1. Take responsibility.
2. Stop running.
3. Make amends to those she'd hurt.

157

Butterflies fluttered in her stomach as the phone rang.

"Lexie?"

"Hi, Pete." Uncomfortable silence filled her ear, stretching until she said, "I'm sorry."

"What happened?"

"I thought you should marry someone who's in love with you." Again silence. "I never wanted to hurt you. I just didn't know how else to stop it."

"You could have said something." His voice grew tight with anger. "Instead of running out on me." He had a right to his anger, but marrying him would have been wrong for both of them.

"I know. I feel really bad. Saying I'm sorry doesn't make up for it."

"You're right."

"We don't really even know each other," she reasoned. "We can't possibly be in love, at least not the kind that sustains a marriage for any length of time. We were just caught up in the excitement of the show. I hope we can both move on from this." She blew out a breath as more silence stretched between them. "Maybe something positive can come from the experience. Maybe in time—"

"I got a two-hour special show out of it," he interrupted.

"Wow." Now it was her turn for silence.

"I'm in Acapulco taping it right now."

"You went to Acapulco anyway?"

"Yeah. The beach is awesome."

Seriously? She'd been in Sandspit and he'd been soaking up the sun?

"I'm on camera more than in *Gettin' Hitched*. So, that's cool."

"What kind of show are you taping?"

"I think they're going to call it *Hitchin' Heartbreak*. I walk around looking sad and meet single women who try and comfort me." He laughed. "This time I picked the women in the cast so I could make sure they're all hot."

"Well . . ." She couldn't absorb it all. "I just called to apologize."

"It worked out, I guess."

"So . . . you're not hurt?"

"I'm still a little pissed off that you ran out on me, but I guess you saved us from divorce. We don't love each other."

He was going to marry her even though he didn't love her, but she wasn't in a position to judge.

"It turned out okay in the end."

For him. He was in Acapulco, lounging on the beach and being served umbrella drinks by women fighting over him. She was stuck in her parents' house.

"I'm surrounded by only hot women. No corn teeth this time."

No matter her feelings for Summer at the moment, the girl had fallen for Pete and deserved better than to be called "corn teeth." That was just mean. A mean side of Pete Lexie'd never experienced, and she was relieved beyond measure that she hadn't gone through with the wedding. "So . . . are we cool?"

Another long silence and then, "Yeah. We're cool."

When Lexie disconnected, her heart felt lighter and she headed for her parents' bathroom. The worst was out of the way. She'd probably have to talk to the producers at some point, but she'd dreaded the conversation with Pete the most.

Yum Yum followed at her heels, then curled up on Sean Brown's shirt as Lexie quickly undressed and jumped into the big shower. She washed the smell of the Sandspit ocean from her hair and skin. Twelve jets of warm water worked tired knots from her back and she felt like she finally let out the tight breath she'd been holding since she'd run from the Fairmont.

Pete didn't seem upset or even mad now. Well, maybe a little mad, but that had more to do with ego than *Hitchin' Heartbreak*.

When she was through, she wrapped a towel around her wet hair and pulled on her own clothes. She felt squeaky clean and headed for the kitchen. Her mother was a gourmet cook and at one time had a catering business with Aunt Mae. She'd taught all her children how to cook everything from beef Wellington to Crock-Pot

160

stew. Lexie sometimes liked to make complicated meals, but her all-time favorite comfort food was chicken quesadillas.

From the Sub-Zero refrigerator, she pulled out everything she needed. Yum Yum sat at her bare feet as she heated oil and grated cheese. She'd cooked more in the past three days than she had in the past three months. Sean had seemed to enjoy her cooking. Geraldine had given modest approval while cleaning her plate. As she sliced baked chicken, she thought about Sean and how little she actually knew of him:

1. He lived in Seattle.
2. His mother lived in Sandspit.
3. He had a secret job.
   a. Probably with the government.
4. Handsome.
5. Smiled and she'd thought "holy crap."
6. Teasing, soul kisses.

Kisses that had made her throw caution to the wind and invite him into her room. An impulse she hadn't acted on since her sophomore year of college, but standing beneath that weak pool of light at the Harbor Inn, it hadn't seemed impulsive. His green eyes had looked down into hers like she was the only woman on the planet. His strong arms were the only things keeping her safe from the madness she'd created. His strong hands pinned her in place as his mouth gave her something to think about besides the looming tempest. Lexie had always been attracted to strong men. Men who didn't ask permission before taking her breath away. Men with knowing eyes and experienced hands.

As Lexie cooked, she figured it was probably best that he'd disappeared, even though he'd told her he'd be back to drive them to the harbor. No uncomfortable good-byes, or awkward lies about keeping in touch.

Still . . . there was a tiny part of her that wouldn't mind seeing him again. The part that disregarded Sunday school lessons about sin and evil temptation. The completely female part that wanted him to desperately *want* to see her again.

The little dog sitting on her feet yipped a few times and Lexie fed her a few bites of chicken before carrying her quesadilla and a bottle of water to her parents' room. She sat cross-legged in the middle of their bed with her dog lying beside her leg. A suspicious hollow, the perfect size of one little dog, created a dip in her dad's pillow.

"Did you do that?" she asked, and pointed. "Papa doesn't like you to sleep on his pillow."

In response, Yum Yum lifted her head to rest on Lexie's thigh, unapologetic and waiting to be fed.

"We won't tell him." Lexie took a bite of the

crispy flour tortilla, then dug pieces of chicken from melted cheeses. "You're such a little love muffin." She was clean and safe in her childhood home and had her dog by her side. The tension from the past two days eased from the back of her neck and shoulders and she completely relaxed for the first time since she'd received a callback from *Gettin' Hitched*.

She took an unladylike bite and turned on her dad's big TV. The news and talk shows would have to cancel their runaway-bride contests now that she was in Seattle. No one would win a free vacation to Cancun or Disney World. Geraldine's dream of visiting Cinderella's Castle was crushed.

After her last bite, she set the plate on a nightstand and curled up next to her dog. Her fingers combed through the fine tuft on top of Yum Yum's head as she pointed the remote at the screen and navigated to the Internet. She Googled her name, and sites like TMZ, Gawker, and PopSugar came up first. None of them had anything nice to say about her, and she clicked on a link to YouTube. Immediately, the image of her running down the docks a few hours ago popped up first. Her mouth dropped open and she sucked in a breath. *That was quick,* she thought as the appalling scene played out on the big screen. Chaotic shouting accompanied footage of her running past reporters, her hair flying from beneath her fish hat. Her Louboutins flashed like disco balls as she sprinted to Marie's silver MINI Cooper. On those rare occasions that Lexie did choose to run, she wore a sports bra with compression panels to keep her boobs from bouncing like in the scene on TV. As her mother had always told her and her sister, "We aren't built to run and work up a sweat. God saved us for better things."

When the video ended, she pulled up a clip from *Gettin' Hitched*. She reached for her water bottle and lifted her head enough to take a drink. She hadn't seen every episode yet, and clicked on the segment of her and several other girls on a sailboat. It had been shot during a group date near Catalina. The sun had been out and the wind blew through her hair like she was a fashion model. What Lexie recalled most about that day was feeling queasy and forcing herself to laugh at Pete's dumb jokes instead of barfing over the side of the boat.

The next episode to pop up was of her and Pete on a date in the backyard of the Hitchin' House. She'd seen this clip, and it made her feel uncomfortable the second time around. Complete with flickering candles and a dozen red roses, the date was supposed to be romantic, but with a film crew less than five feet away and a boom mic just above her head, it had been more annoying than anything.

"I think I'm falling in love with you," Pete con-

164

fessed as candlelight flickered across her face. He'd reached across the table for her hand.

"I feel the same," she'd lied to herself and felt almost triumphant. Almost. There was one word that had kept her from a victory lap with her fists in the air. *Think.* Thinking he was falling in love didn't win in a three-woman match-up.

She carefully took another drink of water and watched herself move in for a kill shot, delivered so skillfully he never felt it. Flirting as well as charm ran through her blood, inherited from her mama's side. On the fifty-five-inch screen, Lexie looked down as if overcome by Pete's declaration. When she raised her gaze to his once more, she kept her eyelids at half-mast, as if she was overcome with desire, too. "It scares me how much I'm growing to love you." Her thumb brushed his wrist beneath the cuff of his sleeve and she tilted her face to the side in complete surrender. "You have the power to make me blissfully happy or break my heart." Then she licked one corner of her mouth and almost smiled when his pulse picked up and he swallowed hard. In that moment, she'd known she'd survive another week.

Lexie watched several more clips and felt like the shittiest person on the planet. Instead of lying, she should have done something to get herself kicked off. Like Desiree from Jersey, who'd crashed Pete and Tonya's date wearing booty shorts and a bikini top and had monopolized the conversation. But Lexie was inherently competitive and had never been a graceful loser. She'd joined the cast for greater business exposure, and her plan had exceeded expectation. Still . . . it was wrong of her to work her charms and calculated flirtations on Pete. She should have let Summer win. Summer was a really sweet girl and she'd actually loved Pete. Lexie wasn't sure how a person truly fell in love with such limited contact, but she didn't doubt Summer's sincerity.

The video continued to the elimination ceremony and Summer getting the pink bootin' pin. The heartbreak in her cornflower-blue eyes filling with tears and her trembling lip made Lexie feel even shittier.

Summer's last interview rolled next. Her face red and blotchy from crying, she said, "Lexie should have gone home. Not me! She doesn't deserve Pete. It's not fair!" That stung, but Lexie couldn't get mad because she agreed. "She's a spoiled brat and has everything handed to her." That wasn't true, but she supposed Summer was just venting. "Everyone in the house hates her. We call her Lex Luthor because she's evil."

Lexie's hand stilled in Yum Yum's tuft. "Hey now."

"I hope Jenny wins. Lexie Kowalsky is a

stuck-up—*beep.*" The network cut off her last word.

"I gave you my Benefits mascara!" Lexie sat up as if she'd been pulled by her hair. "When the other girls made fun of your 'corn teeth,' I didn't shit-talk about you at all! I felt bad and handed you my whitening strips." Lexie pointed the remote at the television. "You're a backstabber, Summer from Bell Buckle, Tennessee." She turned the television off, because she didn't want to hear what the other girls said about her. If Summer called her a bitch, the others would say worse, and she felt beat up enough for one day.

She put her water on the nightstand and curled up with her dog. Her life was a mess, but she'd survived messes before. She'd always been able to talk or charm or work her way out of messes and turn them around. Sure, this mess seemed colossal because it *was* colossal, but Pete wasn't mad any longer. That was a point in her favor. She'd recover and twist this mess to her advantage.

"THERE HASN'T BEEN an online sale for five days."

Those words still echoed in Lexie's mind, and they had the same impact today as they had yesterday when she'd been lounging in her parents' bed and had taken a call from her business manager, Lucy Broderick. "Three hundred and seventy returns since Thursday. Anger is the dominant sentiment in the customer comment box." While Lexie's head had spun, Lucy added, "The only things coming via contact e-mails are rants, marriage proposals, and a few random telephone numbers."

The second day after her return, Lexie sat on the empty KING 5 news set and adjusted the microphone clipped to the collar of her black suit. Her hair slicked back in a simple twist, she looked like a modest businesswoman. Not the scandalous runaway *Gettin' Hitched* bride or the woman in a fish hat, running up the dock, shoes flashing, boobs bouncing. Or, as her dad said when he'd seen the footage, "Two cats fighting to get out of a burlap bag." Both her entertainment lawyer and business manager had suggested an interview to help turn her image around. The sooner, the better.

"Ready in five . . ." the manager said in her earpiece. The light on the camera in front of her turned green and Savannah Guthrie spoke into her ear, "Since last Wednesday, fans of the reality show *Gettin' Hitched* have gone wild with speculations concerning our next guest. Joining us live from our affiliate in Seattle, KING 5, is the runaway bride herself, Lexie Kowalsky. Good morning, Lexie. I'm glad you agreed to be with us this morning."

"Good morning, Savannah." Lexie looked into

the camera and kept her face without expression. Neither happy nor guilty, as her lawyer suggested. "It's nice to be with you."

"I think the first question on everyone's mind is where did you go when you ran from the Fairmont?"

"A friend flew me to a small town in British Columbia."

"What small town is that?"

Lexie couldn't see Savannah but kept her eyes directed into the camera. "Sandspit."

"Sand what?"

Exactly. "It's on Moresby Island in the Hecate Strait."

"That certainly sounds isolated. Was this planned in advance?"

"Planned?" That was a new one. "No. Not at all. I had every intention of marrying Pete when I walked into the Fairmont that day."

"Then what happened? Why did you run out on him?"

"The easy answer is that I panicked." She looked down modestly at her hands. "Everything was happening so fast and I couldn't think straight." She looked back up and managed a little tear in her right eye. "I had to go away by myself so I could get my head together." That was a bit of a fudge. She'd had to go away but she had yet to get her head together. "I didn't want to marry Pete for the wrong reasons. I didn't want to make a mockery of marriage." She paused and swallowed hard. "I want all the fans of the show to know how truly sorry I am for disappointing them. I didn't want to disappoint anyone. I just got caught up in the excitement of it all." She shook her head and looked down at her lap again. "I wanted to take my vows seriously. That night, I realized I didn't love Pete like he deserves to be loved." She looked back up and was pleased with the tear caught on her bottom lashes. "Both he and I deserve a deep love that lasts forever. Not just until the cameras stop rolling." She took a breath and added, "Neither Pete nor I feel that kind of love for each other."

"Let's ask Pete. We've got him on a live feed from Acapulco."

Alarm bells rang in her head and sucked the tear back in her eye. When they'd negotiated this interview, NBC hadn't mentioned anything about Pete.

"Good morning, Pete. You look like you've been relaxing in the sun. How are you feeling?"

"I've been trying to relax and regroup. Trying to get my legs back beneath me."

"You've been listening to Lexie. What are your thoughts on what she had to say?"

"It hurts. I thought Lexie and I did have the kind of love that lasts forever. At least I felt that about her."

Wait, that's not what he'd said the other day.

"I'm supposed to be on my honeymoon with the woman I love, but I'm here alone."

Lexie stared into the camera and tried not to react. He'd said everything was okay between them! And he sure wasn't there alone. He was with "hot" women he'd handpicked to comfort him. She knew he was just pretending to be sad in order to hype his own new reality show.

"I fell hard for Lexie and she ripped my heart out."

The backs of Lexie's eyes stung with real tears this time, and she clasped her hands together in her lap to keep them from shaking. Was he really going to crucify her?

"I don't know if I will ever be able to give my heart to a woman again. It hurts too much."

Like appearing on *Gettin' Hitched* in the first place, she'd agreed to this interview in an effort to help her business. The business she'd worked so hard to turn from a dream to a success. A dream Pete held at knife's point. "When we talked on the phone, I told you that I'm sorry. I thought you understood."

"Just a minute," Savannah cut in. "The two of you have spoken to each other recently?"

"Yes," Lexie answered. The public had cast them into the roles of victim and villain. She couldn't play the first and needed to dispel the second. She had to avoid the slightest appearance of hitting back at Pete while inching public opinion toward the center. "I called Pete to tell him how sorry I am and that I never meant to hurt him. He said things are cool between us."

"What do you say to that, Pete? Are things cool?"

He could save her. All he had to do was tell the truth. He could take the opportunity to promote his new show at the same time. "I don't recall telling her we were cool. All I know is that the woman I love humiliated me on national television."

"I'm sorry," she said just as Pete continued to plunge the knife deeper into her business and kill her dream.

"I don't know if I will ever trust a woman again. Lexie ruined my life."

A fat tear slipped from the corner of Lexie's eye and ran down the side of her cheek. It was over. Her business was gone and she would be the villain forever. "I don't know what to say."

Savannah spoke into Lexie's earpiece, but the words were drowned out by the buzzing in her brain. The light on the camera blinked off, and the stage manager stepped forward to take the microphone from Lexie's lapel. She felt numb and ready to implode at the same time.

Instead of returning to her parents', she drove her hybrid to her condo in Belltown. She'd pick up Yum Yum later, but for now, she wanted to curl up in her own bed and pull the covers over her head. The business she'd poured her heart and soul into was over.

Yum Yum's Closet had started as a simple blog she'd written from her dog's point of view and had grown into a thriving Internet retail business.

The logical next step was to open her first brick-and-mortar store. She'd leased the perfect space in Bellevue and had hired a general contractor to make the renovations. She was supposed to meet with the interior designer next week to pick out wallpaper and open the last week in February. She'd wanted to open on Valentine's Day, but the pink circle banquette wouldn't arrive until the twenty-fourth.

She'd gone on the *Today* show in a last-bid effort to save Yum Yum's Closet and perhaps redeem herself. Neither of those things would happen now. She would forever be cast as a reality show villain. Like Spencer Pratt and Courtney Robertson. Even if she could redeem herself, it wouldn't happen in time to save Yum Yum's Closet. She had ten full- and part-time employees, and that number didn't include her Web designer or the people who worked for the small-batch manufacturer.

It took her a few short minutes to reach her apartment building. The sidewalk outside was reporter-free, and she easily drove through the gates of her parking garage and pulled to a stop in her designated slot.

In a fog of pain, she rode the elevator to the top floor. The doors opened into a condo surrounded with ten-foot panes of glass, insulated to keep the weather out while letting in the sluggish sunlight to spill across lush white rug and gleaming parquet floors. She stepped out of her sensible pumps and left a trail of clothing on the way to her bedroom. She hit a button just inside the room, and shades lowered from the ceiling to cover the windows. By degrees, the room was pitched into varying shades of deeper gray, and Lexie crawled into her bed and pulled the chintz comforter to her chin. She stayed there all day and only emerged from bed when her dad brought Yum Yum to her later that night.

"Here's your worthless dog," he said as she finished tying the belt of her terry-cloth robe. The dog gave him a big lick across his lips. "Jesus!"

"She loves Papa."

"I'm not her papa."

After a brief conversation about what a "tool" Pete was, and the pros and cons of Chinook enforcer Kevin "KO" Olsen meeting Pete after his return from Acapulco, Lexie took her dog and headed back to bed. She couldn't help but replay the last few days in her head. She'd made one bad decision after another. She'd hurled herself and her business into a total free fall. This morning, she'd landed with a big splat on national television.

So much had happened since the night she'd run from the Fairmont, it seemed like five weeks had passed instead of just five days. It had only been five days since she'd jumped aboard the *Sea Hopper* and stared up into Sean Brown's dark face and the question in his green eyes. Two days since she'd pulled him into a small hotel room and stripped naked. Just two days since she'd sworn like a porn star/hockey player during unforgettable sex. Two nights later, her cheeks burned with the memory.

There was one thing that made her feel the tiniest bit better, and that was she wouldn't ever have to see Sean Brown again. A few days ago she'd thought it might be nice to see him and show him the real Lexie. Well, the real Lexie had sunk to the lowest point in her life. She had little hope that things would get better, and the last thing she needed was further humiliation.

TO HER SHOCK, the next afternoon Lucy Broderick called and threw her an unexpected lifeline. Her appearance on the *Today* show hadn't been a total disaster after all. The response had been the opposite of what Lexie had feared—*she'd* somehow managed to appear sympathetic, while Pete's attack had come off as bullying. The fake and real tears she'd shed had made her seem vulnerable and despondent, filled with agonizing remorse for what she'd done to Pete and the fans

175

of *Gettin' Hitched*. Pete had sounded belligerent to the very end. Viewer opinion was shifting against him.

Lexie knew she should feel bad, but she didn't feel the least bit sorry for Pete. He'd done it to himself.

Three days after the *Today* show, the tide was definitely turning in her favor. She did a short call-in interview with *Extra* and was scheduled to tell her side of the story for *Us* magazine next week.

The world didn't hate her. Even Gawker and PopSugar seemed to be finished crucifying her. Her business wasn't totally dead after all. Yum Yum's Closet had been resuscitated and put back on life support. With hard work, she expected it to make a full recovery.

That was until the moment Marie walked into her apartment and slapped the *National Enquirer* on the table between them. Lexie drank a sip of coffee and moved aside her plate of cantaloupe and a bagel. "What's this?" She slid the paper to her and choked. Hot coffee slid down the wrong pipe and her heart stopped.

"Wha—wha?" she wheezed. On the front cover was the headline: *Hitchin' Bride Jilts Groom for Mystery Man*. A picture of her pinned up against the door of room seven at the Harbor Inn took up the entire page. The quality was a bit grainy, but even if she hadn't known it was she, even if she hadn't lived it, even if her eyes weren't blurry from hacking, she was clearly recognizable.

"Who is that?" Marie asked.

Lexie cleared her throat and coughed a few more times, unable to take her eyes from the picture of her pushed up against a hotel door. While her face was clearly visible, Sean's back was to the camera. The only visible parts of him were his hands, wrapped around her wrists and pinning them above her head. "Sean," she choked out. The man with beautiful green eyes and dark hair, who'd felt like the only steady thing in an upside-down world. The man whose kiss made her warm up from the inside out and throw caution to the wind—along with her clothing.

"Sean who?"

"Brown." At least that was his mother's last name. She didn't know for sure, but decided not to confide in her friend, who was acting a little judgmental.

"You look like you were either kidnapped or about to jump this guy's bones."

Lexie cleared her throat once more. "You know I wasn't kidnapped."

"So you hooked up with some random Canadian?"

"It wasn't like that." She looked across the table at her friend, who trolled Tinder. "He was on the plane with me. I was scared and freaked. He took my mind off everything for a while."

"It looks bad."

"I know!"

After Marie left, she checked the online gossip sites. They all had the same picture of her. The caption at TMZ read: *Runaway Bride or Seductress?*

"It wasn't like that," she told her mother that evening. "I helped him take care of his sick mother while we were in Sandspit. I didn't seduce anyone!"

Georgeanne looked across the couch from her and said, "I'm sorry about his mother, but I just really care about you." She shook her head, and her dark hair slid across one shoulder to the front of her red silk blouse. "Cryin' all night, Lexie. I can't believe it. This just keeps getting worse."

"I know. Someone leaked my phone number." She blinked back the tears stinging her eyes, hating the disappointment in her mother's face. "I had to turn it off for a while. I really can't change the number until I notify all my business contacts." Thank God she still had her prepaid phone from Sandspit.

Georgeanne took several deep breaths and said on a sigh, "You're a grown woman. I'm not going to ask you what went on in that hotel room. Although your father might when he gets back from his five-day grind."

Lexie closed her eyes. After a five-day grind, her dad was probably going to be cranky.

She was right.

The next night, her father stood in her open kitchen, watching the television above the fireplace in the living room. *E! News* flashed the now infamous picture onto the screen and Jason Kennedy asked, "Who is the mysterious man with runaway bride Lexie Kowalsky? The world wants to know: Is this a photo of force or fling?"

"This is crazy." She opened a bottle of her father's favorite beer, then reached for the remote control on the counter. She punched the red button three times before the television went black. And yeah, she fudged a bit when she said, "I helped take care of his terminally ill mother."

"That isn't what it looks like in that picture." A scowl pulled at his dark brows as he raised the Molson 67 to his lips. He took several long pulls, then lowered the bottle. "That guy"—he paused to point his bottle at the television where the infamous photo had splashed across the blank screen just moments before—"might be blurry as hell and unrecognizable, but his intentions are real clear. He's either forcing you into that hotel room or he's seducing his way in."

The seducing had been mutual, and she shook her head.

"They're talking about it everywhere. I saw it on TV in a sports bar in Detroit."

This new story was getting even bigger and more devastating than the original.

"If you really weren't being held against your will, I can't exactly hunt this son of a bitch down and feed him my fist." He set the bottle on the counter and folded his arms across his chest. Not a good sign. "You have some accountability in this mess."

"My head hasn't been right since I went on *Gettin' Hitched*." She wanted to show him she was a strong woman and not a child he had to protect. She clenched her jaw to keep her chin from trembling, but a tear spilled from her bottom lash. "I take full accountability for the mess I've made of my life and the pain I've caused everyone. Especially my family." She hated the disappointment creeping into his eyes. "I was confused and scared. He seemed like a good person. I thought I could trust him."

He dropped his hands. "Don't cry."

"Okay."

"Christ." He reached for her and wrapped her in his big arms. "Not all men can be trusted, honey." She rested her head on the one place she'd always felt protected, his shoulder. "Some sons of bitches have little balls and have to coerce vulnerable women just to get some attention."

Sean didn't have little balls, and he hadn't exactly coerced her, but she didn't bother to correct her father. She nodded, relaxing in the warm solace she always found with her dad.

"The guy needs his ass handed to him for taking advantage of you."

She nodded again, because what did it matter? She didn't know Sean. He was a guy she met who probably worked for the CIA. More than ever, she was relieved that she would never see Sean Brown again.

A RAUCOUS WAVE of cheers and cowbells rolled through the Key Arena as "Who Let the Dogs Out" blasted from the speakers. High above the center of the ring, the jumbotron's three screens replayed a blistering one-timer off an Avalanche's blade and into the left pad of Chinooks goalie Adam Larson.

It had been a while since Lexie had donned her Chinooks jersey and stepped foot into the Key. Even longer since she'd sat in the ticketed seats. "I think we might be more comfortable at the Encore," she said, and gazed longingly up to the secluded club on the third tier.

"We're not hiding up there. Remember?" her mother reminded her through a smile. "We have nothing to hide."

She knew her mother was right. They'd debated it and determined that the only way to keep from going into hiding again was to act as if she had nothing to conceal. Once the cameraman spotted them, she had little doubt her face would flash across all four screens on the jumbotron and be beamed out on television.

She'd taken care to appear modest in a gray turtleneck, team jersey, and gray jeans. She'd pulled her hair back in a ponytail and wore minimal cosmetics. She walked a fine line between flaunting herself and appearing guilty. Once the *Enquirer* photo appeared, the good feelings that came out of her *Today* show appearance went down the tubes. She'd gone from sympathetic to villain in no time flat. No amount of apologizing was going to help her out this time, and she couldn't count on another miracle to save her behind. She was seen as a cheater and was back to playing a villainess, only worse. She was now the lowest of lows, the bottom rung, in reality television:

1. Slut.
2. Bitch.
3. Psycho.
4. Slutty bitch psycho.

Lexie took an aisle seat next to her mother and little brother, Jon Jon, in the lower bowl. Her brother took after their dad in looks and temperament. He was protective and ready to do battle for his big sister, which added to Lexie's guilt. It was supposed to be the other way around. She should be looking out for him, but she felt like a coward and had to fight a strong urge to sink down in her seat and shield the side of her face with her hand. She took a deep breath and let it out slowly to keep from hyperventilating, but there was nothing she could do about the sick knot in her stomach.

As a kid, Lexie had loved sitting in the front row just behind the glass. She'd loved the raw energy arcing through the crowd. She'd loved the grunts and thumps and the *shhh-shhh* of skates meshing with cheers and screaming fans. She forced herself to raise her chin and gaze out onto the ice.

"That's the new guy Dad complains about," Jon Jon told her as the puck passed from stick to stick. All she could see was the back of a jersey and short sweaty curls beneath his helmet. "I like him though."

Lexie had more important things to worry about than the Chinooks' newest superstar. Like appearing calm, cool, and collected when what she really wanted was to run away before someone in the control booth recognized her and flashed her face on the jumbotron.

With a hard *thwack,* the puck shot around the boards and was stopped in the corner seconds before players from both sides slammed into each other and shook the Plexiglas. Elbows flew, and thuds and grunts punctuated the air as they all dug for the puck.

A boom and vibration she could feel beneath

her feet, and the number 36 flattened against the Plexiglas. "KNOX" was sewn across his shoulders, and his helmet fell off in the scrum.

"You wanna have a go?" one of them asked.

"On your mother, you tit baby." Thirty-six threw a fist and his big blue glove connected, knocking the player off his skates.

Lexie drummed her fingers on the armrest. Mothers and sisters and tit babies were all fair insults with hockey players.

Whistles blew and two referees entered the fray. They pointed to the biggest offenders, and Lexie leaned forward to look down the boards to where her father stood with his arms folded across his blue blazer. She couldn't see his face, but by his stance, he wasn't happy.

From the other side of the glass she heard, "You're a pussy, Kuch. Go back to the minors with the other girls."

Her brows creased and she returned her attention to number 36. He shoved one glove beneath his arm, then bent forward and disappeared from her view. An odd jolt ran up her spine to the back of her neck. For a split second, she felt as if she'd stepped into an alternate universe where she recognized something that she couldn't possibly know. That split second hung in the air, confusing and bizarre.

"Welcome to the Jungle" blasted through the arena and she raised her gaze to the jumbotron.

Dark hair at the top of his head filled the large screens, then 36 straightened and combed his fingers through a damp lock of hair curling over his forehead like a big C.

Everything within Lexie came to a shuddering halt except the jolt shooting up her spine to the back of her skull. On the huge screens, his green eyes glanced up at the scoreboard and his oh-shit smile tugged at one corner of his mouth.

The screens cut to a loop of him throwing his big fist and the Avalanche player going down. The crowd around Lexie went wild, and the jolt at the back of her skull zapped her brain. The knot in her stomach clutched her chest. On the huge screens, number 36 calmly shoved his helmet on his head. He chewed one side of his mouth guard, and Billy Joel's "An Innocent Man" played overhead as he calmly skated toward the penalty box.

Chapter 9

• i love the way you lie

S EAN GRABBED HIS blue blazer off a hook in his locker and shoved his arms inside. The ends of his just-washed hair wet the collar of his white dress shirt. He'd scored two of the four points put up on the board tonight and secured his worth on the team.

The usual hazing period seemed to be over, although some of the guys still resented the trade. Sean understood that. During the season, players spent more time with their team than anybody else. They were on the road half the season, and the other half was spent working out at the team's clubhouse inside the arena, watching game tapes and practicing for the show. Inevitably, the guys got close. Sometimes closer than their own families, which explained the high divorce rate.

Sean shoved his feet into his calfskin loafers and reached inside the open locker for his wallet. He'd played for several different NHL franchises. He had good friends in all of them, even though it might take him a bit longer to get as close to his teammates as some of the other guys. He wouldn't say they were family. At least not as he understood family.

He stuck his wallet in the back pocket of his khaki trousers and looked across the locker room filled with hockey players. Some half dressed, others completely naked. He'd been around naked guys since he'd played peewee and hardly noticed anymore. A few of the guys sat on a bench, watching an iPad and betting on college hockey.

Left defender Brody Comeau groaned as he tossed his towel on the bench and rolled his left shoulder.

"Still feeling the Russell hit?" Sean asked.

"I hate that guy." Brody was built like a pylon and had a long scar on his right cheek. Since Brody was thirty-five, Sean imagined it was harder for him to shake off the pain.

"He's probably feeling a hell of a lot worse after Kevin put him in the third row."

Brody chuckled. "How's your hand?"

Sean flexed his fingers and made a fist. His middle finger felt a bit stiff. "Fine."

"Next time, you let someone else drop the gloves." Brody reached in his locker and pulled out a pair of boxers. "KO or Letestu or me. One of us will be your shadow. You break your hand and you're fucked." He stepped inside his under-wear and pulled it up. "That means we're all fucked." He looked up. "Got it?"

There had been a time when Sean might have taken offense to another player telling him what to do like he was back in the shinnies. When he'd walked around with a chip on his shoulder the size of a log. When he'd sought attention by glove rubbing his points in everyone's face. When he'd hotdogged to shove the facts home.

"Got it." He hadn't been that guy for a few years now. Not since he'd realized that his talent was overshadowed by his need for attention. He'd also realized that he was more like his mother than he'd ever let himself think was possible. She sought attention through her hypochondria, he through his ability to hit a puck between the pipes. He'd had a girlfriend to thank for the revelation. "You're an attention whore," she'd told him. She hadn't meant it as a compliment or to be helpful. She'd yelled it as she'd kicked his Maybach. He'd broken up with her for denting his car door, but she'd been right. Sure, he might ride his stick when he scored a hat trick, but he let his talent speak for him these days.

Again Brody chuckled. "Decent muck-up though." Ever since he'd returned from Sandspit and hit the road with the team, things were better. No more prank calls to his room at two A.M. or smashed crackers between his sheets. The roster shakeup was now cohesive, and he was getting to know each player and their style and quirks.

"Good game, Knox," Coach Kowalsky said as

189

he passed, even going so far as to pat Sean on the shoulder.

"Thanks." One thing he'd learned about John, the man didn't blow unwarranted sunshine up anyone's ass. A "good game" from him was like excessive praise from anyone else. Despite himself, Sean almost smiled, and retucked his white dress shirt into his trousers. He didn't want to like the guy. John was an asshole, but since his return, he found himself playing smarter. Maybe to prove to the coach and to anyone else that Sean Knox was a team player. He wasn't out for just himself. If they thought otherwise, they were wrong. If they mistook him for a pussy, they were wrong about that, too.

There was only one potential problem with his newfound cohesion. A tall blond problem with the last name Kowalsky. As far as he could tell, her life was one big drama after another, and he'd managed to get himself tangled up in it.

When he'd first returned from Sandspit, he'd tried to get ahold of her in an effort to avoid adding even more drama when she inevitably learned he played for the Chinooks. He couldn't exactly ask her dad for her phone number. He'd asked Jimmy, but the number he'd been given went straight to voice mail. He'd left her a message and e-mailed his number via her business Web site. She hadn't contacted him, and he figured she didn't want to see him again. That was her choice, and after their picture appeared on the cover of the *Enquirer*, he was more than fine with that, too. He didn't want the part of "mystery man" in her never-ending drama.

"Knoxy." Team captain Stephen "Stony" Davis hung one wrist over Sean's shoulder. "Some of the guys are meeting at Quinn's Pub. You should come."

Stony had gotten his nickname because he hit like he had stones in his gloves. Sean could attest to the accuracy of the nickname and was secretly relieved that he wouldn't be on the receiving end of Stony's right hook this season. "Where's Quinn's Pub?" He'd been in Seattle only three months, and half of that had been spent on the road. One of these days soon, he'd have to figure out his way around the city.

"Tenth and Pike."

Sean didn't live far from the Key Arena. He had a fair idea of the city's layout and had a navigation system in his Land Rover. "Sounds good." He grabbed his duffel and moved with Stony through the locker room and lounge and out into the tunnel.

"Quinn's has some cheese fries I'm dying to try."

Sean looked across his shoulder at his teammate. "Are cheese fries on Trina's meal plan?" he asked, referring to the team's nutritionist.

"Not on your plan," Stony said through a

laugh. "I'm a defender. I can bulk up now and again."

Probably not on cheese fries. They talked about several bad calls and questioned the referee's eyesight. "Chucky's toe wasn't anywhere near the crease," Sean said as he turned left toward the outside doors. "Even a blind man could have seen that."

Near the doorway, a woman separated herself from the wall and turned toward him. She wore a gray turtleneck beneath a Chinooks jersey. Gray jeans so tight they looked shrink-wrapped around her long legs, and she was just as gorgeous as he recalled. As one, a surprising mix of lust and dread rolled through him, twisting and fighting and landing in his gut like a ball of hot lead. He'd figured they'd see each other sooner or later, but after the *Enquirer* photo splashed around the world, he would have preferred later rather than sooner.

"Hey there, Lexie," Stony called out to her.

Her deep blue eyes watched Sean approach before she turned her attention to the team captain. "Hey there, Stephen."

Stony opened up his big arms and she stepped inside. "I haven't seen you in ages." He pulled back and looked down into her face. "At least not in person. I've seen a lot of you on the TV."

Her ponytail brushed the back of her Chinooks jersey as she shook her head. "Unfortunately, it seems like the entire planet has seen a lot of me on TV."

"Your dad didn't like those shorts you wore on that show."

"I don't want to talk about *that show*." Over Stony's shoulder, her icy gaze met Sean's.

"No one liked that guy, anyway. Paul's the only one who bet on you making it to the altar."

She took a scandalized breath and stepped out of Stony's embrace. "You all were betting on my wedding?" Her lips turned upside down in an unconvincing frown. "I'm not surprised."

The last time Sean had seen her, she'd been wrapped up in a white bedsheet, her blond hair a mess and one leg hanging off the bed. All warm and sensual, like she was about to pass out after great sex. Her blue gaze warm and satisfied.

Stony waved a hand in his direction. "Have you met our newest right wing, Sean Knox?" She turned her face toward him, her eyes as cold and hard as sapphires. So different from the night she'd played rodeo queen.

"No. I've never met Mr. *Knox,*" she said, and he wondered if Stony heard the slight emphasis on his last name. "I've heard my father talk of him, though."

Yeah. John had called him a nancy-pants and probably worse. He held out his hand, waiting for her next move.

"Sean, this is John's oldest daughter, Lexie Kowalsky."

A big smile split her full lips and her white teeth dazzled like a Crest commercial. He waited to see if she'd expose their connection or not.

"We're all family." She took a step forward and made a point of giving him a big hug. He automatically closed his arms around her. She smelled different this time, too. Like flowery soap and earthy shampoo. "It's good to meet you, Mr. Knox," she said, her warm breath brushing his ear.

She felt the same, though. Like soft, sweet woman, and his body reacted. "Thank you."

Beneath his blazer, her hand slid across his chest, and for one insane second he wondered if she was going to unbutton his shirt like she had a week ago. For one insane second, he wondered if he should let her, right there in the concrete tunnel of the Key Arena. Instead of undressing him, she slipped something in the pocket of his dress shirt. She gave his chest a pat for good measure before she stepped away, taking with her the scent of her skin and feel of her body. A week ago, he would have pulled her right back against his chest. A week ago, they'd been strangers in a strange environment, under strange circumstances.

"You might have seen Lexie on TV," Stony

194

said, as if he hadn't noticed the exchange or the slight pull of Lexie's brow.

"Maybe a time or two." Although he knew her body intimately, they were still strangers.

"I said I don't want to talk about that." She folded her arms across her jersey.

Kevin Olsen rounded the corner and laughed when he saw Lexie. "There's our little runaway bride!" His voice boomed through the tunnel.

"Shhhh." She tried and failed not to smile. "Stop shouting, and before you get started, I don't want to talk about *Gettin' Hitched.*"

"I don't blame you." Brody gave her a quick hug and kept one big hand on her shoulder as he bent forward to look into her eyes. "No one liked that Pete guy. Paul's the only one who bet on you making it all the way to the altar."

"That's what I heard. You boys will bet on anything."

"Next time, go on *American Ninja Warrior.* You'd kick butt on that one." He straightened. "Win yourself some cash instead of a wuss."

Her arms fell to her sides. "Tell the guys to get a new hobby because I'm not signing up for any more television shows or interviews. No more magazine articles." Her brows lowered and she looked at Sean out of the corners of her eyes. "Or pictures in a gossip paper for the world to talk about."

He'd have to be deaf not to have heard the

195

widespread speculation regarding that photo; everything from she'd run off with a lover to she'd been kidnapped. The corner of his mouth twisted up. *Kidnapped. Yeah, fucking right.* That was funny given that she'd dived headfirst into the *Sea Hopper.*

"Me and Chucky talked about it," Kevin said as he dramatically slammed one meaty fist into an equally meaty palm. "You just give us the word, and we'll find that guy and shove a stick up his ass."

Sean turned his attention to the two big men next to him. There was nothing funny about the fire in his teammates' eyes. They were actually serious, and he asked, although he was afraid he already knew, "What guy?"

"The guy in that photo. The one who'd coerced Lexie."

Now it was his turn to look at her from the corners of *his* eyes. "Coerced?"

Lexie raised a hand and covered the top half of her face. "I don't want to talk about that, either."

"Jesus, KO. You're an insensitive jerk." Once again Stony wrapped his protective arms around Lexie. "She's been through enough without you bringing up that jackass who forced himself on her."

Jackass? Forced? What the hell?

"Sorry, Lexie. I just want you to know that I'm

196

right here. If you ever see that guy again, promise you'll call me. I have a hockey stick with his name on it."

Sean looked at her, waiting for her to correct his teammates. To clear things up and set the record straight.

Instead, a slight smile curved her pink lips. "I promise." She patted Stony on the shoulder and stepped away. "But I doubt I'll be seeing much of Mr. Brown." She turned to Sean. "Meeting you was . . . interesting. I have a strange feeling we've met before."

He looked into her blue eyes and the crease across her smooth forehead as if she was deep in thought, trying to solve a mystery. Was she going to point an accusing finger at him now that KO was dying to shove an Easton up his ass, or was she playing a game? "I have one of those faces." The only game he liked to play was played on ice.

"That must be it." She gave another dazzling smile, and he had his answer. She was playing with him, and he didn't like it. "See you guys around," she said as she turned on her heels and moved toward the door. As the others watched her walk away, Sean dug into his breast pocket and pulled out a folded piece of paper. He glanced at the address and the code to a secure elevator written in blue. The word "tonight" was underlined. By the chill in her eyes, he doubted she wanted to scream in ecstasy and call him a cement head again.

"She's such a sweetheart," Stony said as she disappeared out the door.

That was not the first word Sean would have used to describe Lexie. He crumpled the note in his fist and shoved it into the pocket of his blazer. "I'm going to have to take a rain check on those cheese fries."

FIFTEEN MINUTES LATER, Sean entered the elevator of a swanky apartment building in Belltown. His anger shot up incrementally with the rise of each floor. He hadn't coerced or forced himself on Lexie. He'd never coerced or forced himself on anyone. Ever. He'd never even thought about it. If she said no, then she meant no. He had plenty of offers of yes. Women threw themselves at him, or in Lexie's case, fell at his feet.

She wanted to meet and he wanted to know her plans. No games. No manipulations. No implied innocence on her part while condemning him with her silence and pouty lips.

The elevator doors opened and he stepped into an open space constructed of walnut floors and glass, stone, and overstuffed purple furniture with big fuzzy pillows. The far wall consisted of a window so big and clear it appeared as if he could just step from the white carpets and into the lights of the Seattle skyline.

"Hello, Sean." She stood in the middle of the room, the city behind her, lighting her up as if she'd walked in from the skyline. She'd removed her team jersey and held some sort of creature in her arms. It might be a dog, but he wasn't certain. The only thing he could tell for sure was that it wore something pink and fluffy. "Your name *is* Sean, right?"

"Right." She still had on those tight gray jeans he'd noticed earlier, and her feet were bare. Unlike the last time he'd seen her, her toes were painted red instead of pink. "The kidnapping, rapist jackass."

"Don't be so dramatic."

"I'm dramatic?" He put a hand on the front of his jacket. "You're crazy as a bunny boiler."

"You say that like it's a bad thing." She laughed and turned toward the kitchen. "Relax. I would never boil a bunny, and I never said you were a rapist."

"If you tell people you were coerced and forced against your will, that's rape."

"I never told anyone that." On closer inspection, the thing in her arms was indeed a dog. A hairless dog, and she set it on the floor by her feet. "I guess they just assumed it from that picture." A black tongue snaked out and licked the pink tutu around its naked body.

"Do you know who took the photo?" If he

hadn't been preoccupied, he would have noticed the flash.

"Not a clue." She opened a stainless-steel refrigerator and pulled out two beers. "I never knew it was you, the real you, in the photo until a few hours ago." The door shut behind her and she looked downward. "Watch out, Yum Yum precious baby."

Yum Yum precious baby? He might have taken a moment to swallow back some vomit if he wasn't so pissed. "Then who made up that coercion bullshit?"

"Not me!" She shrugged one shoulder and reached into a drawer for a bottle opener. "People just filled in the blanks." She popped the tops and handed him a beer without asking if he needed one. "I didn't correct them."

Obviously.

"Kind of like when I thought your last name was Brown and you didn't correct me." She clinked her bottleneck against his. "Cheers."

"I'm not feeling the cheer."

She chuckled and raised the beer to her lips.

"And I'm not laughing."

"No?" Her deep blue eyes watched him over the brown bottle as she drank. She lowered the Molson and bent down to pick up her ugly dog. "But I bet you had a real good laugh in Sandspit when I thought you were a super secret spy like Perry."

From *Phineas and Ferb*? "I never told you I was a spy."

"I never told anyone to shove a hockey stick up your ass, either." She looked down at her dog and said, "I never would have slept with you if I'd known you're a hockey player."

"But sleeping with Perry the spy is okay with you?" Were they really talking about a cartoon platypus? She nodded as she took a drink, and it was his turn to laugh. "I was there that night. You can't lie to me or yourself. When you had your legs around my waist, you wouldn't have cared if I was a serial killer."

She lowered the bottle and said, "I never lied to you."

"I didn't lie to you, either."

"Maybe not outright." She shrugged one shoulder and looked down at her dog. "A lie by omission is still a lie."

"Exactly."

With her dog cradled against her big breasts, she walked from the kitchen. "You knew who I was the moment we met. I didn't keep it a secret."

"Princess, it was obvious the moment Jimmy shoved you into his seaplane." He pointed his bottle at her. "No way you could keep that a secret."

"KO is right about you. You *are* a jackass."

"Then why am I here?" He took a long drink,

201

irritated with people calling him a jackass. Irritated by his inability to control his gaze from wandering from the swing of her ponytail, down her back, to the curve of her waist and nice round butt. Irritated by the pure lust pouring through his stomach and sloshing around in the bottom of his gut. Mostly, irritated by the chaos she created below his waist, specifically, and his life in general. "If you want to pick up where we left off in Sandspit, we need to get busy. I have a four A.M. flight to Arizona," he said, not bothering to keep the irritation from his voice.

"Don't flatter yourself. It wasn't that memorable."

He could remind her that he'd made her scream from pleasure, but he wasn't *that* big a jackass. Instead he smiled and walked across the room. "Who's lying now, sweetheart?" He took a seat on a purple velvet sofa, cluttered with fussy pillows.

She set her beer on a glass coffee table, sat down, then pulled one bare foot beneath her thigh. Her fingers ran through a patch of long hair on her dog's head, her red cheeks the only indication she'd heard him. "Why didn't you tell me you play for the Chinooks?"

If she wanted to change the subject away from that night, fine with him. "It never came up."

She finally looked up at him. "That's a deke, not an answer, but you're good at it." Her ugly

202

dog jumped up on the top of the couch and shook out its tutu. "Much better at it than your wrister."

He was good at both and chose to ignore her comment. "I didn't realize that you had no idea I played for the Chinooks until we were somewhere over Vancouver." The dog stretched out on its belly with its furry paws in front. The thing had black beady eyes that stared at him through strands of white and black hair falling from the wild topknot on its head.

"That was the first hour."

The little dog scooted toward him. "At the time, I thought it was probably best if your father never found out I'd ripped your wedding dress off of you. Even if it was at your request." That was half the truth. He took a drink, then set the bottle on the coffee table.

"Believe me, that's something I never want Dad to find out about, either. You still should have told me."

He looked at the dog as it inched toward him. Its big furry ears and Flock of Seagulls hair, combined with wrinkly skin and a sharp pointed nose, made probably the ugliest dog he'd ever seen. Certainly the most bizarre.

"You could have mentioned it the next morning at the Waffle Hut or later at your mother's when she was dying to call Wendy." A frown wrinkled her brow. "Or when I brought you lunch in your weight room and stuck around to clear my head of the description of your mother's bowels. Or when I told you that my dad thinks you're a nancy-pants."

"Which time?"

"Any of those times." Another wrinkle creased her forehead as if she couldn't recall talking about it more than once. "Or when you had your hand down my shirt."

"I wasn't thinking about it when I had my hand down your shirt." He was focused on the soft weight of her breast in his palm.

"You could have mentioned it before you snuck out of the hotel room in the middle of the night."

"I didn't sneak. I thought I'd see you on the *Sea Hopper*, later that morning." He glanced at her shifty-eyed dog, then back at her. "It shouldn't have even gotten to that point, but the whole situation just kept snowballing until it got out of control. You have experience with something snowballing out of control."

"You could have contacted me when you returned home."

"I tried. Your voice mail box was full." He pointed to the dog. "Does that thing bite?"

"She's not a thing, and no. She doesn't bite." She paused. "At least not yet."

He glanced at Lexie. "What is it?"

"Yum Yum isn't an 'it' either. She's a Chinese crested." Lexie brushed her fingers through the long hair on her tail. "Please watch what you say in front of her. She's very sensitive, and her feelings are easily crushed."

"What the fuck?"

"And no cursing. She doesn't like it."

"Does she have a fucking swear jar?"

"No, but that's a good idea. You and Dad can help contribute to her chew-toy fund."

"Jes—sus."

A big frown wrinkled her brow again. "Harsh voices upset her."

"But that pink thing you make her wear isn't upsetting?"

"It's from my Woo-Hoo Tutu line of dog couture. Hot pink makes her feel better when she's sad."

He wasn't about to ask how she knew her dog was sad. Mostly because he didn't give a shit, and because he was already sorry he'd asked about the stupid tutu. "It's getting late." Was he really having a conversation about a dog's sad feelings? "Let's cut through the bullshit. Why did you stuff a note in my pocket?"

"We need to talk about the picture."

There was only one picture she could be referencing. "What about it?"

"It's ruined my life."

"I doubt your life is ruined." What a drama queen. "And if it is, you ruined it the day you ran from your wedding."

She shook her head, and her little dog inched

205

closer. "Before the picture came out, I'd managed to repair my reputation and salvage my business. Now it's all ruined again because of you."

"Me?" The dog whipped out her thin black tongue and licked her pointed muzzle. "I wasn't the only one standing outside that motel."

"Now you have to fix it."

Sean had never responded well to demands. He kept his eyes on the dog and said, "I don't have to fix anything. I didn't leak that photo to the press." He could swear the thing was licking her chops in anticipation of snacking on his jugular. He wasn't afraid. He could take her out, but she was unnerving.

"I have a proposition that is mutually beneficial to us both and will fix everything."

He couldn't imagine anything that would benefit both of them. Not unless she changed her mind and wanted to get naked. He pulled his gaze from her dog and gave her his attention. "What is that, princess?"

"You have to convince everyone that you are madly in love with me."

Nope, he wouldn't have imagined that. Her eyes looked into his, steady and serious, and he started to laugh.

"It's the only way that I get my reputation back and you don't get a stick up your ass."

His laughter turned into a deep chuckle.

Her brows lowered and she got all squinty-eyed like her mutt. She might have looked unattractive if she wasn't so damn pretty. "I'm serious."

"I can see that." He rubbed the lower half of his face and tried to wipe away his smile. "How long did it take you to think up this ridiculous scheme?"

"It's not ridiculous." She sat back against the couch and folded her arms across her breasts.

"That's what I thought. You've given it the same scrutiny you did when you agreed to marry a man you didn't know." He leaned forward and grabbed his beer. "Even less than you did when you signed on to the show that fucked up your life."

"It's going to solve our problems."

"I don't have a problem." He pointed the bottle to himself, then took a drink. He wasn't worried about anyone on the hockey team literally shoving a stick or anything else up his ass. He took a few swallows and lowered the beer. He was more worried about a figurative stick. The one that could skewer any progress he'd made with the Chinooks and especially John Kowalsky. Maybe he and Lexie could come up with something. Something about them having met and being friendly. Nothing about being forced or coerced into anything. Maybe he could work it and come out looking like a hero.

"How's your mama doing?"

"Why?" The hairless dog caught his attention as she crept even closer.

"Just wondering."

Sean doubted that as he watched the mutt belly-crawl, tutu and all, close enough to put her pointed nose next to his shoulder on the couch.

"Some elderly people flock to Florida or Arizona this time of year. It's better for their health."

Geraldine was exactly where he needed her to stay. "My mother's health is just fine." In fact, the last time he'd spoken to her, she'd made a miraculous recovery. He figured he had another six months before she was facing certain death again. Six glorious—chaos-free—months that he needed to focus on the Stanley Cup finals.

"Sandspit can't be good for a woman in your mother's delicate condition." She sucked air between her teeth as if in pain. "Her heart palpitations are worrisome. Not to mention her skin lesions."

"My mother would never move someplace where she doesn't have friends or family to complain to. She could never be a little fish in a big pond. It's just not in her." She didn't have much family left, just a cousin or two in Saskatoon. She did seem to have a few friends left in Sandspit—for now. "She doesn't know anyone in Florida or Arizona."

"She knows someone in Seattle, though. Admittedly, Seattle isn't as warm as Sun City, but it has great hospitals and access to wonderful health care, too. I'm sure she would love a long visit with her only child."

Sean's gaze met hers. Her eyes were no longer squinty from anger, but filled with the triumph of a poker player who'd just shown a royal flush. He'd been about to give some thought to her plan. Rework it a little. Negotiate terms so that he'd come away looking like he kept her safe from the media horde. There had been no need to drop the gloves.

"She already thinks we're soul mates." She reached for her beer and smiled. "Thanks to you."

"How long?"

"Have we been soul mates?" She shrugged. "Since before I signed on with *Gettin' Hitched*."

That wasn't what he'd meant.

Lexie took a drink, then looked up at the ceiling as if she was giving it some thought. As if she didn't have it already worked out in her pretty little head. "We were star-crossed lovers. Fate was against us. My father is the Chinooks coach and you played for the Penguins. We didn't believe it would work out and we didn't have enough faith in our love." She returned her gaze to his and smiled. "I was so heartbroken when we broke up, I acted too impulsively. You didn't know I'd signed on to do *Gettin' Hitched*, and I

209

didn't know you accepted the trade to Seattle so you could be near me."

That was so sappy and really did make him look like a nancy-pants. "Let me guess, I got ahold of you before you could walk down the aisle and declared my undying love."

Her grin got bigger. "Isn't it romantic?"

The little dog lifted her head and placed her nose on his shoulder. He got a strange whiff of corn chips and roses as her beady eyes stared at him through the part in her hair. He figured both owner and dog were pushing him to see how far he'd let them go. "As romantic as a slap shot to the groin."

"I prefer Romeo and Juliet."

For now, he'd let Lexie think she had him by the short and curlies because it was to his advantage for people—specifically his teammates—to think they'd known each other before she'd ended up in Sandspit with him. It was to his advantage for her father to believe he had feelings for her beyond irritation. And lust. Lust and irritation were an odd combination he'd never felt for a woman. Usually it was one or the other. If he could tamp down the lust and use the irritation, he could work it to his advantage. "Romeo and Juliet killed themselves."

"The good news is that you don't have to drink poison and I don't have to stab myself."

If he played out this charade, he'd probably

want to kill her. Or himself, he thought as he folded his arms across his chest.

She took his silence for acquiescence. "It'll all be painless, I promise." She returned her beer to the table, and her ponytail fell over one shoulder.

"What about your father?"

"I'll talk to him."

"No." He couldn't let John think he was a pussy more than he already did. "I'll talk to him."

"*We'll* talk to him and my mother." She straightened and turned toward him, her eyes still shiny with victory.

"Before a word of this goes public." He glanced at the dog licking the shoulder of his navy blazer like he'd dropped food on it.

"No problem." She stood as if her proposition was a done deal. "I'll get a notepad and we can outline terms."

She could outline all she wanted, but that meant nothing to him. "Hold on there." She didn't exactly have the best track record when it came to schemes. "I have one condition before I even start to consider your plan."

"What is that?"

"And it isn't up for negotiation." He stood and stared down into her deep blue eyes.

"Okay."

"No shit storms."

"No problem."

He watched her turn and walk across the room.

211

"Just relax," she said over her shoulder. "We'll work it all out beforehand. I have a plan."

"No offense, but I don't trust you to plan anything for me."

"I'm an excellent planner," she said as she opened a kitchen drawer. "I learned to outline for term papers and business plans at Kent State."

He didn't know she'd gone to Kent State, but he didn't know much about her.

"It's kind of my thing." She took out a notebook and a pen. "We need to plan different scenarios in order to mitigate risk," she said as she walked toward him.

His gaze slid from the top of her blond hair and down her pretty face. The only scenario he wanted to work out was putting his mouth on her lips and running his hands all over her body, but not bad enough to mess up his career with the Chinooks. Sex with any woman wasn't worth that, but especially not with Lexie. She was beautiful and tasted sweet. A beautiful, sweet package that tempted a man to take a risk, even when he knew it was bound to blow up in his face.

Chapter 10

• no love lost; no love found

THE FIRST SHIT storm blew the next morning while Lexie spoke with the contractor renovating her store. Before Sean set foot in Arizona, an "anonymous" source contacted the *Seattle Times* with Lexie and Sean's star-crossed-love story. Within an hour of the "leak," the story appeared on the paper's online site and was quickly picked up by the gossip sites. Each added their own brand of snarky commentary with headlines like:

Sean Knox Out Pete Dalton
Hitchin' Bride Ran Away With Hockey Star
Pete Dalton Put on Ice for Sean Knox
Lexie Kowalsky Scores With Hockey Player

TMZ stoked the flames and fueled the story with a photograph of Sean stepping onto the ice at Gila River Arena in Glendale.

Before Sean had left her apartment the night before, he'd reminded her of their agreement to talk to her parents first. He didn't want any distraction while on the road and demanded that the news not happen until the Monday after his return. Lexie tried to negotiate the leak date, but he'd been totally stubborn and wouldn't budge.

Too bad everything got mixed up.

She'd put her *anonymous* source, Marie, in charge of the leak, and Marie being Marie overthought her assignment. Her friend insisted that they needed a layer of plausible deniability and had handed it off to *her* anonymous source, Jimmy. Jimmy being a nincompoop jumped the gun five days before Sean's return. From the road, he'd sent a "What the fuck?" text to her prepaid phone. She'd explained the mix-up but wasn't sure if he believed her. She'd received pretty much the same text from her mother and father. She'd texted them back with a lie, "I love him," and they'd agreed to table the discussion until the team returned that Sunday night, giving Lexie time to make a detailed memo. Of course they'd discussed the plan, but she always felt better when everything was written out. She created sections and subsections, complete with highlights and bullet points, then she'd sent it in a file to Sean's phone. By the time the Chinooks returned from the road, and she met Sean in the belly of the Key Arena, she was feeling almost confident of the plan. The only weak link was Sean himself, but as long as he stuck to the script, everything would turn out fine.

"Has my dad been hard on you?" she asked

next to Sean's ear as they embraced the night of his return. His hair smelled like woodsy shampoo and fresh air, and if anyone was watching, they looked like a couple in love. "Has he yelled or cursed at you?"

"No more than usual." They stood just outside the Chinooks locker room. "But the I'm-going-to-pound-on-you glare has returned to his eyes." He pulled back and looked down into her face. "The guys on the team discovered Gawker and TMZ, and their chirping is relentless."

That was bound to happen with hockey players, who considered chirping a moral obligation. "Did you read the memo?"

"I glanced at it."

The memo needed to be absorbed, not glanced at. The anxiety pounding in her heart kicked up a notch. She took his hand and tried not to look worried as they walked into her father's office. She didn't know what scared her more, the frown on her father's face or that she and Sean might contradict each other.

"Explain this to me." John Kowalsky waved a hand toward them as she and Sean took the chairs across his desk. "The story on the Internet is crap."

Looking at her parents added a heavy dose of guilt to her anxious heart. "It's not crap." Section one outlined the story they would tell her parents. It was always best to stick as close to the truth as

215

possible. Unless the truth needed to be covered with a big fat lie. "I love Sean." She turned to her mother sitting beside her father. "We met in Pittsburgh, and it was love at first sight." She squeezed Sean's hand so he paid attention to the story. Instead he untwined their fingers and loosened his blue striped tie.

"The two of you?" Her father pointed at her, then at Sean. "You want me and Georgeanne to believe this fairy tale?"

It wasn't *entirely* a fairy tale, at least not like the one she'd carefully detailed and planned to tell the press the next day. She turned her gaze to her mother. "You fell in love with Dad the first day you met." She'd been conceived on that day, too. Very few people knew that her mother had once been a runaway bride, too. A runway bride who'd jumped into John "The Wall" Kowalsky's little red Corvette, but now wasn't the time to talk about the first seven years of her life and the impact her parents' own bad choices had made in her life.

Her mother's green eyes worried over Lexie's face and piled on even more guilt. "I don't understand why you didn't tell me that the man in the picture played for your dad."

Because she hadn't known. "I'm sorry. Everything was so crazy and confused." That much was true, and she glanced at Sean to see if he was paying attention. He looked straight ahead as he

216

unbuttoned the collar of his blue dress shirt, and she couldn't tell. "I didn't know if my feelings for him were real." That was close to the truth if she stretched it a bit. "Then Sean sent a note to me at the Fairmont and I just knew I was still in love with him." She hated lying to her parents, but needs must. According to the terms and conditions she had sent Sean, they'd "break up" in May but remain amiable. She'd wanted to give the story time and credibility, but in one of the few texts Sean had actually returned, he'd insisted on the third week in March, three weeks before the Stanley Cup playoffs. He didn't need any distractions and wanted enough time for the story to completely die before he and the Chinooks made a race for the cup.

Lexie had agreed because she didn't have a choice. She needed Sean more than he needed her. One more lifeline had been tossed her way. She wasn't about to let this chance to save herself and her business slip through her fingers. This time she gripped it in a stranglehold and wasn't about to let go.

"We love each other." She reached for Sean's hand resting on the arm of his chair. Their declaration of love might be more believable if he didn't look like a dead man walking and she was the executioner leading him to the gas chamber.

The legs of her father's chair hit the floor and his gaze locked on Sean. "I've heard Lexie mention love a few times now. I haven't heard Sean mention it. In fact, Knox, you haven't said much of anything."

If he blew it, she *would* punch him. Knee him really good, too.

"It happened pretty much like Lexie said," Sean finally spoke up. Now, all he had to do was recite subsection two from the outline. "I waited aboard the *Sea Hopper*, not knowing if she'd even show up. Then I saw her running toward me, and I just knew. I checked her in to the Harbor Inn so she wouldn't feel pressured and took her to meet my mother the next morning." It wasn't exactly what she'd outlined, but close enough. He covered her hand with his and gave a little squeeze. "The two have a lot in common and really hit it off."

The last was not part of section two and set off alarm bells in Lexie's head.

"You haven't mentioned the word 'love,' " her father persisted.

Sean looked down at her and smiled. "There are so many things to love about Lexie." That wasn't in any section or subsection, either. She'd made it simple and really didn't think she could have made it easier:

1. I love her.
   a. Never stopped loving her.
   b. Our love brought us back to each other.

    c. My heart beats for her.
2. Lexie is
    a. Fun.
    b. Smart.
    c. Big-hearted.
    d. Beautiful.

A tic pulled at the corner of the smile she kept glued on her face. She looked up at the amusement shining from the depths of his dark green eyes. She'd blackmailed him into playing her boyfriend. Either he was exacting revenge, or he just wasn't smart enough to follow a simple outline. Both were problematic.

He rubbed his hand up and down her bare forearm, warming her skin with his big palm. "What's not to love about Lexie?"

"I always say that, too." Her mother laid her head on her husband's big shoulder. "Don't I, John?"

"Yes, Georgie," he answered, and kissed the top of her head. "You say that about all the kids."

No one but Lexie seemed to notice that Sean hadn't directly answered the question.

"That was messed up," he said as they walked to the parking lot half an hour later. "I don't like lying to John and your mother."

She looked up at him out of the corners of her eyes. Dusk settled on his forehead, and a chilly breeze tousled locks of his dark hair and turned his cheeks red. He'd put on a long wool coat but left it open enough for the wind to ruffle his tie. "It's okay if you decide to lie to your mother about us, but not okay if I decide to lie to my parents."

"It's not the same. I lied to save your ass from Hoda and Kathie Lee."

Her car lights flashed twice as she pressed a button on the keypad. "And I literally saved your ass from a hockey stick."

"That was just talk. It wouldn't have happened."

"We will never know that now." She stopped by the driver's side door. "Do I need to resend the memo?"

"Nope." He patted a side pocket in his gray overcoat. "Got it right here in my e-mail."

"You went a little off script." Several strands of her blond hair blew across her face, and she shoved them behind one ear. "It's important that you stick to the bullet points tomorrow. Sylvia pounces on the slightest inaccuracy. Real or perceived," she said, referring to the *Seattle Times* reporter.

"You just worry about Lexie." He wrapped an arm around her waist and pulled her against his chest. "In case the world is watching," he said, but kissed her like they were alone. Warm and wet, sucking the breath from her lungs and starting a fire that burned from the tips of her toes, all the way to the top of her head. Just as suddenly he released her, leaving her in stunned silence as he walked away. The wind kicked up the single vent at the bottom of his coat as she raised a hand to her lips. Her fingers felt especially cool against the hot imprint of his kiss, lingering on her lips long after he faded into the dusky evening.

THE *SEATTLE TIMES* had a daily circulation of over two hundred and thirty thousand, with three times as many online views. The morning after the leak had first appeared, the views had almost doubled. By the time Lexie and Sean sat down in his condo, the anticipation had grown so big, the story was being held for the cover of the local section of the Sunday edition, circulation of over eight hundred thousand.

"It was love at first sight," she gushed to reporter Sylvia Navarro. Lexie placed a hand on the front of her cashmere sweater, made from the underbelly of cruelty-free Mongolian goats. "Too bad I didn't trust it at first." She and Sean sat on his gray leather couch, one of his arms wrapped around her shoulders, with the observation deck of the Space Needle in full view in the windows beyond. The perfect setting for the star-crossed lovers. "We just thought the odds were stacked against us." The condo was decidedly modern, inside and out. Cold steel, stark white walls, and slate tiles that definitely could use some color.

"You say you two met in Pittsburgh when Sean was playing for the Penguins." Sylvia's slick black hair fell over one shoulder as she glanced at the notes in her lap. "When was that exactly?"

"September," Sean answered, just as she'd outlined in section three. He wore a green dress shirt and charcoal slacks, the perfect complement to her deep blue sweater and black pants. If Lexie had been allowed to stage the apartment, too, she would have added touches of red and sunny yellow and several area rugs made of long, toe-curling shag.

"What day in September?" The reporter looked up, and if her dark gaze seemed to linger a bit in Sean's direction, Lexie couldn't really blame the woman. He was big and handsome, his cheeks shaved smooth of his usual daily scruff. The color of his shirt made his eyes seem a deeper green, and he smelled like musky soap, rich and intoxicating.

"Sixteenth." And Sylvia didn't appear to be immune to his certain brand of intoxication. "A full month before I agreed to do *Gettin' Hitched*." She paused as if in deep reflection. "I've had time to take a good hard look at my actions, and I know now that I was running from my feelings for Sean. When I agreed to do the show, I'd convinced myself that our relationship was over. My feelings were raw and our relationship seemed so impossible, and the show was a distraction from the pain I felt inside." She laid her head on his big shoulder. "When I signed the contract, I honestly thought I could fall in love with Pete, but my heart still belonged to Sean. I never should have participated when my judgment had been so clouded with pain."

"What did you think when you saw Lexie on reality TV, competing to be the wife of another man?" Sylvia asked Sean as she checked the battery life on her digital recorder.

"Shock. Anger." He chuckled. "But I never thought she'd actually win."

Lexie lifted her head and looked into his face. "I'm very competitive."

"I know. Inherited from your dad's side."

How did he know that? It wasn't in the memo. If she wasn't careful, she might actually believe he had feelings for her. Other than anger and annoyance. She might actually believe she had feelings for him, too. Other than suspicion and a growing fascination with his kiss.

"You shouldn't have competed so hard to win a man you didn't love." He squeezed the top of her arm.

That wasn't part of the script, either, and she felt like she was in Sandspit again, sitting at the Waffle Hut and being judged by him. "If you'd tried a little harder to *win me,* I never would have pulled on a pair of Daisy Dukes and

223

climbed down from a tractor." That wasn't in the memo, either, but honestly, being lectured by the hypocrite who'd lied about his identity when they'd first met added irritation to her list of feelings.

Sean laughed. "If I'd known you were going to win a husband on the set of a fake farm, I would have hog-tied you, baby."

Sylvia's laughter joined Sean's, and Lexie could feel a crease pull her brows. *Baby?* They hadn't discussed terms of endearment and she hadn't thought to include them. "You're so romantic." One unauthorized endearment was probably okay, but this was her life. One wrong move could put a pin in her last chance. She'd have to include some in her memo just to be safe.

"It does sound romantic," Sylvia agreed. "When did you realize that you couldn't let her marry Peter Dalton?"

"When I saw the last episode." Sean removed his arm from around Lexie and sat forward with his forearms on his knees. His green eyes stared across at the reporter, blasting her with his mega-watt charm. "I'd signed with Seattle in late October. Mostly so I could see Lexie, but when I got here, I couldn't find her. I don't watch a lot of television, and I'd never even heard of *Gettin' Hitched*. I'm from Canada. Her father wasn't my biggest fan, so I couldn't ask him."

"That must have been difficult. You have your

career on one side and the woman you love on the other."

"It was, Sylvia." He paused, as if remembering that difficult time. "I searched for Lexie behind the scenes, but no one seemed to know where she was. She'd just vanished on me and I was very concerned."

Wow, he'd gone off script again and made himself look like a great guy? And what did being Canadian have to do with anything?

Sean looked down at his leather shoes. "I don't watch a lot of television, but I was on a spin bike one night at the Key and I looked up and there she was. Rolling in the mud with a pig."

He was purposely ad-libbing, and Lexie got that familiar panicky palpitation in her heart. "That was the lipstick-on-a-pig competition. We had to catch a greasy piglet and put lipstick on it." She paused to put one hand on her chest and explained, "No pigs were harmed during the episode, and I wouldn't normally exploit an animal like that. The poor little pig's heart was beating like crazy. I felt horrible."

Sean glanced over his shoulder at her. His eyes settled on her lips, and he said, his voice deep and intimate as if they were the only two people in the room, "You're so sweet." The palpitations pinched a corner of her heart. This wasn't real, she reminded herself.

"Did you win?" Sylvia wanted to know.

"Of course." Lexie ducked her chin to hide the warmth rushing her cheeks.

Sean laughed and sat back. "We should probably add cutthroat to the list of your charms." Once again he wrapped his arm around her and dropped a casual kiss on her lips. He was good at that. So good at making a casual kiss seem like so much more. If she wasn't careful, she might start to like it too much. If she wasn't careful, she might start to like him too much, and that was impossible.

Sylvia looked down at her notes as if she was intruding on a private moment. "How did the plan to run away from one man to the other unfold, Lexie?"

Impossible. She didn't even like Sean. Not very much, at any rate. "I got a note from a mutual friend that Sean was waiting for me at the docks off Fairview." After Jimmy had messed up the "leak" they'd decided to leave his name out of things as much as possible. "The note said he still loved me and would wait for me until seven-thirty." Then, because he was rubbing her arm and purposely confusing the palpitations in her heart, she added, "He signed it with a little heart." He squeezed her against his side and she smiled up at him. "Wasn't I supposed to mention the hearts?"

He lowered his face and whispered next to her ear, "You're going to pay for that."

"Ahh . . . now who's being sweet?" She laughed at the color rising up *his* cheeks. "I was terrified that I'd miss him," she continued, returning her attention to Sylvia. "But there he was, standing at the end of the dock, waiting for me with open arms."

"It reminds me of Carrie and Mr. Big." Sylvia smiled as if she was reliving the last ten minutes of the *Sex and the City* movie. This was nothing like Carrie and Mr. Big, and Lexie looked into Sean's puzzled green eyes. He clearly didn't know what Sylvia was talking about. Maybe he should watch some TV.

"Except for the closet and the Manolos." And just about everything else.

The reporter laughed at the little joke. "Sean, did you worry that she might have fallen in love with Pete and not show up?"

"No. I was only concerned that she wouldn't get the letter in time. There was no question in my mind that she'd choose me over that guy."

Okay. That was a good answer.

"Pete's a loser," he added. "What kind of man goes on national TV to find a wife?" Lexie opened her mouth to answer, but Sean answered himself, "A sissy who can't get women on his own."

Now he sounded like a jealous lover, which was good but confusing. If she didn't know this

227

was all an act, she might start to believe he cared. "I don't want to talk about Pete."

"I don't blame you. He's a weasel."

Staring at the amusement in his eyes brought her back to reality, reminding her that:

1. He didn't have feelings for her.
2. She didn't have feelings for him.
3. He didn't want a relationship.
4. She didn't want a relationship.
   a. She'd almost married the wrong guy.

"Why Sandspit, British Columbia?" Sylvia asked.

"Two very good reasons," Sean answered, and turned his attention to the reporter. "I wanted my mother to meet Lexie." He pulled her closer against his side again. "No one would think to search for us there, and we needed some serious alone time. If you know what I mean." She elbowed him and he took it further, squeezing her even tighter. "I needed to put a smile back on my baby's face."

"Did he?"

Once again, a warm flush rose up Lexie's throat and heated her cheeks. To the casual observer, it might appear tender and loving. For Lexie, it reminded her of his warm breath on the side of her throat. His big hands on her breasts and her legs wrapped around his waist. They'd never really discussed that night at the Harbor Inn. She didn't want to talk about it now. Nor did she want the little tingles gathering at her wrist, just above her pulse.

"Don't be embarrassed," he said into her hair. His breath warmed her scalp and sent more tingles down the side of her neck, just like that night they'd spent in the small Canadian hotel. "Making love is the best part of being in love. Isn't that what you always say?"

Sort of. While she hadn't included a section on suitable endearments, she had given him a list of answers to questions about love. She'd done the work for him and thought he'd find subsection five useful:

1. Part of love is taking the risk.
2. Love heals all wounds.
3. I saw her smile and I just knew.
4. Making love is *one of* the best parts of being in love.

She'd come up with a few more that she couldn't recall at the moment. He had her flustered and nervous and unable to think beyond the memory of the night he'd spread scattering tingles and chased them with his mouth.

Sylvia turned her questions to Sean and the five years he'd lived in Pittsburgh before he'd "fallen in love with Lexie" and moved to Seattle. His thumb idly brushed her arm through her sweater as he answered.

She knew that he'd played hockey in Pittsburgh from a Google search of his name. Of course she knew that his mother lived in Sandspit, and she knew that he liked his vodka cold and sex hot. At the moment, he was a huge part of her life. She was hanging on by her fingernails. She was depending on him to help save her, yet she knew next to nothing about his life.

"Where do you see yourself in twenty years?" Sylvia asked Sean, pulling Lexie's attention from the man against her side.

"Surrounded by six kids."

"Six kids!" Lexie put a hand on her chest. "With me?"

He squeezed her tight against his side. "I can't wait to get started."

There it was again. The little pinch in her heart that confused truth and lies and made her remind herself that none of this was real. He was acting, and who knew he would be so good at it?

"Where do you see yourself?" the reporter asked Lexie.

Lexie couldn't see that far ahead. There was so much she had to do in the present, she could hardly see past tomorrow. This newspaper article was just second on her list of missions she had to accomplish before she could even begin to think of the future. "Happy and still in love." She held up her index and middle fingers. "Two kids. Maybe three. My business, Yum Yum's Closet, a household name and a franchise of physical stores." As long as she had a reporter in front of her she had to add, "I'm having an opening for my first store at the end of next month. I'll send you an invitation." She flashed the man beside her a smile. "Sean will be there. Who knows, we might have some surprising news by then."

One brow lifted up his forehead. "Really?"

"What news?" Sylvia wanted to know.

The last time she'd gone after free publicity, it had backfired. She was more cautious this time. "I'll call you first. I promise."

"I'm going to hold you to that."

Before Sylvia shut off her recorder, Lexie hurriedly added, "We're asking people to bring a bag of dog food to the opening, which we will donate to our local animal shelters. March is National Animal Poison Prevention Month, and we always donate a portion of that month's profits to the ASPCA. Animal cruelty hurts everyone and must be stopped."

"You're one of those," Sean said.

Lexie looked up into Sean's green eyes. "Of those?"

"Responsible for all those horrible commercials of abused animals on television."

"I thought you didn't watch TV."

"Not usually, but I swear to God, every time I

231

turn it on there's a commercial of a dog with its ribs sticking out and limping down the street."

Sylvia shut off her recorder. "Most people just turn the channel."

"There's no way you can turn it fast enough to avoid seeing a cat with a messed-up eye."

Lexie tried not to judge, but in his case, she didn't try that hard. Abused animals were helpless and broke her heart. She was very disappointed that Sean changed the channel instead of reaching out to help starving dogs and sick kitties.

"I had to give them my credit card number just so I don't feel hammered by guilt each time I change the channel."

THE THURSDAY AFTER the interview, Lexie relaxed with chardonnay in her seat on the third deck at the Key. On the ice below, the Anaheim Ducks skated from end to end enduring the boos of Seattle fans.

"You probably need to say that you have complete respect for the directors and producers," Marie said from the seat beside her.

"I agree." Lexie scribbled on a yellow legal pad as she brainstormed scenarios and crafted a plan for the *Gettin' Hitched* reunion show that was scheduled to tape next month. "And the fans." She wasn't looking forward to the reunion show. She'd rather face a swarm of yellow jackets than the hive of hitchin' brides. She'd stand a better chance of dodging the sting of wasps than the barbs of twenty pissed-off contestants. She'd seen all the episodes and follow-up interviews now. She knew what they'd said about her during the show and in the days afterward.

"And you should probably think of something nice to say about the other women."

Lexie's pen stopped. She opened her mouth to ask if Marie had lost her mind when the arena dimmed and T.I.'s "Bring Em Out" blasted through the speakers. Blue and green lights swirled on the ice below, and the announcer said over the music, "Get ready, Seattle, for your Seattle Chinooks!!!" From the decks below, wild cheers filled the arena as the team stepped from the tunnel and onto the empty ice. They skated from end to end, tightening the circle with each pass. Lexie's gaze landed on number 36 as he stopped at the players' bench and stepped inside. She bit her lip to hide a smile as the lights came back up and the music died. The announcer listed the names of the referees and linesmen, then called out the Ducks starting lineup.

"Boo!" Marie yelled. Like Lexie, Marie had been raised around the Chinooks and knew all the insults. "You suck pond water."

The roar of boos and insults turned to cheers when Seattle's front line was announced.

"Number 36 . . . winner of the Conn Smythe and Art Ross trophies, Sean Knox!"

His team picture and stats flashed across the jumbotron as he skated to the centerline.

"Impressive." Marie pointed her glass of wine toward the ice. "But I noticed he's never won the Lady Byng for sportsmanship."

A live feed replaced the photo, and he raised one hand in a single wave. His green eyes looked upward, and the usual dark scruff covered the lower half of his face. Lexie's tongue stuck to the roof of her mouth.

"Holy balls, Dale," Marie uttered.

Sean was handsome and could take a girl's breath with just a smile. His touch made her skin tingle and made bad thoughts bounce around her head. "Holy balls" pretty much covered it all, and there was only one thing left to be said, "You're Dale. I'm Hank Hill."

"Call me Rusty," Marie laughed.

Everyone rose for the National Anthem, and Lexie put her hand over her heart as it played. She'd discovered that Sean was an ASPCA member, and he liked Yum Yum enough to let her lick his jacket. More importantly, Yum Yum liked him enough to rest her head on his shoulder and stare up into his face. People thought Lexie and Sean were in love and made a perfect couple, but it was a lie. One she needed to remember.

"Where were we?" Marie asked when they took their seats again.

"When?" If she ever forgot, she was afraid she just might end up beneath him again.

"When you were outlining your memo."

"Oh." Now she remembered. "You think I should say something nice about the other women." She took a sip of her wine, then added, "I'd rather get stung by bees."

"Yeah, but you gotta do it or you'll seem like a bitch." Marie took a drink of merlot as she watched the puck drop. "I mean, look at it from their point of view. You didn't have sex with him, yet you still won anyway. You got the ring and the big puffy dress that they all wanted. Then you ditched the groom at the altar and ran away with a superhot hockey player. For all they know, he swooped you up and flew you off to get reacquainted on the night you were supposed to start your honeymoon with Pete."

The idea of starting up anything with Pete made Lexie's nose wrinkle, and she highly doubted she would have consummated the marriage. As for what went on when they were taping the show— her lawyer had gone over every bit of the contract she signed before she appeared, and there hadn't been anything in it saying she had to ever have sex with Pete.

Her thoughts were interrupted by action on the ice below. Paul Letestu passed the puck across the ice. In one fluid motion, Sean skated forward, pulled back his stick, and one-timed it on Badaj's stick side. The Ducks goalie deflected it and the whistle blew.

"Try and think of one thing nice about each girl." Marie pointed to the notepad. She was clearly not letting this go. "Create a subsection under *Gettin' Hitched* bitches."

Of the many things that Lexie and her best friend had in common, their love of detailed memos was near the top of the list.

Lexie figured that title was apropos. She'd been hurt and astonished, actually, by some of the things the other women had said behind her back and didn't believe she owed them anything at all. "I don't know where to even start." Marie was right, though. Being nice cost her nothing. Looking like a bitch could cost her a lot.

"Start with Cindy Lee from Clearwater. Find something nice to say about her."

Hmm. Cindy Lee had said Lexie never worked a day in her life. "How about, 'Cindy Lee isn't as big a bitch as Davina from Scottsdale?'" Davina had told the confession cam that Lexie looked like Sasquatch with dark roots. "Or that Summer's teeth aren't quite as yellow as corn."

Marie frowned. "You're not getting the point of this on purpose."

Once more the whistle blew and it was game on again. Lexie's gaze skimmed the ice, but she didn't see number 36. "I get it. I just don't like it." She looked toward the Chinooks bench and saw him sandwiched between other players, their attention rapt as they pounded their sticks on the board, chewed on their mouth guards, and spit between their feet. Her dad stood behind them with the other coaches, their arms across their chests, their gazes lasered in on the players passing the puck and dumping it behind the goal.

The two men in her life. She counted on them both. One she loved and trusted with her life. The other she wasn't even sure she liked. She couldn't even trust him to follow the carefully outlined, super-easy memo she'd given him.

The whistle blew and the game stopped. "Crazy Train" pumped through the arena and the camera operator panned the crowd, stopping on Lexie and Marie and zooming in on their faces. *All aboard, hahaha,* Ozzy laughed. On all four fifteen-foot screens, she gave a little wave and smiled.

Another mission accomplished.

Chapter 11

• love is a battlefield

THE RETROFITTED DC–9 took off over Seattle within a blinding ball of morning light. Almost at once, seventeen window shades lowered on the aircraft as it headed into the rising sun and a five-game, nine-day road trip. Twenty minutes into the flight, the seat belt light went off and coats and blazers were stowed in overhead bins, ties loosened, and breakfast was served from the catering service hired to provide the special diet for twenty elite athletes, coaches, and staff. While some of the hockey players ate omelets and bacon and hash browns, Sean stuck to a bowl of oatmeal, Greek yogurt topped with blueberries, and a vanilla whey shake. Each loaded up on carbohydrates and protein to begin the game-day process toward an optimal energy build. Their individual diets were dictated by years of conditioning and team nutritionists, but most of all by superstition. Adam Larson ate sausage but wouldn't think of allowing bacon to pass his lips, on account of the 2010 final against the Rangers when he'd been carried off on a stretcher from a groin injury after the pre-game meal of a bacon sandwich. KO didn't eat dairy, and Sean refused Gatorade on account of a neutral zone spew at the Air Canada Cup Nationals when he'd played in the midget league.

After breakfast, Sean pulled out his phone and watched game tapes of the Red Wings defensive line. When Howard was hot, he locked low and wide and committed with split-second timing. When he was cold, he hung out in the blue ice and lost angles and opened up holes. The question was, how to make a hot Howard turn cold?

"Hey, Knox."

Sean lowered his phone and tilted his head to the right and glanced a few rows down the aisle into left defender Butch "The Butcher" Ferguson's red-bearded face.

"Look what I found on my porch before I left this morning." He handed something to Brody in the seat behind him. Brody passed it along to Adam, and he dropped it on the table in front of Sean.

Love on Ice. He looked down at the local section of the *Seattle Times* and the bold title just above the picture of him and Lexie. The photo of them sitting on the couch in his condo took up half the page. They both smiled into the camera, looking relaxed and natural. Seeing it, no one would notice the underlying tension or guess that it was all a lie. No one but him knew that he'd tried and failed not to think of her naked the whole time. His arm around her shoulder had made him remember how she'd felt against his chest. Sitting next to her reminded him of how she'd looked sitting on top of him, the dip of her waist, her big breasts, and the deep blue of her eyes. Wild and the sexiest thing he'd ever seen. He'd remembered how she'd felt, too. Soft and warm, their skin sticking together in the best places. She'd felt so good and tasted even better.

The photographer had captured a beautiful angle of her face, and Sean was relieved that he had a goofy look on his face. He unfolded the paper and read the caption beneath the photo: *"I got a note from a mutual friend that Sean was waiting for me." Lexie on why she left Pete Dalton at the altar. "He signed it with a little heart."*

The blood rushed from Sean's head and the corners of his eyes pinched. Fuck.

"Sign my copy with a little heart," the left defender said before his booming laugh filled the plane.

"Eat me, Butch." Sean shoved the paper back down the row. It got as far as two seats before Tim Kelly paused to read it. "I never met a celebrity before."

Just when he'd passed the new-guy hazing phase, this. He glanced toward the front of the plane to see if John had overheard the conversation. The only thing he saw was the sleeve of the coach's shirt and part of one hand flipping through game tapes on his laptop.

"I met Adriana Lima at a Victoria's Secret show," Chucky bragged. "Never did get an article written about my love life, though."

This wasn't his love life. Sean pushed a big grin on his face like he wasn't the least bit bothered by the story or the razzing. "Maybe you're not as pretty as me."

Brody upped the ante. "I met Scarlett Johansson after a Kings game a few years back."

"Was that when she was dating Sean Penn?" Stony wanted to know.

"Why does that matter?"

"He put the dirty hippie taint on her," Stony said. "It's hard for a girl, even a girl like Scarlett, to recover from something like that."

Several players laughingly agreed.

"Are you saying you wouldn't do her because she dated Sean Penn?" Brody asked.

"No. I didn't say that."

"I met Milla Jovovich," Adam boasted.

"She's badass in *Resident Evil*," KO said, and the conversation turned into a competition of who'd met the hottest celebrity.

Henrik Frolik, so fresh from the Czech Extraliga, said something, his accent so thick, no one understood a word. No one but ten-year veteran Martin Rozsival, who looked at everyone and said, "Petra Němcová."

"Ah."

"She's hot, Henrik."

Henrik nodded, and it was the next player's turn. "I met Emma Stone at the last *Spider-Man* premiere."

"I met January Jones when I played for the Rangers." Paul upped the ante by adding, "And Kate Upton."

"Kate Upton's hot."

"Did you see the picture of her cutting off her own shirt?"

"Yeah. Jesus."

"I met Gordie Howe."

A reverent hush fell over the plane. Meeting Mr. Hockey was better than meeting Gretzky or Messier or both. Better than three courses of Petra, Emma, and Scarlett, with a side of Kate Upton.

For the next few hours, the team settled in with their electronic devices, watching movies or game tapes or playing Big Win Hockey. The plane touched down in Detroit just before eleven A.M. A freezing wind whipped the tails of Sean's coat and stung his cheeks as he walked from the plane to the waiting bus. A light snow flurry swirled around his dress shoes and he lifted his shoulders against the cold.

"Knox." John Kowalsky caught up to him, his coat open and collar unbuttoned, seeming impervious to the cold.

Sean stopped and turned toward Lexie's father, waiting. He and Lexie had stuck mostly to the truth the night they'd talked with her parents, but he was sure the newspaper article had dredged up a few more questions that Sean didn't feel like answering. Mostly because he hated lying to John.

"Howard is sitting at 1.8," he said over the wind as they moved toward the bus. "Decent. He's worked blocker saves, but when he goes paddle down, he leaves his five open."

"I saw that, too."

John looked across his shoulder at him, creases fanning the corners of his eyes, with something that looked like a bit more respect. "I think if you go top shelf, you'll find air up there."

Sean liked this John a hell of a lot more than the man who'd called him a hotdog to his face and a nancy-pants behind his back. Guilt twisted and coiled inside his chest as he waited for the coach to mention the newspaper article and Lexie.

"That thing that happened the other night in my office."

Sean had been waiting for this and mentally squared his shoulders.

"You keep your head in the game. We're going to table that other thing." John cleared his throat. "For now."

The team loaded on the bus and John didn't mention it. He didn't say a word about Sean and

Lexie when they all met for lunch and loaded up on pasta before the game.

Taking the ice in Detroit always tested a player's ability to focus. The wave of boos and pelting insults surging from the Red Wings fans threatened to get inside a guy's head and knock him off his game if he let it.

The insults from the players weren't much better, but at least could be addressed.

"You want this? Huh?" the Detroit enforcer asked Sean as he tied him up against the boards. "You don't want any of this."

"You should have retired already." Sean pushed back, fighting to keep his eyes on the puck. "You're embarrassing yourself."

In the second period, the Chinooks were up a point and the insults got more personal. "You know the difference between your girlfriend and a walrus?" a Red Wing chirped as he jostled for position in the face-off circle. "One has a mustache and stinks like fish, the other is a walrus."

Sean laughed as he easily hooked the puck and sent it cross-ice to Chucky. Sean knew for a fact that Lexie didn't have a mustache and smelled like peaches.

Over the next two games, Sean took a few more insults directed at Lexie. It was part of the game and didn't bother him. The same could not be said for Ozzy Osbourne and "Crazy Train."

Each time the song pounded through the arena, it filled his head with the memory of Lexie's big beautiful breasts.

On day seven, the team landed in St. Louis, winning by two points but losing Butch due to a high stick to the cup that doubled him over and dropped him to the ice. As he lay curled on the ice, whistles blew, gloves dropped, and players mixed it up in the corners, resulting in a combined fifteen penalty minutes and a four-on-three advantage. Sean took three shots on goal, each deflected by Rask.

He took his place in the face-off circle in the end zone and crouched with his stick across his knees, waiting for Paul to get situated inside the circle across from the Blues center.

Blues defender Marty Holt bumped Sean's shoulder as he took the spot next to him. "I almost didn't recognize your girlfriend with her back shaved."

If Sean had been in a good mood, he would have laughed. Lexie had a beautifully smooth back. Too bad he was pissed off, frustrated, and feeling the pressure to get one in the net while they still had the advantage. "You're a slow dusty fuck." He put his blade on the ice and kept his eyes on the puck suspended in the referee's hand mid-circle.

The puck dropped and Paul dug it out from the other man's stick and fed it to Sean. He passed it behind him to Chucky just before Hutchison hit him hard, but if he thought he could knock Sean off his skates, he was doomed to disappointment. Sean pivoted free in time for Chucky to shoot it back. He cushioned the puck in the curve of his blade, faked a wrister, but pulled a backhander out of his bag of tricks, finessing the puck between the goalie's pads. The red light flashed and the goal horn blew. Some of the pressure lifted from Sean's shoulders as he lifted his stick in the air. At once, his teammates surrounded him and slapped him on his back and shoulders with their big gloves. "How'd you like that one?" he called out to Hutchison as he skated to the bench, bumping gloves with the other Chinooks.

"Suck it, you overrated pigeon."

Sean laughed and looked up at the scoreboard. They were up by one point. He'd feel a lot better if it was two. He sat between Paul and Jay Lindbloom, a rookie so fresh his game beard looked moth-eaten.

"That was a beauty, boys," John said from behind him.

Sean squirted water into his mouth and looked over his shoulder. The coach's attention was fixed on the ice but a smile curved his lips. Sean swallowed and bumped knuckles with Chucky.

Being up by one wasn't enough to satisfy the Chinooks' bloodlust. The hits got harder, the verbal abuse more caustic.

"Good one, Lenny," Stony called out, heckling the Blues winger when his pass bounced off his teammate's left skate.

"Yeah, if you're trying for the worst pass of the year," Brody added.

With a minute left in the game, KO hit the Blues front-line forward, who had the misfortune of falling on his ass in front of the Chinooks bench.

Paul hit his stick on the board as the whistle blew. "Are you going to sit there and cry, little girl?"

Sean leaned forward and looked down at the guy, who'd raised himself to one knee. Before playing for the Chinooks, Sean had been on the receiving end of a KO hit and knew what it was like to have the enforcer knock the breath right out of his lungs. That didn't keep him from saying, "Show some class. Get up, you fucking sissy."

"Yeah. Show some class, you donkey baby."

Sean looked across his shoulder at Jay. " 'Donkey baby?' "

The rookie shrugged his shoulders inside his big pads.

Sean and Paul laughed as they stood and scissored their legs over the board, onto the ice. Thirty seconds later, the horn blew and Sean was more than happy to put the game behind him. In the locker room, he took a hot shower, warming his muscles and soothing the hard hits to his body. The team's assistant coach informed everyone that Butch was on the injured list and was expected to stay there for at least two more weeks.

Sean lagged behind and had the Chinooks massage therapist work out the kinks in his lower back and rub out the pain in his shoulder from the hit Hutchison had put on him. By the time he got dressed in his tie and blazer and grabbed his coat, most of the boys had left the Scottrade Center. The sun had set over the Gateway Arch lit up in blue, and the temperature rolling off the Mississippi had dropped to forty-five degrees as he walked the two blocks to the hotel alone. The team wasn't flying to Boston until the next morning, and Sean looked forward to room service and a good eight hours of sleep. As he entered the Hyatt, his phone vibrated with a text message from Lexie, letting him know that she'd sent him an updated memo and he should check his e-mail and get back to her "ASAP." His back felt better and his shoulder wasn't as sore, and the last thing he was going to do was read her damn memo and give himself brain damage. He hadn't been able to get through the others she'd sent, and he'd rather stab himself in the head than read any more of her sections, subsections, and bullet points.

"Knox."

Sean looked up at Lexie's father standing by the bank of elevators. He returned his cell phone to his blazer pocket. "Hey, Coach."

"What's put that pained look on your face?" John asked as if he already knew the answer to his question.

"Your daughter and her memos." The doors slid open and the two waited for a mother and three children to exit before they stepped inside.

"She gets that from her mother's side. What floor?"

"Ten."

The doors closed as John punched the ten and eighteen. "I never would have picked you for Lexie." Sean looked across his shoulder at the older man. "It's nothing personal, I never would have chosen a hockey player for Lexie. I would have chosen someone normal."

"You don't think hockey players are normal?"

He glanced at Sean. "You know the life. It can be hard on a family. I always thought Lexie should marry someone safe. Preferably a dentist. He's home every night and our family gets a dental plan at a discount. And we need it. My son plays junior triple A and he's only fifteen. You know he's bound to lose a few teeth." Both men almost cracked a smile. "I thought I had her convinced she needed a normal guy. Then she turns up on that damn TV show and ends up winning herself a husband."

"Pete's a jagwagon." Compared to that guy, Sean probably didn't look so bad right about now.

"Yeah. While she was picking out a wedding dress, I was picking out ways to kill him and get away with it." The elevator stopped and number ten above the door blinked off. "For a person who likes detailed memos, she can be impulsive, and it gets her in trouble."

The door slid open and guilt rushed in at Sean. "Good night, Coach," he said, and stepped into the long hall.

John put a hand on the door to keep it open. "The other night at the Key, you didn't come right out and say you love my daughter."

Sean guessed they weren't tabling the discussion and now was the time. He knew what John wanted to hear and thought of one of Lexie's handy-dandy lists of pat answers. "The first time I saw her smile, I knew." At least that's what he thought it said. Then he swallowed past that lie and heard himself say, "I love her more with every breath, truly madly deeply." Jesus, had he just quoted Savage Garden? He didn't even like that damn song.

John's brows pulled together across the creases in his forehead as if he was trying to figure out if he'd heard the lyrics and just couldn't place them. Either that, or he was trying to figure out if Sean had turned into a girl. "That's good," he

251

said, and stepped back further into the elevator. "That's what a father needs to hear." The doors slid shut on John's puzzled face, and Sean felt heat rise up his neck and burn his cheeks.

He'd never quoted mushy love songs in his entire life, and he'd just poured out the most embarrassing sap to the person whose respect had slipped through his fingers. A man he'd admired growing up. A hockey legend, John "The Wall" Kowalsky.

He moved down the hall and pulled his key card out of his pocket. It was because he'd been rattled about the lie, he told himself as he unlocked the door and walked inside. If not for that, he never would have humiliated himself. If he wasn't careful, he was afraid he'd go full Michael Bolton, or worse, Justin Bieber.

His roomie, Adam Larson, sat on one of the queen-sized beds with his feet crossed, watching television. The goalie glanced at Sean as he took off his coat and tossed it on the back of a desk chair. "Your cheeks are red. You must have been outside. Colder than a penguin's balls out there."

"Yeah." That was it. He loosened his tie, and his phone vibrated in the pocket of his blazer. He pulled it out and read another text from Lexie.

The Gettin' Hitched reunion show is taping the day after you play the Kings in LA. The producers asked if you were coming with me.

Sean wrote, You told them no. Right? He buttoned the collar of his shirt and removed his tie and blazer.

Not exactly, she answered back.

What exactly did you tell them? He tossed his cell phone on the nightstand and tossed his garment bag on the bed.

She took a few moments to answer. I informed them that you'd consider it.

Of course she had. She was as pushy as her mutt. If he wasn't careful, in her memo under public displays of devotion she'd write, "carries purse and buys tampons."

Inform them that I considered it and said no. I'm not going to appear anywhere near that show. He pushed send and thought that was the end of the subject. Apparently, he was wrong. Two days later, he agreed to meet her at a trendy bar in Post Alley. She sat at a pub table and he had to push his way through a crowd of hipsters in skinny jeans and heavy beards, baggy plaid, colored tights and combat boots.

"Hello." Not to be outdone by her surroundings, she wore ripped jeans, Nirvana T-shirt, and black leather jacket. She'd pulled her hair back, and she stood to greet him and offered her cheek for a kiss.

"Hello, baby," he said above the noisy bar, and lowered his face to her dark red lips. Her mouth opened below his, as if she might have something to say. He took advantage of her parted lips and gave her a wet kiss. A publicly acceptable kiss that hinted at the kind of pleasure they enjoyed in private. He slid his hand up her back, under her leather jacket, and pressed her breasts against the front of his hooded sweatshirt. He wanted to catch her off guard and rattle her. He hadn't planned on being rattled himself, instantly frustrated by the thick clothing that separated her naked breasts from his bare chest.

He lifted his head and looked into her eyes filled with surprise and a hint of sultry frustration. At least that's what he liked to believe. He'd hate to think he was the only one feeling like they should move the party of two a few blocks away to his condo and get reacquainted.

He stepped back, and his hands fell to his sides. That kind of thinking was crazy. That kind of thinking led to doing, and doing led to more problems. Problems he didn't need.

"This is my friend Marie," Lexie introduced him to the other woman sitting at the pub table. "Marie, this is Sean."

Lexie slid into a chair and Marie stood, or hopped down really. She was short, had dark hair pulled back in a stubby ponytail, and wore black glasses with little rhinestones at the corners. While Lexie wore hipster chic like a fashion choice, Marie's Doc Martens, plaid skirt, and "Feminist As Fuck" T-shirt were clearly a lifestyle. She wore no makeup except deep red lipstick, and still managed to look cute as hell, in a feminist-as-fuck sort of way.

"Hello, Sean." She shook his hand, and he noticed the crease between her blue eyes as if she was sizing him up in case she might have to kick his ass. Funny given that she was about five feet, two inches and weighed next to nothing.

"Marie drove me to the dock the night we took off in the *Sea Hopper*."

Ah. The driver of the clown car. "It's nice to meet you."

She let go of his hand. "Thank you, Sean." She retook her seat and he turned toward the bar and signaled a waitress. "What are you ladies drinking?"

Lexie took the last sip from her cocktail glass. "Golden Shower." She smiled like she was going to enjoy hearing him order up one of those.

Marie held up a frosty mug and grinned. "Horny White Girl."

Jesus. Within seconds a waitress stood in front of him with a big smile on her pretty face. If it wasn't for the nose ring and lip piercings, and of course if he wasn't pretending to be Lexie's boyfriend, he might have seen if he could get more than a smile from her.

"Hello, Sean," she said, and took a small note-pad from her apron pocket. "I'm a huge Chinooks fan and was at the Anaheim game the other night. You guys are looking good this year."

"Thanks. Hope you can make it to every game. We love to hear our fans getting rowdy."

"What can I get for you tonight?"

"I'll have an Amstel." He motioned toward the table with his hand.

"Sean!" Lexie called out. "No."

"I've got this one, babe. My girl would love another Golden Shower." He waved in Marie's direction. "And our friend is down for another Horny White Girl?"

"Can I interest you in truffle popcorn or chicken and lamb skewers?"

"None for me." He turned toward the women. "Are you ladies interested in food?" They shook their heads and ducked their faces. "Is something wrong?"

Lexie said something he didn't quite catch. He took the chair next to her and leaned in. "What?"

"This is a Lemon Drop and Marie is drinking Diet Coke." She looked up at him. "We were joking!" Her cheeks were a nice scarlet color, and bright red rose up Marie's neck.

"You should have told me!"

"I tried!"

He looked from one to the other and started to chuckle. Laughter from deep in his chest built and rose, rocked him back in his chair, drawing the attention of people around them.

The whispers of "It's Sean Knox and Lexie" rose and grew louder until their table was surrounded. Just as Marie's Horny White Girl arrived, she grabbed her leather backpack and said, "I'm out of here."

"We'll talk later," Lexie told her friend as she slid her hand in his, resting on the table. It was for show. All for show, and he brushed his thumb back and forth across her knuckles.

"We're happy in love, now," Lexie answered a question thrown at them. "But yes, running from my wedding to Pete was scary as heck. I wasn't sure what would happen. Only that I couldn't marry one man when I loved another. I was anxious and frightened and uncertain what the future looked like for me and Sean." Lord, she was a good liar. She gazed up at him, looking like she'd fallen so hard for him, it had turned her soft in the head. She was such a good actress; if he didn't know better, he'd fall for it, too. "Then I saw him at the end of the dock, and I knew."

The look bothered him more than the lie. Maybe because he couldn't recall a woman looking at him like she was so deep in love she'd never find her way out. He'd had his share of girlfriends, and none had looked at him like that. Not even after he'd coughed up expensive gifts.

A question got lobbed at Sean and he pulled his gaze from Lexie. "Pardon me?"

"Didn't it trouble you to see her in a wedding dress meant for another man?"

"No. I'm secure enough not to get bothered over a dress." Which was true. He recalled her rolling around in that ridiculous dress, then buttons pinging around the fuselage as he ripped it down the back. "But I did have trouble getting her out of that damn dress." He held up his free hand. "My fingers were too big for all those slippery buttons."

"He says such romantic things to me." The smile at the corners of her lips dipped a bit and she squeezed his hand. "Just last night, he told me he wished he could reach up into the sky and pull out the brightest star just for me."

Jesus. She'd obviously OD'd on romantic quotes. She was making him look like he was soft in the head, too. A real lovesick wimp.

"I told him I don't need stars. Just him to stand under them with me forever."

"Ahh," a few women sighed.

"And—"

"Baby." He lowered his face and silenced her with a soft kiss. His hand slid up her arm to the back of her neck. "You'll ruin my reputation in the league," he whispered across her lips. She opened her mouth as if to respond, and he silenced her with a kiss, because God knew what she might say next. A long, deep kiss that tasted of lemon and sugar. A kiss that was meant to suck the breath from her lungs and give her something to think about besides those damn romantic sayings she'd probably found in an Internet meme. A kiss meant to slip inside and heat up the pit of her stomach, to make her heart beat a little faster, and leave her wanting more.

When the kiss ended, she opened her eyes wide and licked her lips. She wasn't the only one heated up and wanting more. "Ready to go?"

She nodded, and he once again took her soft hand in his. They wove their way through the bar and out onto the street. Inky patches of overcast sky hid the stars she'd said he wanted to pull out just for her. A thick chill hung just above freezing and seeped through the weave of Sean's hooded sweatshirt and jeans. Damp air clung to his cheeks and exposed neck and nipped at the tips of his ears.

"Are you planning on going to the Biscuit in the Basket fund-raiser?" she asked. Multicolored lights from storefronts shone in her blond hair and on the side of her face.

He'd heard something about the fund-raiser but hadn't given it much thought. "Maybe."

"All the money goes to youth hockey, but it's a strictly twenty-one-and-older event. There's lots of booze and gambling."

He wouldn't mind playing poker with the guys.

"I'll get the tickets. It'll be a good place for us to be seen together."

Of course. They needed to be seen together. That shouldn't bother him, but for some reason it did. "Where are you parked?"

"Parking lot down a block." She dropped her hand from his and shoved it into her pocket. "Do you need a ride?"

"No. I jogged here." The cool night air chilled his palm where it had pressed into hers. "I'll jog back."

"In this weather?"

"It's only a mile or so." He stuck his hands in his sweatshirt pocket. "I still get lost in this city, and it's actually easier for me to get around on foot."

They moved past a seafood restaurant and a coffee shop.

She looked up at him and her shoulder bumped his arm. "I could show you around." She thought a moment. "Have you been to the Chihuly Garden? It's by the Key and your apartment."

"No. I really haven't had a lot of time since I was traded."

Her lips pursed as she paused in thought, and he wondered if she was trying to drive him crazy. "We're limited this time of year," she said, as if they'd still be pretend dating. "And I refuse to have anything to do with the zoo. Captivity is sad and mean."

He could suggest a Woo-Hoo Tutu, but thought better of it.

"I help raise money for the endangered species, but that doesn't mean I approve of warehousing animals. It's just wrong."

He didn't like cruelty to animals as much as anyone, but he wasn't opposed to a fur rug beneath his feet.

He grabbed her elbow and walked to the curb. He looked one way and then the other, then stepped into the street between a Prius and a micro car.

"The producers of *Gettin' Hitched* contacted me today."

He looked down the street at a headlight in the distance as she threaded her arm through his and hurried beside him. "They offered to move the taping to the Fairmont here in Seattle."

"Still not interested."

She cozied up to his side, and a lock of her hair rested on his shoulder. "They even moved the day to make it convenient for you."

He looked down at her, getting all snug against him in order to warm him up. "I'm not getting anywhere near that drama."

"It'll be painless."

"That's what you said before."

"That wasn't my fault. It's hard to find reliable leakers these days." She shook her head and stepped up onto the curb beside him. "Please say

261

you'll come to the taping. Yum Yum and I could really use your support."

They moved into the dark parking lot. "Sorry, you and your little dog are on your own with this one." He was a nice guy, but he had his limits. He wasn't nice enough to appear on that stupid show.

"The other girls are going to gang up on us. They can be really mean."

They moved into the pitchy darkness between two cars, and he glanced down into the smooth shadows of her pretty face. She was a hell of a lot stronger than she appeared at first. More determined, too. "I put my money on you and your dog. You're smarter than all those girls put together."

She shook her head and pulled her keys from her pocket. "They're going to ask me questions about you and that picture taken outside the Harbor Inn." The car behind her made two beeps and the lights flashed twice as the locks popped up. "Personal questions that are going to make me look bad."

"What happened that night is no one's business but ours." He didn't need to see her face clearly to cup her cheek in the palm of his hand. "I had a good time. You had a good time. No one was hurt."

"How can you say that? My business suffered."

"Your business suffered the second you decided

to run from the Fairmont. Don't get it twisted."

"I'm not. That shouldn't have happened."

But it did.

"They're going to try and make me look skanky. I'm not like that. That night was . . . was . . ." She struggled for words.

"Was good." He kissed her forehead and temple. "We're adults, Lexie. You're beautiful and hot, and sex with you is something I still think about." Her mouth found his in the dark. Unlike the earlier kiss in the bar, there was no reason to hold back. No one was watching or acting or playing at anything. The instant her mouth touched his, everything got real hot real fast. No sweet kisses for the camera this time. With his free hand, he unzipped her leather jacket and slid his hand inside. Her ribs were warm against his palm, her breasts warmer. She moaned into his mouth and he backed her against the car door and shoved his pelvis into her belly. Her nipples were so hard, he felt them through her shirt and bra. He remembered the taste and softness of her, and he wanted that again. Right here. Right now. In a parking lot in Seattle.

She fed him another long, sweet moan and rocked against his full-blown erection. Hard and painful, craving the soft pleasure of her body. He grabbed the backs of her thighs, and she readily wrapped her long legs around him. Just like that night at the Harbor Inn, her fingers combed through his hair and he fanned her puckered nipple with this thumb, back and forth, feeling it grow harder beneath his touch. He wanted her. He wanted to slide his mouth all over her and make her his. At that moment, he couldn't recall anything he wanted as much as he wanted her. By the sounds in her throat and the crotch grinding into him, she wanted it every bit as much. There was a part of him that knew he was only causing more trouble for himself. More chaos. At the moment, he didn't care.

She pulled back and took a huge gulp of air. Without a second of hesitation, he slid his open mouth to the side of her cool neck.

"Sean."

"Mmm." He kissed her throat, feeling the varying degrees of temperature as he lowered his face.

"Sean!" She placed her hands on the sides of his head and brought his face to hers. Through the pitchy darkness she said, "Someone just walked into the parking lot."

His hand squeezed her. "Then we'll have to be quiet."

The car behind him beeped twice, the lights flashed, and Lexie's feet hit the ground before the locks popped up. His hand slid from her breast and she looked down at the ends of her jacket.

The threat of getting caught dry humping like a teenager did nothing to alleviate his hard-on.

"Come home with me tonight," he spoke to the part in her hair.

She shook her head and zipped her coat up practically to her chin. "Sex will just complicate things."

Not for him. Sex was just sex. Sometimes fast. Sometimes slow. Not complicated unless someone wanted to make it complicated.

The phone in his hoodie vibrated and saved him from an argument he knew he would lose. "Yeah," he answered without checking the number.

"I'm here."

"What?" He actually pulled the phone from his ear and looked at the number. "Mother?"

"I'm here," she repeated herself. "But I don't have a key and the guy at the desk won't let me in."

"Where?" A bad feeling landed in the pit of his stomach. "Where are you?"

"Here."

"In Seattle?"

"Yes. Where are you?"

Hell. "How did you get here?"

"Your friend with the frog plane."

"Jimmy?" He glanced down into Lexie's dark face. "Why are you here?"

"I'm your mother. Who else should help you plan your wedding?"

"Wedding?"

"I heard it on *Wendy Williams*!"

He looked out into the parking lot and the glassy rain puddles. "You shouldn't get your news from Wendy."

"I have experience planning weddings, you know."

Yeah, she'd planned three of her own.

He looked at Lexie for help.

"Lexie's a pretty girl, but you can't expect someone special with a dusty attic to do it on her own," his mother said.

Lexie slid into her car, and the dome light turned on just long enough for him to see the smile on her face and the laughter in her eyes. She probably wouldn't be smiling so big if she knew his mother thought she was "special."

"That trip just about killed my small bladder."

He imagined she'd complained the entire trip. It served Jimmy right. "Hand the phone to the guy at the front desk." One of the last things he needed was for Geraldine to chat it up with people in his building. Lexie gave him a little three-finger wave as she drove from the parking lot, and the taillights of her small SUV disappeared into the dark Seattle night. He instructed the front desk to let his mother into his apartment, then shoved the phone inside the pocket of his hooded sweatshirt. A water droplet hit his forehead and ran down the bridge of his nose. Just as he looked up into the heavy night sky, inky clouds opened up and pelted him with cold rain.

He raised the hood over his head and ducked his face against the stinging downpour. By the time he'd jogged three blocks, his sweatshirt and shoes were soaked. At the corner of Broad Street and Second Avenue, a minivan raced through a yellow light and sent a spray of water up his legs to the crotch of his pants.

Fabulous. He was soaking wet, freezing to the marrow of his bones, and his mother waited for him at his apartment. He didn't think his life could suck any harder.

"WOULD YOU LIKE more tea, Geraldine?" Georgeanne Kowalsky lifted a china pot with tiny pink flowers painted on it and wrapped her hand around one side. "The water is still warm."

"Yes, please." Sean's mother set her little matching teacup on the matching saucer and handed it over. She hadn't mentioned the dog at the table, yet. Sean hoped she'd keep her rant about disease-spreading, filthy animals to herself.

"We serve a pink tea at several local retirement communities each year. The residents look forward to it, and we love it," Georgeanne explained as she poured. "It's a family tradition."

Georgeanne's Southern accent clung to her words like golden honey. If Sean listened close enough, he thought he just might hear "Dixie" playing in the background.

"Not my family," John said as he reached for his tea and took a chug. His big hand dwarfed the delicate cup and looked as ridiculously out of place as Sean imagined his own did.

"John?" Georgeanne motioned toward her husband.

"No. Thank you, love."

"Sean?"

"I'm good. Thank you."

A bowl of pink roses and lilies sat in the center of a round table covered in pink linen. Next to the bowl, fussy a two-tier stand was filled with girl food.

"Cucumber sandwich?" Lexie asked him as she picked up a pair of silver tongs. She stood beside him, looking beautiful in a pink dress that hugged her in all the right places. A pink headband held her blond hair from her face. If they'd been alone, he might have messed it up for her. She leaned a little toward the tray, and the back of her dress inched up her thighs. If they'd been alone, he might have inched his hands up her thighs, too. "I've got petits fours and cream puffs?"

"Sure." Why not? He was in hell. He sat at a pink-covered table with John and Georgeanne, thinking about sliding his hands up their daughter's thighs. His mother sat on his right, her pinkie out like she was the queen of England. Why not eat the tiny food? Maybe he'd choke to death and put himself out of his misery.

268

"You may notice that we are missing a few cream puffs." Lexie pointed to an empty space on the tray. "I'm not sure where they went"— she paused to look across at the ugly dog sitting in John's lap—"but someone had cream on her nose." She set a small plate in front of Sean with two crustless little sandwiches; three pink squares, each with a red rose; and two cream puffs. The dog was dressed in a tutu again, and her beady eyes stared across at Sean as her black tongue snaked out and licked the tip of her nose. He reached for a pink square and pushed the cream puffs to one side.

"Did you do that?" John "The Wall," Chinooks coach and hockey legend, asked the hairless mutt. The dog yipped and was rewarded with a piece of pink cake.

"It's been a long time since you joined us for pink tea, Daddy," Lexie said through a laugh as she sat next to Sean. She raised a cup to her lips and took a delicate sip.

"If I'd known John and Sean were joining us, I would have more to offer." Georgeanne slid Geraldine's cup toward her. "You should have given me a heads-up," she told her husband.

Kicking back in his chair, dog in his lap, he shrugged. "When Knox mentioned his mother was here at Lexie's, I thought I should drop in and say hello. Sean asked to tag along."

Yes, so he could head off his mother if John

asked too many questions, or if she happened to mention their daughter's dusty attic. She'd been in town two days now, and he was fairly certain he'd convinced her that there wasn't going to be a wedding anytime soon. He hoped she didn't bring up her miraculous pancreas cure or her latest—diplopia. Or double vision.

"I've never been to such a fancy occasion." Geraldine picked up a pair of silver tongs and placed a cream puff and a cucumber sandwich on her plate. For the "fancy" occasion, she wore a green pantsuit and yellow blouse. She'd curled her brown hair and put on some lipstick. If not for the eye patch, she would have passed for normal.

"We're leaving in the morning, and I'd hate to miss the opportunity to meet Sean's mother." John tipped his chair back and looked across the table at Sean. "You met my daughter when she and Sean hightailed it to your place."

"Oh yes." Geraldine dipped a bag of Earl Grey into her cup. "It was all very romantic."

"Huh."

John still wasn't totally buying the whole story and looked like he was gearing up to interrogate Sean's mother. If that was the case, he and Lexie were screwed.

"John." Georgeanne placed a hand on his shoulder. "We didn't invite Mrs. Brown to tea so you could grill her about what took place in Canada."

The legs of the chair hit the floor. John combed his fingers through the dog's topknot. They'd agreed to shelve this discussion until after the season. When they talked hockey, they were on common ground. But this wasn't hockey. This was about Lexie, and he still didn't like the idea of Sean dating his daughter.

"I saw they were in love right away. That's why I didn't call Wendy and get that trip to Disney World. Or Hoda and Kathie Lee. Of course, I could never go to Cancun." She paused to take a sip of tea. "I have sun sensitivity."

Still with the Disney World. "Give it up, Mom." But what did he expect from the most embarrassing woman on the planet?

"I'm still grateful for that." Lexie leaned forward and looked at Geraldine. "You gave up a trip of a lifetime for true love."

"Jesus. Pass the bucket."

"Now, John."

"Daddy!" Lexie reached for Sean's hand on the table and entwined their fingers.

Yum Yum lifted her nose in the air and barked while Geraldine scooted as far from the dog as possible without falling on the floor.

Sean looked at the big man, the legend, surrounded by frilly, fluffy pink chaos, and he didn't appear in the least threatened or miserable. He reached for a little square cake and tossed it above his head. He easily caught it in his mouth

271

and chewed through a grin as if he was real pleased with himself. As if he'd maneuvered Sean into the perfect position for a slap shot to the nuts.

Sean wasn't intimidated by anything. Least of all an explosion of tiny pink teacups and tinier food. He looked across the table at his coach and raised his and Lexie's entwined fingers to his mouth. Sean fed him a one-timer and kissed the back of his daughter's hand. Game over.

"Sean?"

She said his name, a hitch of surprise and a catch of wonder. He turned to look into Lexie's deep blue eyes, and it would have been the most natural thing in the world to kiss her pink lips. To hover there for several breaths, teasing them both but giving in to neither. Within those teasing breaths, this game they played with each other suddenly felt real. So real, her eyes looked bluer and deeper. So real the edges of his solid world threatened to unravel. So real he felt held together by a thread so fragile he was afraid to breathe.

"More petits fours, Sean?" He let go of his breath and the feeling was gone. He shook his head and turned his attention to Georgeanne. "No thank you." His throat felt dry, and he picked up his teacup in the palm of his hand. So fragile he could easily crush it. He downed the tea in two swallows and returned his attention to Lexie.

She'd turned away, and all he could see was the shell of her ear, the single pearl in her lobe, and a tinge of pink climbing her throat. He'd seen color flush her neck before. When she'd been embarrassed or lying or making love. This flush in her throat and catch in his lungs wasn't love, but it was more than desire. It was confusion and chaos.

It wasn't a game anymore.

Chapter 12

• love: subtle as a sledgehammer

A RE WE ALMOST there yet?"
From behind the frames of her black sunglasses, Lexie gave a quick glance across her car at Geraldine. Sean's mother held the armrest so tight, Lexie wouldn't be in the least surprised to discover nail marks in the leather. "Almost."

"Is there always this much traffic?"

"This isn't bad." It was one o'clock on a February afternoon. "Wait until five. That's bad traffic."

"I don't know how you live like this." She wore a blue parka and mukluks. Perfect winter gear for an island just south of Alaska, but a little overdressed for Seattle's fifty-degree weather. "Too many people."

Sean had been right about his mother. She didn't like feeling like a little fish. "Wait until you see my store," Lexie said to change the subject. "It's fabulous."

As if on cue, Yum Yum barked from her pink mesh car seat in the back. "That's right, Yummy Cakes," Lexie gushed as she slowed and merged into the center lane.

"You call your dog Yummy Cakes?"

Lexie looked at Geraldine, who wore an identical expression as her son when talking about Yum Yum. "It fits her and she likes it." Discussion closed.

They turned into the high-end strip mall not far from Bellevue Square, and Lexie was relieved to hear silence from the passenger seat. The only sound to fill the car was her gasp as she pulled into a parking slot of her first store. The backlit dormer and Venetian awnings were up and Lexie paused to look at the deep red storefront. She'd worked so hard, and her heart gave a little hiccup of pride. The physical store had been purposely branded with Yum Yum's Closet online, but it looked so much richer in real life. On the dormer, "Yum Yum's Closet" was painted in bold black letters lined in gold. It looked so fabulous tears pinched the backs of her eyes.

"Your dog is weird-looking."

Evidently the discussion was not closed. "Yum Yum has tender feelings." She turned off the car and unbelted herself. "She knows when you say hurtful things about her."

Geraldine turned to Lexie. "How?"

"She is very intuitive and gets sad."

This time Geraldine looked at Lexie as if she'd lost her mind. Coming from a woman who'd put her patch on the wrong eye, Lexie wasn't all that bent out of shape over her opinion.

"Sorry," Geraldine mumbled, and reached for her seat belt.

"Thank you." The front doors of the store were open, which was always a good sign, and when Lexie got out of the car, she heard the glorious sounds of power tools. Dog in one arm and Geraldine in tow, she walked into the building. Sawdust filled the air toward the back and settled on the plastic covering the front counter and several white tables. In her four-inch pumps, Lexie picked her way toward the back, stepping over boxes of nails and parts to the shelving system. She wore a white blouse and pinstriped skirt. Whenever she met with the general contractor, she always liked to look professional. She was the Owner/President, CEO, Director of Products, and sole designer of Yum Yum Inc. She'd discovered that people sometimes needed to be reminded that she was the boss, but of course the contractor wasn't on scene. She spoke with the site manager instead. The crystal chandelier hadn't arrived, nor had the freestanding wardrobe closets. The manager assured her everything would be ready for the grand opening in two and a half weeks. Looking around, Lexie wasn't convinced.

"All this is for dog clothes?" Geraldine asked.

"Not just clothes," she answered as they picked their way back toward the front. "Accessories, treats, bedding. Whatever a dog could possibly need, and a few things the owner hadn't thought of needing."

On the way back to Lexie's apartment, they stopped off at Whole Foods and bought fresh fruits and vegetables and meat. Lexie was going to overdose Geraldine on healthy food, even if it killed her. Lexie always watched what she ate, but could always eat more veggies.

Once they were home, Lexie put away the groceries while Geraldine watched the television above the fireplace; from the sounds of it, *Ellen*. If Lexie leaned back just far enough, she could see Geraldine's left hand, stroking the ponytail Lexie had put in Yum Yum's hair. From her reaction at the pink tea and today in the car, Lexie wouldn't have thought the woman even liked dogs.

Crazy. Crazier still, Lexie had somehow become Geraldine's keeper again. Sean had been gone two days and his mother had moved into Lexie's condo the night before. According to Geraldine, Sean's apartment was too noisy and the neighbors looked at her funny, which was no doubt true.

While Geraldine watched daytime TV, Lexie worked on the fall line for Yum Yum's Closet. She'd been inspired by the rich fabrics of the latest *Beauty and the Beast* movie. The one with Emma Watson. She designed everything from leashes and collars to soft bedding and cavalier vests.

Just after four, her entertainment lawyer got back to her regarding a few stipulations she wanted added to the *Gettin' Hitched* reunion contract: No, she couldn't storm out after five minutes and not return. Yes, she could refuse to answer intimate questions.

At five-thirty, Sean texted an inquiry after his mother: Has Mother driven you insane yet?

Yes, she replied. You owe me.

Within moments he texted back: What do you want?

A kiss was the first thing that popped into her head. A kiss like the one he'd given her in a downtown parking lot. Like the one she'd wanted him to give her at the pink tea as he'd looked across their hands.

Before she could answer he texted: I have a few suggestions.

She thought of a punishment commensurate with his crime. Something beneficial for her, yet miserable for him at the same time:

1. Pink tea at Bay View Retirement Home.
2. Heels for Meals marathon.
3. *Gettin' Hitched* reunion.

It took him an hour to return her text, and she didn't even like to think about how many times she'd checked before he wrote:

1. Probably not.
2. Maybe.
3. Give it up.

When he learned that he'd have to run in a pair of pumps, she felt certain he'd choose a tea with seniors. She smiled at the memory of Sean drinking from a teacup and his bewilderment at the petits fours and cucumber sandwiches. She wasn't certain why her father and Sean had crashed the tea, but it had been interesting to watch them watch each other. It was like a battle of testosterone. A game of *quien es mas macho* surrounded by pink frills and delicate china. She wasn't sure of a winner, though.

At five, she made chicken and spinach Cordon Bleu, and they sat down to dinner at six.

"I don't drink," Geraldine said as Lexie set two wineglasses on the table, but when Lexie popped the cork of a chardonnay perfectly paired with the meal, she changed her mind. "Well, maybe just a sip. Sean will never go hungry with you around cooking for him. I can see why he kidnapped you away from Pete."

Lexie wasn't sure if that was a compliment, but it did make her feel guilty. She hadn't been kidnapped and she was only going to be "around" another month.

By the time dinner was over, Geraldine's plate was cleaned, the bottle was empty, and the woman was feeling no pain, for a change.

"I used to dance," she told Lexie as they did the dishes together. "My mother took me to lessons every Wednesday. I could have been really good if I'd stuck at it."

"Why'd you quit?" Lexie asked as she loaded the plates.

"Off to other things, I suppose. I'd get bored with piano or ballet or painting and I'd take up something else." She handed Lexie a mixing bowl. "I was the only girl and very spoiled. I loved it. I almost died when I was born, and my mother and father carried me around in a shoebox filled with satin. They were so afraid I'd break." As Lexie hand-washed the wineglasses, she kept quiet and let Geraldine talk. Something she had no problem doing. The more Geraldine talked, the more Lexie gathered that Geraldine had been the center of her family's universe. Which made sense, she supposed.

"My two older brothers are deceased now, but my brother Abe practically raised Sean. He was such an unusual child."

Lexie's ears perked up and she reached for a dish towel. Ever since he'd kissed her hand and looked into her eyes at the pink tea, she found herself thinking about him at odd and random times of the day. She knew a bit more than she had the night she'd had sex with him in the Canadian motel, which wasn't saying much since she hadn't even known his real name, but when she'd looked at him across their entwined hands, something happened. Something changed. Her world tipped and she'd caught her breath waiting for it to right itself again.

"I watched you at your store today. Ordering those men around and telling them what you wanted done. You're a smart girl."

Lexie was still, waiting. "Thank you."

"Pretty, too."

"Again, thank you."

"You're not at all dusty in the attic like Sean said."

"Excuse me?" She guessed she didn't have to wait any longer. Sean was still a jerk. "He said what?"

"That your attic is dusty." Geraldine folded her arms across her skinny chest and thought she should further explain, "You know, not very bright. Special. Like special-needs special."

"Really?"

Sean didn't think she was smart. That just showed he didn't know her at all. "When did he say that?"

"Sandspit." She looked at Lexie and shrugged. "I think he just said that so I wouldn't ask lots of questions."

"I noticed he doesn't like to answer." She set the glasses on the counter, then walked down the hall to the laundry room. She guessed she did know more about him than she'd thought. He didn't like questions and he thought she was stupid. She was going to remind herself of that the next time her world felt all tippy.

"It's the way he was raised," Geraldine said from the doorway. "Kids would ask him about me and he'd get embarrassed."

Lexic turned with a clean T-shirt in one hand.

"After a while he quit bringin' kids around."

There had been a time in her life when her world had changed so dramatically, she hadn't wanted to talk about it, either. When old friends and new friends asked questions that she didn't want to answer. That hadn't made her a secretive liar, though. Well, maybe she had gone through a fibbing period.

"He was alone most of the time and kept to himself. He wouldn't tell me when there were other kids' birthdays or school plays or nothing." Geraldine shook her head. "So we went to live with my brother Abe 'cause I thought he needed a man's influence. I meant for us to stay for one summer, but Sean didn't leave until he was eighteen and went off to play hockey in Calgary. I missed him but was too sick to follow."

Sean probably hadn't wept buckets about that, she thought as she folded the shirt and put it in a basket.

"He avoids any kind of drama. Although I

283

swear he's paranoid about the smallest things sometimes."

No shit storms. No drama. No questions. His refusal to take part in the *Gettin' Hitched* reunion made perfect sense. That was going to be a shit storm of shit storms, and she wasn't looking forward to it.

Shortly after Lexie finished folding clothes, Geraldine went to bed. Lexie stayed up making outlines and lists and possible *Gettin' Hitched* scenarios. She fell asleep grumpy and got up cranky. Her eyes were hardly open a crack when she walked into her kitchen to the sight of Geraldine and the sound of her sputtering Keurig.

"What are we doing today?" Geraldine asked, all bright-eyed and happy.

"I have to pick up dog food." Lexie scrubbed her eyes and she yawned. "It's my donation day at the pet rescue downtown. I have to go to PetSmart, fill up the back of my car with food, and drop it off at the shelter where I adopted Yum Yum." She yawned again and added, "It's sad and I wish there was more I could do to help."

"I have bursitis in my left shoulder, but I can lift with my right arm."

Through the slits in her scratchy eyes, Lexie looked across at Sean's mother and her flat bed head. At least the woman was off the couch. "I didn't think you liked animals."

Her bathrobe hung off the one skinny shoulder

and she shrugged. "Maybe I like 'em. Last night, your little dog curled up next to my neck like a little heating pad and my fibromyalgia pain went right away."

That's where Yum Yum had disappeared. She should have guessed.

Geraldine's nose wrinkled. "She kinda stinks though."

"Just when she sweats."

"I can't help with only the one arm, though."

Lexie had been kind of hoping to get a break from Geraldine. No such luck. Three hours later, and weighted down with hundreds of pounds of dry food, Lexie pulled to the back of the shelter and reversed to the door. Geraldine wore a shoulder sling to make sure no one accidentally mistook her for an able-bodied worker, and she instantly disappeared as the big bags of food were unloaded. Lexie didn't need the help or want to be responsible for Geraldine accidentally contracting a rare and unidentifiable illness.

As she wheeled the last bag inside, she found Geraldine sitting in a chair by one of the grooming stations, Buddy the three-legged bichon frise curled up in her lap. Two-year-old Buddy had been found on the 405, his right front leg so mangled there had been no choice but to amputate. Lexie had sponsored his care and rehab, and he was well enough now to find a special home.

"She's soft." Geraldine's free hand stroked his fur.

They made quite the picture. A disabled dog and a hypochondriac. "His name is Buddy." No one knew his real name, but everyone at the shelter had started calling him that because he got along so well with other dogs.

"He's hot with all that hair."

"That's because he has a dense coat and doesn't shed much, like a poodle. He's hypoallergenic and . . ." He needed a more subdued family where he didn't have to run around a lot. "Buddy is a special-needs dog." Maybe Geraldine could benefit from thinking about something other than herself all the time. Lexie knelt on one knee beside the chair. "He's a sweet boy and never smells when he sweats." She smiled and told a little fib. "He's a therapy dog. In training."

"How about that."

LEXIE SAT ON a love seat made from a claw-foot bathtub. Now cut in half, it was tricked out in a coat of red paint and outfitted with tuck-and-roll leopard cushions. The rest of the *Gettin' Hitched* set had been shipped to the Fairmont, and the ballroom now resembled the inside of a barn, complete with the tractor they'd all climbed down from on the first episode. A small studio audience sat on bleachers behind the cameras, blacked out of sight from the stage.

The show had been taping for several segments before Lexie was brought out and shown her place on the love seat. She wore a cobalt turtleneck dress that clung to her like a second skin and blue suede heels. The perfect touch of modest and sexy. Of class and in-your-face sensuality.

Across the stage, the more memorable members of the cast sat on hay bales while the hostess of the show, Jemma Monaco from *The Young and the Restless*, sat on a leather buggy seat on Lexie's left. The wheelbarrow chair where Pete sat while Lexie had been backstage was empty. For now. Lexie would have to face him on camera, but the hitchin' brides wanted a piece of her first.

"Welcome Lexie to the show," hostess Jemma Monaco greeted after the light on the main camera turned green. The audience alternately booed and cheered, but Lexie couldn't see them so they were easy to ignore.

"Thank you."

"Have you brought the infamous Yum Yum with you?"

Yum Yum was curled into Lexie's lap and shook from nerves. "Yes. She's a little shy." Lexie pulled one side of her long hair behind her shoulder and ran a soothing palm down her dog's back. "She'll warm up in a few minutes." She looked across the stage at the ten or so of the hitchin' brides poised on bales of hay. They all looked cleaned up and polished for the show. They wore stilettos, short skirts, and phony smiles with nasty intentions. Lexie almost felt bad that they had to have itchy hay up their butts. Almost but not quite. During the first segments, she'd sat in her dressing room while Pete and the women had really piled on the insults.

"What is your dog wearing?" The tone of Jemma's voice implied that she might not be on board with animal couture.

"A blue dress and white pinafore from my Alice in Wonderglam collection." The mumblings from the hay bales across the set made her smile. "She loves the little bow in her hair," she said, and adjusted the ribbon on top of her dog's head. "It's sold out online." Which was thankfully true. "We're taking preorders and hope it will be back in stock for the grand opening of my Bellevue store in two weeks. We'd love to have everyone stop in."

"I don't think the other girls will hang around." Jemma turned her legs to one side, attempting to figure out her best angles beneath the studio lighting. "I'm sure you've been listening to what the other girls had to say."

"Yes. I heard them."

"Do you have a response?"

Lexie gave them the smile she'd always reserved for church. The I'm-bursting-with-God's-holy-love smile. "I understand they're

288

upset. We all went on the show to find love, and rejection is never easy. Some people strike out at others instead of dealing constructively with their own disappointment."

"You shouldn't have been allowed on the show," Davina from Scottsdale said. "You obviously weren't there to find love like the rest of us."

Lexie turned up her smile instead of rolling her eyes. Davina was an actress and had figured reality television would make her a star. A chance that was as fat as her head. "I'm sorry you feel that way."

"God, I'd like to smack that smile off your face," Davina added, followed by a smattering of applause that Lexie couldn't ignore.

"No one is getting up from their seats," Jemma warned. "Violence is never the answer."

Lexie straightened her little dog's pinafore. "Yum Yum is a pacifist. So am I."

"You're a sneaky liar!" Mandy from Wooster pointed at her.

"You think you're better than all of us," Desiree from Jersey said, triggering full-on tirades from the other girls on the set.

"You spent most of your time on the pig phone."

"You stole my lip chap!" Whitney from Paducah claimed, and the audience howled with laughter.

Oh God, not Lip Chap–Gate, again. Whitney's Chap Stick had gone missing around week three and she'd turned it into a huge ordeal. As if it was worth a million dollars instead of costing around two bucks.

"You told Jody I walk like a poodle. What the hell does that mean?"

"Well, it—" Lexie tried to explain but was interrupted by Jenny from Salem, who pointed at her. "You tripped me in the chicken-and-egg contest. That's the only reason you won." Jenny scooted to the edge of the bale. "I should have gone on that hayride date with Cindy Lee and Pete. Not you."

"I didn't trip you." That wasn't an outright fib. She just hadn't *tried* to trip her. "Your running in five-inch wedges through a chicken coop tripped you up."

"Speaking of the chicken coop challenge, you all had your share of trips and falls." Jemma pointed at a big overhead television. "Let's take a look."

On the screen ran a montage of various challenges, starting with the pig chase and ending with Lexie winning the obstacle course, pumping her fist in the air and hotdogging the hell out of it. "Booya, suckers!" she said into the camera as the other girls struggled to get over the last wall.

The lights came up, and Lexie shrugged. "Perhaps I am guilty of excessive celebration."

"Lexie and Pete will come face to face for the first time since the ring ceremony." Jemma smiled into the camera. "We'll be right back."

A red light signaled the commercial break, and the makeup artist appeared to reapply Lexie's lipstick. The cast gave her evil looks as they vacated the hay bales, and Pete took the wheelbarrow chair on Jemma's left. Lexie glanced at his face but couldn't tell if he was going to play the part of the wounded groom or get real.

"We're back with Pete Dalton. Welcome back, Pete. How does it feel seeing Lexie again?"

This was the moment where he either manned up or threw her under the bus again. "You look nice," he said.

"Thank you. You look good, Pete," she said, which was true. Blond streaks in his hair made him look like a surfer.

"What do you feel now that you see Pete again?"

Relief. Joy. A bit of guilt. "That we experienced something unique together, but it didn't work out."

"Did you ever think you were in love with Pete?"

"At the time, yes. I was caught up in the show." She put a hand on her chest, then motioned toward Pete. "I think we were all caught up in it, but once I went back to my real life, reality hit me

291

and I realized that it takes more than ten weeks, and half that many dates, to know a person well enough to fall in love. Let alone get married."

"What do you have to say to that, Pete?"

"My heart was involved."

He was all tanned and healthy from his show in the Acapulco sun, where he got to pimp a whole new batch of women.

"It hurts," he added.

If Lexie believed him for one minute she might feel bad, but they both knew the only thing she'd hurt was his pride. "I've apologized to Pete repeatedly. I know that an apology doesn't assuage his pain, but I am very sorry." There, that sounded sincere. And it was—mostly.

"I was there to find my soul mate," he said. "All Lexie wanted was her face on television." A smattering of applause broke out from behind the cameras.

That was true, but no truer for her than for any of the rest of them. Even Pete.

"You were on the rebound from your hockey player and you used me to get back at him. As soon as he showed up again, you went running back to him."

"It wasn't quite like that." In fact, it was nothing like that. "I should have handled things differently. I wish I had."

"Pete mentioned something that I wanted to get into with you, Lexie." Jemma turned to her and said, "You told a Seattle newspaper that Sean Knox got a note to you moments before you were to walk down the aisle with Pete. If Sean hadn't sent you the message, would you have married Pete?"

That was easy, since the message was a lie. "No. I knew I couldn't go through with it before Sean contacted me," she confessed, which earned her a wall of boos from the audience.

"Quiet down." Jemma held up one hand. "Tell us where you went when you left the Fairmont."

Yum Yum shifted in Lexie's lap, and she ran a soothing hand over her dog as she repeated the story she and Sean had told the *Seattle Times*. When she was through, Pete looked ready to explode, and Jemma said, "We'll be right back."

The makeup artist appeared again and this time brushed Lexie's hair as well as retouching her lips. As the woman worked, Pete's wounded-guy veneer slipped and he laughed and joked with some of the crew. She had two more segments to go before the reunion was over. Two more segments that were bound to be worse than the previous segments combined. The cast only had twenty minutes to get in their last minutes of fame. They all knew the most outrageous behavior would be showed on commercial clips to hype the show, and she braced herself for the inevitable.

The first and second runners-up for the

Gettin' Hitched title were brought out next and sat next to Lexie's bathtub in a pair of rawhide chairs. Cindy Lee from Clearwater, Florida, and Summer from Bell Buckle, Tennessee, cried huge tears as clips from the show replayed snippets of each woman's private "dates" with Pete in the Pig Pen, and him leading each girl to the Hog Heaven bedroom. Lexie thanked God she hadn't been filmed anywhere near Hog Heaven or the subsequent walk of shame the next morning. The clip ended with Cindy Lee's and Summer's tearful exits from the show.

"You didn't choose either Cindy Lee or Summer," Jemma pointed out to Pete when the camera returned to them. "They cared enough about you to sleep with you in Hog Heaven."

Pete shrugged a nonchalant shoulder. "In the end, it came down to how I was raised. I'm an old-fashioned guy."

"Are you saying you didn't choose them because they had sex with you?"

"It was a consideration, Jemma. Someday I hope to have children, and wouldn't want any of my future children to see their mother being promiscuous on television."

The women beside Lexie gasped.

"I loved you," Summer managed through her tears.

Cindy Lee crossed her arms over her chest. "I thought we had good chemistry."

Lexie frowned. "You're a jerk, Pete."

Summer and Cindy Lee turned toward Lexie, and instead of agreeing, they turned on *her*. By the time the final segment started, Lexie was tired. She had a headache. Her face hurt from smiling and her stomach was twisted into a knot.

The other hitchin' brides returned to their hay, and a crew member took Yum Yum to her pet carrier. As soon as the cameras turned off for the last time, Lexie planned to run as fast as her Manolos could take her, and put this chapter of her life in the rearview mirror.

"What are your plans now?" Jemma asked the other women. The first few cast members answered, but after a few minutes, the question got turned and twisted back on Lexie. She was called Lex Luthor and heartless and an entitled bitch, again. Davina threatened to smack her in the face and charged across the stage. A crew member detained her, and the audience cheered and booed at the same time.

"I'm not heartless or entitled." Lexie put a hand on her chest and felt her heart pound. "I am comfortable with who I am, and if you think that makes me a bitch, that's your problem."

"No, that's your problem," someone countered, and the conversation warped into everyone's problem with everyone else. Mandy and Desiree almost came to blows. Summer and Whitney cried big weeping tears, as Pete sat back, loving every last minute.

"Everyone calm down," Jemma spoke above the bickering.

"Someday you're going to get what's coming to you!" Davina yelled, and even though Lexie knew it was all for ratings and an attempt at ten extra minutes of fame, her heart pounded and she swallowed hard.

"Speaking of getting what's coming to her, we have one last guest," Jemma announced.

Lexie tried to recall which cast member wasn't on the set today. Rhonda, the girl who was kicked off on the first episode, maybe. But she was fairly certain she'd never done anything to Rhonda.

Jemma looked offstage to her left. "Come on out, Sean, and tell us what you think of all this drama."

Right. Lexie hadn't spoken with Sean since the last text. Even then he'd made it very clear that he wanted nothing to do with the reunion show.

A smattering of applause started toward the front and grew louder as a knot of production crew members moved from the left wing. In the middle, Sean's dark hair and face towered above them. Lexie's heart felt like a five-point star and got stuck in her windpipe. He wore the blue dress shirt and gray trousers the Chinooks always wore on the road. He'd loosened the striped tie around his neck and unbuttoned his collar like he'd been about to undress when he'd been interrupted.

Applause and a few whoops broke out as Lexie stood and straightened her dress. A strange sob clogged her throat just above her stuck heart. He looked so good, she wasn't positive he was real. Maybe she was suffering from some sort of stress-induced delusion. A delusion of dark scruffy beard and big shoulders that made her feel a little light headed. Then he stood before her and wrapped her up in his arms. It was all for show, but she didn't care. He was warm and solid and she felt protected. "You're here."

"I just got in." He pulled back far enough to look into her face.

"You're here," she repeated herself.

"What my baby wants, my baby gets." Then he lowered his mouth to hers and kissed her several seconds past a simple hello. For all the world, and especially the television audience, they looked like two young lovers, their lips clinging in anticipation of more. Lexie's sore stomach got hot and squishy, and the sob clogging her throat came out as a breathy sigh.

Sean pulled back and softly pinched her chin. "You look beautiful."

She opened her mouth, but all that came out was a weird garbled sound.

He bent forward and whispered in her ear, "You're supposed to say, 'You make me feel beautiful,' or 'I want to feel our beautiful love forever.' " She recognized the sayings she'd sent him but she was too shocked to respond at all. "And my personal favorite, 'I want to be filled with your beautiful love lance forever.' "

Lexie's neck and face caught fire and her throat closed. She'd never added that last one to the list. Ever! "Love lance?" she managed.

He pulled back and laughed.

"Ahh . . ." Jemma said, "I think we caught some of that on Lexie's hidden mic."

"Sorry." He dropped a quick kiss on her lips but he didn't look sorry at all.

"Why don't you take a seat with Lexie," Jemma suggested. "We only have about five minutes, and I'm sure viewers would love to hear your thoughts and what's been going on."

Clearly, she and Sean couldn't fit comfortably in the tub, and a stagehand brought back the two rawhide chairs. Silence fell over the hay bale section, and Pete went from looking smug to looking very uncomfortable.

"We know that you've been on the road, but we're glad you could join us at the last minute."

"Anything for Lexie." He took her hand as they sat next to each other.

Lexie looked up into his face. "I appreciate you coming."

Amusement creased the corners of his green eyes as his gaze met hers. "Sorry I didn't shave first." A lock of his hair fell over his forehead like a big comma and touched his dark brow. "But I couldn't let you face the wrath of those other girls all by yourself."

Her poor heart grew bigger, the points sharper, her breathing impossible. This was bad. Really really bad. He'd rescued her again, and she hadn't even had to blackmail him this time.

"Have you watched the show?" Jemma asked.

"Bits and pieces here and there. Watching my woman compete to be another man's wife wasn't high on my TV viewing list." He looked down at her hand and played with her fingers. It was the day. The whole emotional day was playing tricks on her. "It's over now and we've moved on."

"Pete, do you have anything you'd like to say to Sean? Now's your chance."

That had to be it, because, God help her, falling in love with Sean Knox was impossible.

"No," Pete answered. "Not really."

Jemma looked at Sean. "Anything you want to say to Pete?"

"No. I think he's suffered enough without my opinion."

"What is your opinion?" Jemma wanted to know.

If Lexie had her wits about her she might have intervened before Sean answered, "He must have a small dick if he needs a TV show to get women."

But her wits were nowhere near the Fairmont Hotel, and she could only gasp, "Sean!"

"Luckily that will get bleeped out in production." Jemma gave a bark of laughter and was joined by a few of the girls across the stage.

"That's not true!" Pete defended himself and turned red in the face. "I didn't need the show to find women."

Sean looked at him and grinned like they were standing in the face-off circle at the Key, and he was going to drop his gloves the second the whistle blew. "Some of us don't need a TV show. We're good on our own."

If Lexie didn't know better, she might think he was jealous, but she did know better. This was all an act. One she'd outlined for him, including sections, subsections, and bullet points.

He squeezed her hand and said against the side of her forehead, "You know it's true."

Lexie didn't know what was true anymore. Not him or her or her pointy heart.

Jemma cleared her throat and continued, "It sounds like you don't like reality TV."

"It's fine."

"Sean doesn't like chaos and drama," Lexie provided for him. He glanced at her out of the corners of his eyes and she added, "I've given him both and I am sorry for that."

"You two look like a couple in love," Jemma said with a sigh.

"Yes." She'd really done it this time. Despite her notes and memos and knowing better, her heart twisted and turned and gutted her from the inside out.

She was in trouble. Deep, deep trouble. She sat between her fake ex-fiancé on one side and her pretend boyfriend on the other:

1. She'd tried to love Pete
   a. That had ended in disaster.
2. She'd tried *not* to love Sean
   a. That was a disaster waiting to happen.

It didn't matter. She'd gone ahead and done it. She'd gone ahead and fallen in love with Sean Knox.

Chapter 13

•love to love you, baby

T HAT LOOKS LIKE a good bush." Sean pointed to the shrubbery outside his apartment building. "Take a leak on that." The white dog sniffed and moved to a different shrub altogether. Sean still couldn't believe there was an actual dog at the end of the blue leash. Let alone one with only three legs. Growing up, he'd never had a pet, no matter how many legs, because his mother thought all animals were filthy.

Now she was upstairs with a "migraine" and he was on poop duty with Buddy. The dog kind of hopped and walked at the same time, and Sean did feel sort of sorry for the little thing. Together they moved down the street a little ways, stopping when Buddy sniffed a tree.

His mother had told him that the idea for a "therapy dog" had been hers, but he had his doubts. She'd spent a few days with Lexie and came back with a disabled dog. This had Lexie's fingerprints all over it.

Buddy circled the tree and Sean followed. After the reunion show yesterday, he'd wanted to put his fingerprints all over *her*.

"Come home with me," he'd whispered in her ear as they once again found themselves in a parking lot. When they'd first made their agreement, they'd decided not to have sex. Well, she'd mostly decided and he'd gone along with it because he hadn't known that almost every time he was near her, his body would react. He wanted her again. Naked like before, and she could deny it all day, but she wanted it, too.

"I can't go home with you." They'd stood at the back of his SUV and he'd had to fight an urge to open the hatch and stuff her inside. "We'd end up in bed."

"It's gonna happen sooner or later." Her eyes hid behind black sunglasses and he pushed them to the top of her head. "I vote for sooner."

"We can't," she said, but with little conviction. He pulled her long body against him and pressed her into his chest and belly. He let her feel how much he wanted her, and he took advantage of her gasp and opened his mouth over hers. Everything about Lexie turned him on. The touch of her hands sliding up his chest. The smell of her neck and taste of her lips. She opened her warm mouth a little wider, and her slick tongue tangled with his, drawing him in deeper. The suction got a little tighter, the kiss a little wetter, the world around them a whole lot hotter.

Raw lust pulsed through his body and hers. So good he slid his hands to her behind and pressed her into his erection. She felt so good and he could hardly control the sharp edge of desire slicing through him.

He lifted his head and gasped for air. "Let's take this to a bed."

He looked into her eyes, hazy from passion. "Come home with me."

She blinked and her brows drew together. The wrinkle on her forehead wasn't a good sign. "I can't do that, Sean."

"Yes, you can. All you have to do is get in my car."

She took a few steps back, and his arms fell to his sides. "There's too much at stake now." As she turned away, he thought he saw a tear spill from the bottom of her lashes. At the time, he'd been too turned on and too frustrated to care. He hadn't been able to think past his throbbing hard-on.

Buddy sniffed a light pole, and apparently it was a better spot than the shrubs or tree. He lifted one leg and finally went. Sean had a little poop baggy, but he didn't know the rules for where a dog could whiz and where it couldn't. The light pole looked as good a spot as any. Instead of taking the time to slowly walk back to his apartment, Sean picked Buddy up, careful not to touch any wet spots on his fur. The dog licked his chin and mouth when he made the mistake of looking down. "Stop," he commanded, but

Buddy didn't. He licked Sean's throat and the front of his Pabst T-shirt from halfway down the block, up the elevator, and into his apartment.

"Your dog's back," Sean called out down the hall.

He expected to hear moaning or some other sound of distress. When he didn't, he set Buddy on the hardwood floor, then followed after his little walking hop.

What he didn't expect was to see his mother fully dressed and her open suitcase on the bed. "What are you doing?"

His mother looked across her shoulder at him as she tossed her clothes in the suitcase. "I have to take Buddy home. He needs to get used to my house. I have to be careful of his front paw, and a sidewalk is no place for a dog to do his business. He needs a yard."

"You're leaving now?"

She nodded and zipped up her suitcase. "I called Jimmy, the fella with the flying frog."

He couldn't say that he was sorry to see her go. "I'll take you to the dock," he said, and picked up her one suitcase. He'd easily been replaced by a three-legged dog. Strangely, he couldn't say how he felt about that.

Later that night at the Key Arena, he couldn't say how he felt about seeing Lexie on the third tier. Or the next night, either. He had three back-to-back games in Seattle, and each time he glanced up, she was there. And each time "Crazy Train" boomed through the arena, the flash of her smile made him chuckle.

On the road, she sent him daily texts. Part memo, part schedule, and chatty comments about her day. He told her about his hat trick against New York and that his mother had called to report on Buddy's progress, as if he was an actual member of their family. One of the things she always mentioned was her store and the planned grand opening. So the night he returned to Seattle, he plugged the store's address into his GPS and drove to see for himself.

"What do you think?" she asked as she showed him white and gold tables and red velvet chairs. He hardly noticed anything but the way she looked in yoga pants and a maroon shirt with mesh cut-outs in the back.

"Beautiful," he said, looking at her.

"Thanks. I've worked really hard." She pulled a stretchy tie from her ponytail and combed her fingers through her loose hair. "The office is back here," she continued, and he followed her into a stark white room, filled with a desk, several chairs, and a red velvet lounge chair wide enough for two. The business smelled of new wood and fresh paint. "We'll move this to the front window once the painters have finished up there." She talked about her fears with opening a physical store and the net profits between e-sales and retail. "A store on the Internet can get lonely. I want to be around pet lovers."

Sean watched her gather her hair into a tight ponytail and thought of the first time he'd seen her. Running down the dock, white dress flowing behind her, shoes flashing like disco balls. "You are full of surprises, Lexie Kowalsky. You're different from the woman who dove into the *Sea Hopper*."

With her chin on her chest, she looked at him out of the corners of her eyes. "I'm the same woman. You just met me at my worst." Her hair secure, she turned to face him. "Your mother told me what you said about my attic."

He moved to the center of the room, close enough to reach for her. He thought a moment, then began to laugh. "I had to throw her off track." He grasped her shoulders and looked into her eyes. "There is nothing dusty about you." Then he kissed her because he'd been waiting long enough. Waiting for her soft mouth and slick tongue. Waiting to pull her against him and feel the rise and fall of her breasts against his chest.

She'd been waiting, too. Her hands slid up his ribs and across his shoulders to his hair. The waiting was over.

He slid his hands to her backside and cupped her cheeks through her thin pants. He pressed his erection into her and she sucked in a breath.

Sean's testicles drew up tight against his body, and his rock-hard erection ached. He looked down into her gorgeous face and blue eyes, her lips wet from his kiss. "I've been thinking about this since I left Sandspit." He curled his fingers into the bottom of her maroon shirt and pulled it up. Up past the waistband of her pants and navel, up her flat stomach to the bottom of a blue bra, holding the plump undersides of her breasts. Her ponytail swung across her bare back as he pulled the shirt over her head and tossed it aside. "I thought about this." He brushed the tips of his fingers across her voluptuous breasts and the lacy edge of her bra. He wanted to take his time and do all the things he'd been thinking about for weeks now. All the places he wanted to kiss. He wanted to draw it all out until neither could stand one more touch or kiss or whispered breath against sensitive skin, but the moment he unhooked her bra and her soft breasts filled his hands, those moments were forgotten, and all that occupied his head were thoughts of getting completely naked in as little time as possible.

He pulled off his shirt and kicked off his pants and shoes. He picked her up long enough to carry her to the lounge chair. Within seconds he'd stripped her completely naked and lay between her legs, keeping his weight on his elbows. Her soft skin pressed into him, her hard nipples scoring his chest. He placed his hands on the sides of her face and kissed her long and deep. The head of his penis touched between her legs where she was warm and wet and slick, all the things he craved. She moaned into his mouth and ran her fingers through his hair. Her short nails scraped his skull, sending shockwaves of fiery lust down his spine to his feet. She rocked her hips, sliding the apex of her thighs against his hard-on. He pulled back and looked into her eyes, deep blue and filled with desire. She wrapped one leg around his waist and moved against him, pleasuring herself and him.

He remembered how good she felt inside, and he wanted that again, as many times and as many ways as possible.

"Sean," she whispered between little pants of breath. Then she said one word that sent him spiraling and fighting for control. "Inside."

A deep groan was torn from his chest as he pushed into her incredibly soft flesh. She was tight around him, so luscious and slick, he remembered the condom in his pants pocket. Too late. Much too late to think of stopping. He pulled out and slid into her twice before he buried himself deep.

"That's good." He felt each of her fingers pressed into his back and she whispered, "Give me more."

He looked at her face, and the fire in her eyes, and a little moan escaped her lips. He kissed her mouth as he drove into her, unhurried, taking his time, feeling the pleasure build within him and her.

He watched her face, the lust in her eyes and the pink of her cheeks. "Faster," she said through a whisper, and he matched the thrust of his hips with hers. The sounds of her pleasure heightened his pleasure and drove him faster.

"Talk to mc, Lexie."

"Can't," she said, then she called his name as the first pulse of her body drew tight around him. Her back arched and her orgasm squeezed him so tight he could hardly breathe. He pulled air into his lungs as an intense climax hit him and knocked every last bit of oxygen from his lungs. It started at his toes and worked through him. It lasted too long but not long enough, and when it was over, he felt like he'd been cross-checked and fallen to the ice on his knees, the wind knocked out of him and too weak to get up.

He swallowed hard and croaked next to her ear, "Are you okay?"

"No."

Alarmed, he raised his head and looked into her face. "Did I hurt you?" Then he saw her satisfied smile and hung his head with relief.

"I don't know that I'll ever be the same," she said. "That was amazing."

His smile matched hers. He knew the feeling.

Chapter 14

• love stinks

"D ID I THANK you for Buddy?" Sean asked as he and Lexie entered his dark apartment. "I think he's the best thing that's ever happened to my mother. Even better than the time she was cured from double-certain death."

Lexie chuckled and set her red handbag on the table next to the front door. "He gives her something to think about besides skin lesions and kidney failure." They'd spent the evening playing darts at a local sports bar. He'd won, but barely. They were both so competitive that it was probably a good idea that they not play any game that contained sharp objects . . . it was too tempting.

Sean turned on the lights and helped her out of her red jacket. "My entire life, she hated dogs."

"Well, she doesn't hate Buddy, at least she didn't when I talked to her yesterday." She unwove her red scarf and followed him into the living room.

"You talked to my mother?" He tossed her jacket on the couch, then moved beside her to look out at the city lights and the Space Needle

313

in the foreground. "The thought of you two colluding behind my back makes me nervous."

She doubted anything made him nervous. Tonight they'd looked like a couple in love. The laughter and lingering touches on his big shoulder, and the warm palm in the middle of her back, weren't real. "She called with a question about Buddy." But they weren't in love. At least not both of them.

"What's wrong with the mutt?"

"She thinks he has gout."

Sean looked at her across his shoulder and laughed. He wore jeans and a simple black T-shirt, and he turned heads with his dark hair and handsome face. She loved everything about him, but she might like his laughter the most. She didn't hear it all that often, but it was big like him and filled with amusement and, when not directed at her, infectious.

"I made the mistake of telling her that he might be prone to arthritis as he gets older."

"He's only two weeks older than he was before!"

Thirteen days. He'd turned a week older on Valentine's Day. Lexie only knew because Geraldine had called to ask if Buddy could eat chocolate. Sean had been on the road and hadn't mentioned the one day every year set aside for lovers. She purposely hadn't anticipated an acknowledgment from him, and at the end of the night when she'd heard nothing but a joke KO had told him, she texted him three simple words, "Happy Valentine's Day." He hadn't responded and she'd felt foolish. "Look on the bright side. At least she doesn't have gout."

"She's already had that." He moved behind her and wrapped his arms around her just beneath her breasts. "I don't think there's an illness she *hasn't* had."

Lexie looked at his reflection in the window, his face just above her head as he stared out at the city. His warm arms made her heart go all squishy even as her spinning head reminded her that it wasn't real. For the sake of her squishy heart and spinning head, she should grab her purse and run. "I used to be a hypochondriac." She did neither. She loved him. It wasn't the smartest thing she'd ever done, but it hadn't happened on purpose. "I think I wanted attention—and Band-Aids. Band-Aids were big in my life. My first dog cured me, though. He gave me something to think about besides cuts and bruises." And who knew what would happen in the future. He wasn't going anywhere for three more weeks. A lot could happen. He could find her simply irresistible and fall in love with her, too.

"Oh, I don't think anything can cure her for long. Although I think she's just about run out of illnesses."

She thought of Geraldine the first time she'd

met her, all wrapped up in an eye-crossing afghan and skullcap. "When I was six, I thought I had Ebola."

"What?" Through the glass his gaze met hers. "You're kidding."

"No." She shook her head, and his chin brushed her scalp. "I didn't know what it was, but on the news they talked about an outbreak in Kikwit. I thought they said Kennewick. My aunt Mae and I had visited her parents in Kennewick the week before, and I thought for sure I was a goner." She thought about the night Geraldine had been liquored up and talked about Sean as a boy. "People think hypochondria is funny, but it's not if you have to live with a hypochondriac."

"Tell me about it."

She waited for him to say more. When he didn't she said, "I can only imagine how hard it might have been to be raised by Geraldine."

He took a step back and dropped his hands. "I raised myself, Lexie."

She turned to face him. "You did a fairly good job."

"Fairly?"

Her lips twisted in a smile. "Well, you're kind of obnoxious, but you're an okay hockey player."

"I'm more than okay," he corrected her, but he didn't dispute being obnoxious. "I started playing late, compared to other boys, but I caught up and kicked ass. Now no one puts goals in the net like

I do." He turned and said over his shoulder as he walked into the kitchen, "I won the Art Ross trophy two years in a row."

"Not to brag or anything."

He pulled two bottles of Vitamin Water from the refrigerator. "It's only bragging if you can't back it up." He tossed one to her. "Otherwise it's just stating facts." He unscrewed his cap and tilted the bottle toward her. "I've got skills."

She shrugged a nonchalant shoulder and opened her bottle. "You have a decent wrist shot. I'll give you that."

He lowered his water and laughed. "My wrist shot is clocked at a hundred and ten and my slap shot at a hundred and fifteen. Bobby Hull's slap shot was a hundred and nineteen and big bad John 'The Wall' Kowalsky's was a hundred and five." He smiled. "But who's counting."

"Every NHL player in history." She took a drink and tried not to make a face. It tasted worse than Gatorade. "My uncle Hugh hated slap shots. He said that no matter how thick the pads or how he stacks 'em, a hundred-mile-an-hour puck hits like cannon fire."

"The goalie, Hugh Miner?" A wrinkle crossed his brow. "You're related to him, too?"

"Not by blood. He's married to my aunt Mae." She leaned one hip to the granite cooking island and wondered how much to tell Sean. Her life wasn't a secret, but it wasn't something she talked about with just anyone. "Aunt Mae isn't my aunt by blood, either, but she and my mom are as close as sisters. She helped raise me." She was talking about it with Sean; she trusted him. From the moment she'd jumped on the *Sea Hopper*, she'd trusted him. Even when he'd let her believe he was a government spy. "Mae practically lived with Mom and me until I was seven and met my dad."

His brows lowered and he slowly set his bottle on the counter. "Say that again."

It was no big deal. At least not anymore, but there had been a time when it had bothered her. "I never met my dad"—she paused to swallow—"my real dad, John Kowalsky, until I was seven."

The recessed light in the ceiling shone down on Sean's head and lashes but he didn't blink as he stared at her.

"It's kind of a long story," she said, and looked down at her hands. "And involved and weird . . ." She looked back up and shrugged one shoulder. "Basically, I'm the product of a wild weekend between my mom and a hockey player she met while running away from her wedding to an old guy." She picked up her water, decided against a drink, and set it back down. "John discovered me when I was seven. My parents married when I was eight, and that's it." Except that wasn't it. Not really. "It's not a secret but we don't really talk about it outside the family."

He finally blinked then said, "Your mother ran away from a wedding to an old guy?"

"Yeah." He'd been the owner of the Chinooks at the time, but no need to complicate things. "My mom and dad spent what would have been my mother's honeymoon weekend with someone else, together. Then he dropped her off at the airport without looking back."

"Wait . . ." Sean held up one hand. "First things first. John didn't know about you?"

"Not until I was seven."

"You all seem so close. Like you have the perfect family and live perfect lives."

"We're far from perfect." Especially her. "We're close now." But there had been several teen years when she'd acted out of anger toward her mother. "I used to be really jealous of my younger sister and brother because they always knew my dad from the time they were born and I didn't. I acted out and got into trouble."

"What kind of trouble?"

"Sneaking out. Driving my parents' car when they were out of town."

"That doesn't sound so bad."

"I didn't have a driver's license." She took a breath and let it out. "Now you know all my secrets."

"I doubt that." He laughed and took her hand in his. "Don't you think it's ironic as hell that both you and your mother ran away from weddings?

Her from an old guy and you from Pete."

More than he knew. Her mother had jumped in a car with a hockey player, Lexie aboard a seaplane.

"And you both spent your honeymoons with men other than your fiancés?"

"I guess we're alike." They'd both run from men they didn't love, only to fall smack-dab into it with men who didn't love them back. "My mom and dad have been married almost twenty years now, so it worked out for them, I guess. I got a little sister and brother whom I love very much." Now. She waited for him to judge her or her mother and father. Some people did. Instead he put his hands on her shoulders and smiled down into her face.

"I finally have a brother," he said. "But I think my mother is more fond of Buddy than she ever was of me."

He hadn't judged her and she fell even more in love with him.

"I'm sure that's not true." She thought a moment, then added, "Although I wouldn't bet a lot of money on it. Buddy is very cute and better groomed than you." Placing bets reminded her of the Chinooks fund-raiser. "Do you want to meet me at the Biscuit in the Basket?" she asked as if they were a regular couple on a regular date. "You have a game against Anaheim that afternoon. It might be easier."

"I'll pick you up." He pulled her close and rested his forehead against hers. "You think my brother is better groomed?" Obviously he wasn't through with the Buddy topic.

"Are you fishing for a compliment?"

"Maybe." His silent laughter touched her face. "I've never been compared to a three-legged dog."

"You're cute and fairly well groomed."

"Thank you."

She smiled. "But Buddy is better behaved."

"I behave when I want to behave." He lifted her chin and said against her lips, "And right now, I don't want to behave."

She opened her mouth for his kiss. It warmed her all over and made her heart beat hard in her chest. She loved him, and there wasn't anything she could do about it except hope that maybe he'd love her, too.

She followed him to his bedroom and poured her heart into every kiss from her mouth and touch of her hand. Her love spread like fire through her, burning up her chest and pooling in the pit of her stomach.

"I'm going to make love to you," he said as he stripped her naked and pushed her down on his bed. All she heard was the word "love" and her heart answered, *Yes.*

"You're all I've thought about all day." He slid his tongue across her tight nipple, then raised his head and looked into her eyes. "I think I'm addicted."

He slid into her, hard and massive, and she closed her eyes. Her pulse beat so hard she couldn't hear above her pounding heart. She kissed him and touched him and made love to him with her body. This time was different than the times before. This time her heart and soul were involved, consuming her, overriding every thought in her head but him. "Sean," she gasped as the first flush of orgasm gathered between her legs and burned her inside and out. "Sean."

"Talk to me, Lexie." He pushed her further, harder, and a hell of a lot hotter. "Talk to me, princess."

"Oh God!" She arched her back as a second orgasm scorched the first. "Don't stop." Her eyes popped open and she thought she might die from pleasure. "I love you, Sean."

Only after their breathing calmed and the sweat on their skin chilled did she realize what she'd said.

"Sex with you gets better every time," he said, and rolled to lie next to her. "You're amazing."

That wasn't the response she expected to her blurting that she loved him. She was quiet for a moment, then asked, "Did you hear me?"

He closed his eyes. "Hmm," he sighed with content.

"Did you hear me say I love you?"

"Yeah. That's just your orgasm talking. It happens sometimes during good sex."

Not to her. "Has it happened to you?"

"Hmm."

He sounded like he was about to fall asleep, and she elbowed him. "Has it happened to you?"

"No, but orgasms don't make me emotional."

She sat up and looked down into his closed eyes. "Really?"

"Don't worry about it. Women just get caught up in the glow." He yawned. "We'll forget it happened by morning."

Impossible. "I'm not caught up in anything, and I know the difference between love and *glow*. My attic isn't dusty. Remember?"

"We can talk about it later." He cracked an eye open. "Why don't you curl up next to me?"

"You don't believe me." She hadn't meant to blurt it out, but she had, and he didn't believe her. He wanted to dismiss her like the other women he'd been with who'd suffered from "glow." She scooted to the end of the bed and reached for her underwear. She knew he didn't love her. The little tear in her heart made her realize that she'd hoped he felt the same, but she didn't expect it. Nor did she expect to be treated like just another woman who'd said she loved him. She wasn't special and didn't know why she expected more.

He cracked open both eyes. "Where are you going?"

"Home."

"Why the rush?" he said through another yawn. "I'll take you in the morning."

"I'll call a cab." She hooked her bra and reached for her shirt on the floor.

That got his attention and he sat up. "What are you doing?"

"Getting dressed."

"I can see that. Why?"

She had to leave. To get away. As fast as possible before she slugged him and burst into tears, undoubtedly like all the other women. This was her fault. She'd fallen in love with a man who was only pretending to love her.

"You're better than this, Lexie." He gathered the sheet around him and stood. "You're better than the women who get mad and act this way."

She'd thought so, too. She guessed not.

He paused as if struck with thought. "Are you about to start your period?"

Her jaw dropped and she drew in a breath. "Tell me I didn't just hear you say that."

"Sorry, but you're getting all emotional for no reason."

And he wasn't. Not at all. Not for any reason.

"I think you're just confused."

"You're insulting."

"What you're feeling isn't real. You'll realize that tomorrow."

"You don't get to tell me how I feel or what I'll

324

realize tomorrow." She pulled her shirt over her head and jumped on one foot and then the other as she got into her pants. "I know how I feel. I know how I feel when you walk into a room and I see you smile at me. I know the touch of your hand in the small of my back makes my heart swell up and pound really hard at the same time. I know you like to tell yourself that you're a good guy for the obvious things you do, but what makes you a good guy are the things that aren't so obvious. Maybe not even to you." She zipped her pants, then looked back into his face. "But I see *you*, Sean." His brows and lips were drawn tight as if she'd seen deep down into him and he didn't like it. "You don't have to love me back. That's fine." It wasn't. "I mean, I never expected that from you. We had a deal. That's it, but don't tell me I'm confused like all other women who've had the misfortune to say they love you." She pushed her hair from her face. Whether from exertion or emotion, her breathing was fast and choppy. "Instead of blaming my period—which is so typically *guy*, by the way—the least you could do is say, 'Gee, Lexie, that's nice.' "

"Gee, Lexie, that's nice."

Her hands fell to her sides as she watched him wipe all expression from his handsome face. "Maybe you could fake some emotion."

"Sorry. Next time write it down for me in one of your annoying memos."

Now he was just adding insult to injury. "You're being a jerk."

"And you're being overemotional."

"Well, I'm sorry." She picked up her socks and shoes. "I told you that I love you and you said I'm confused."

"You are." He fought with the sheet and gathered it in one hand. "For God's sake, you thought you were in love with Pete Dalton two months ago."

She stuck her chin in the air and gathered as much dignity around her as possible. "That was low."

"It's true."

She stuck her shoes under one arm. Her heart pinched and her eyes stung, and before she shattered completely, she said, "Thank you for all you've done to help me out." She should end it all right now, while she still had a shred of pride, but God help her, she couldn't force her heart to say good-bye. Not yet. "It's best if we just keep this strictly business from now until the middle of next month."

Chapter 15

•love me like you do

T HE SYCAMORE ROOM inside the Four Seasons glowed with golden candlelight. Gold tablecloths and fine white china adorned round tables with centerpieces made of exotic flowers. Hockey legends crowded the tables, paddleboards in hand. "Next up we have an all-inclusive trip to Honolulu," the auctioneer announced. "Let's start this off at two thousand. Two thousand—can I hear twenty-two."

As the bidding escalated around him, Sean glanced at the woman pretending to be a statue by his side. A beautiful statue in a red dress. Waist cinched in, cleavage spilling out. "You look beautiful."

"Thank you."

He hadn't seen Lexie for two days. Not since she'd stormed out of his apartment.

"Your dress is too low on top."

She held up her paddle. "I don't care what you think."

She was pissed off? So was he. She'd done that thing women do when good sex made their heads all soft and mushy. He'd thought Lexie was smarter than most women. "Is that one of those standard responses you write in your memos?"

"Yes." She lowered the paddle without even glancing in his direction. "Section one, subsection b, under 'leave me alone, Sean.' "

He didn't know what she was the most mad about. That he hadn't gone soft in the head, too, or that he'd reminded her of how many times she'd thought she was in love recently. "Love is never angry," he pointed out. "Section five. Random bullshit." He'd tried to contact her repeatedly, but she'd returned only one of his texts. I'm going with Marie to the benefit, she'd written. I don't need you to pick me up. He'd debated on whether to even show up tonight. In the end, he'd put on a suit and tie because he was expected to show. Not because he hadn't been able to stay away.

He was exhausted, Lexie was pissed off, and to top it off, her friend Marie sat at a table behind him, her eyeballs burning holes in his back.

"I'm going to the bar. Need anything?" he asked the statue.

"No thanks."

Sean set his paddle on the table and stood. He and Lexie were good together, in and out of bed. When she realized that what she felt was lust, not love, she'd come around. He just hoped it was sooner rather than later and she didn't waste any more time on her temper tantrum. They had only a little over two weeks before the whole fake breakup thing.

Two weeks, he thought as he moved into the next room and sat at the bar. And she was wasting it. "Vodka. Splash of tonic," he told the bartender, and pulled out his wallet. Yeah, it was a vodka kind of night.

"Hey, Knox." Chucky patted him on the shoulder and ordered a Bud Light. "I just lost out to Olsen for that vacation." The left wingman then said, "Lexie looks hot tonight. Damn."

Sean had an irrational urge to punch Chucky in the head.

"Hey, Knox and Chucky." Butch hobbled up to the bar, still walking slow after the high stick incident. "Lexie is looking hot tonight."

Sean stuffed the tip jar. "How's your dick, Butch?"

"It's my groin."

He stood. "Same thing." Drink in hand, he moved out into the hall. There were several former Chinooks and hockey greats at the Four Seasons. Sean purposely chatted up Sam LeClaire, Ty Savage, and old-school enforcer Rob Sutter. None of the three men knew anything about him and Lexie. Their fake relationship was the last thing he wanted to talk about, and he could relax and shoot the shit with guys who knew what it was like to play in the finals and win the cup. He swallowed half his drink and felt the tension between his shoulders ease. He laughed at jokes that only men in their positions understood. Lexie would come around. If not, there were plenty more beautiful women in the world.

"Paul's out with a torn rotator," he said as they talked Stanley Cup strategy. Out of the corner of his left eye, he caught a flash of red. He looked past LeClaire's shoulder, and his gaze landed on the tight waist of Lexie's dress and full skirt. She moved into the women's restroom, and he excused himself before he thought better of it.

He pulled up the cuff of his shirt and glanced at his watch. Eight-thirty. He could leave without appearing to dip out early. He shoved a shoulder into the wall and waited a few moments for her to appear. There were plenty more beautiful women in the world, but he liked Lexie. Her life interested him. She interested him.

"Lexie." He straightened and stepped in front of her. "I'm leaving."

"Okay."

She looked beyond him, and he raised a hand to the side of her face. "Come with me."

"No." Her gaze finally met his. "That's impossible."

"No. It's not." His hand dropped from her soft cheek. "All you have to do is put one foot in front of the other."

She shook her head.

"If you can't walk, I'll carry you."

Her blue eyes filled with tears.

Shit.

"I don't want to cry here in front of everyone." She blinked and blew out her breath.

She was crying. That meant he should apologize for something so she'd stop. "I'm sorry I blamed your period, the other night." That was true. He shouldn't have said that. "Come with me and I'll make it up to you."

Her nose scrunched like he'd just made everything worse. "I can't do this anymore. I can't be your pretend girlfriend."

"Sure you can." He looked at her mouth and bare throat. She said she loved him. She said he was a good guy. He wanted to back her against the wall and put his hands on both sides of her head, kiss her breathless, and show her how good he could be. "For two more weeks."

"Sean, I can't—"

He cut off her rejection with his mouth and pulled her against his chest. She stood stiff within his arms as his lips teased and coaxed, trying to warm her up and turn her all soft like the Lexie he knew.

"No, Sean." She stepped out of his arms and raised a hand to her lips. One big tear rolled down her cheek. "Don't do this to me. I love you and I can't pretend that you love me, too."

"It's only for two more weeks," he repeated.

She shook her head and wiped the moisture from her face. "I'm going to announce our breakup."

That wasn't what he wanted, but he couldn't do anything to stop her. "When?"

"At the grand opening of Yum Yum's Closet. Sylvia will be there, so it might be big news for a few days." She shook her head. "Then it will all be over."

"It's not the middle of March yet." He wanted to argue. To convince her she was just over-reacting. The emotion pooling in her blue eyes stopped him.

"I'll say we had an amicable split and are going our separate ways."

He didn't want to hurt her. That's the last thing he wanted, but he was so pissed off he couldn't think straight. "Are we going to be pretend friends now?"

"I don't think that's possible." She stepped around him and moved in the direction of the front door. He wanted to go after her and shake her and hold her against his chest. What he wanted didn't matter, and he watched her walk away.

THE NEXT MORNING, the Chinooks' DC–9 took off for a three-game stretch. Sean wasn't in the mood for chitchat and stuck his headphones over his ears. Lexie was going to end things.

332

Fine by him. The minute she'd launched herself into the *Sea Hopper*, she'd caused drama in his life. He didn't need it. He didn't want it, and he was positive that by the time they touched back down in Seattle, she'd be nothing to him but a distant memory. One he could forget because he needed to get his head in the game. His dreams of Stanley Cup glory were more important to him than a pain-in-the-ass runaway bride. More important any day of the week, but getting her out of his head was harder than he anticipated. She was stuck front and center as he took the ice against the Sharks, and her memory didn't fade when the jet touched down in Columbus or Tampa Bay, either. And certainly not by the time he returned to Seattle six days later. The whole team seemed to feel his mood and made a wide path around him.

"Is something wrong?" John asked him as the team waited to take the ice in the Key Arena for a match-up against Buffalo.

"No." He shoved his helmet on his head and stepped onto the ice when his name was announced. What else could he have said to Lexie's dad? *Your daughter's drama is fucking with my head?* He took off skating from one end of the rink to the other, then sent up a spray of ice as he took his place on the centerline. The fans whistled and chanted his name. Number 36 was at the show and it was time to do his job.

Time to put points on the board. He adjusted his shoulders beneath his pads and looked up into the third tier. Her seat was empty. He knew it would be, but that didn't keep the disappointment from his brow or extinguish the angry flame burning in the pit of his belly.

Several times during the first frame, he forgot that she was no longer a part of his life, and he caught himself glancing up, expecting to see the flash of her white smile. Each time, his brow furrowed a little deeper and the flame burned a little hotter. It didn't help that Buffalo's defender, Ed Sorenson, kept his gums flapping and his hits late and from behind. A solid defense was a part of the game, and a good, big, solid defenseman was worth his bulky weight in gold. Then there were instigators like Ed.

Halfway into the second period, Sean had just about enough of Ed's stick in the small of his back. The whistle blew for an offsides and Sean skated to the face-off circle.

"Having a bad night?" Ed asked as he took his place next to Sean.

He'd been pretty much having a bad week. "It'll take more than you, Special Ed, to make me have a bad night." He bent forward, his gaze focused on the ref's hand, waiting for the puck to drop. Inside his head, he went over the next play. If Paul got the puck, he'd shoot it to Sean. Sean would one-time it center ice to Brody and get in position to take a shot. He needed to keep his head in the game. It would take more than Special Ed's insults to make him lose control.

"Hey, Knox, what's it like to have Pete Dalton's sloppy seconds?"

Sean's stick fell to the ice and he swung even before he turned his head to see where to plant his fist. A low buzzing shot up his spine and blew out his ears. For one of the only times in his life, he didn't even bother to control the anger blasting through him. Before Ed could recover, Sean slammed a shoulder into the bigger guy's chest and punched him in the side of the head. The defender staggered and swung, landing two good blows before Sean got him in a headlock and fed him lunch. Punching as the bigger man flailed, Sean felt hands on his arms and back, pulling at him, but he didn't stop until someone pushed him hard and a ref trapped him in a tight bear hug from behind. "I'm going to kill you the next time I see you," he yelled as he got a glimpse of Ed, the guy's jersey half off and his face bloody.

"Are you done, Knox?" a referee screamed in his face.

Sean blinked a couple of times and looked around him. The buzzing receded and he flexed his sore hand. The ice around him looked like a yard sale filled with hockey gear. The benches for both teams had emptied, and KO and a Buffalo player were still throwing punches in the corner.

"Yeah," he said between big panting breaths, and the arms holding him fell away. Blood dripped from Sean's nose and he wiped it on the back of his hand.

"This isn't over, Knox someone," Ed yelled as his teammates skated with him off the ice.

"Bring your mom next time, Ed!" Sean wiped blood from the side of his mouth and winced. "She has a better right hook than you."

By the time the ice was cleared of players and gear, a variety of penalties were called; the most serious ejected Sean from the game. The adrenaline that had pumped through his veins as he'd whaled on Ed began to fade as a team trainer stuck a plug up his nose. The corner of his left eye stung, and a trail of blood had dried on his neck and the front of his jersey. Someone handed him a towel and he hung it over his head. He looked down at his right hand packed in ice and couldn't remember how it got there. That whole fight had been stupid. So damn stupid. Chaos.

"What the fuck was that?"

He pulled the towel from his head and cracked open his good eye. John Kowalsky stared down at him as if he wanted to finish him off. "I don't know."

"What do you mean you don't know? That dance of yours resulted in thirteen penalties. KO and Marty are cooling their asses in the box for twenty-five minutes." His scowl got more thunderous by the second. "That's some kind of fucking record! You were brought on this team to add points, not empty benches!" He folded his arms across his chest. "Explain that to me."

"He said Lexie is sloppy seconds."

All the air went out of John and his hands fell to his sides. "Jesus, Knox." He sank to the bench next to Sean. "I was afraid of that."

FOR INSTIGATING THE fight with Ed Sorenson, Sean sat out the next game, too. It was the first time in his life his name had been dropped from the roster for misconduct. These kinds of things just didn't happen to him. He was a franchise player; he put points on the board. Unless he was dog-sick and unable to lift his head from his pillow, he played every game. He'd never been dropped, ever, until he'd met the runaway *Gettin' Hitched* bride.

He'd always known Lexie would cause trouble if he let her. He'd known she was drama and chaos. He'd known it all along. He'd known she could mess up his career, too. He'd been right about everything, and he'd let her into his life anyway.

For the first time in his life, he'd let his personal life interfere with his career. For the first time in his life, he'd let a woman mess with his head. He didn't know when or how Lexie had slipped into his brain and taken over, but it had to stop. He had to stop it.

When he was eligible to return to game-day practice, he was more focused. More determined and ready to give the Chinooks one hundred percent.

He felt good as he stepped on the ice for the first time in two days. His passes were sharp. His shots perfectly timed. His attention focused . . . then he remembered that it was Monday. He glanced at the big clock on the scoreboard. In an hour, Lexie would officially open the doors to her new store in Bellevue. At some point during her grand opening, she'd announce that he and Lexie were no longer together.

I'll say we had an amicable split and are going our separate ways, she'd said. *Then it will all be over.*

The two of them would be done for good. The charade over. *I can't be your pretend girlfriend,* she'd told him. She said other things, too. She'd said that he made her heart pound really hard. She'd said that she saw *him*. No one had said that to him before.

"Are you going to shoot that thing or stare a hole through it?"

Sean glanced across his shoulder at Stony standing on the centerline beside him. She'd said she loved him. Ridiculous. No one fell in love in so short a time. It took more than two months.

Six at least. Maybe even a year. Not that he was an expert, but two months was just crazy. Like the woman herself. Lucky for him, she was some other man's crazy now. Without a word, he loaded and fired three pucks into the net.

"You look like someone ran over your dog."

Some other man's crazy. The thought of her being some other man's crazy felt like a big truck ran into his chest. The thought of any man but him touching Lexie suddenly made *him* feel crazy. It spun his head and made his face hot.

He took off toward the other end of the rink, dangling a puck in the curve of his blade as he skated a familiar pattern between orange cones. He wanted peace. He didn't want crazy. Not in his life. Not in his head. Not hitting him like a truck.

The cool air brushing his cheeks and pushing his hair from his forehead felt good against his flushed face. He shot into the net, then skated around the boards and picked up another puck on the goal line. This time as he approached the cones, he plowed over the first and tripped over the second, almost falling on his ass. Chaos and crazy rushed across his hot skin, squeezing his chest and making him drop his stick. He'd never felt so muddled in his life. So out of control, not even when he'd listened to Lexie's schemes or read her bossy texts. Not when he listened to her laughter or crazy stories of making clothes for chickens or chasing pigs.

He shoved one glove in his armpit and picked up his stick. He would never hear her laughter or wild stories. He would never touch her face or kiss her lips. The thought of another man looking into her eyes as he made love to her made him stop in a spray of ice. The thought of Yum Yum jumping in another man's lap and crunching his nuts as she searched for the perfect place to lay her hairless body brought him upright.

Lexie was crazy but his life without her was the worst kind of crazy. It made him want to beat his head against a wall. In two short months, she'd caused him nothing but drama. Hot, sweet chaos that he couldn't imagine living without.

The thought of her never waving to him from the third tier squeezed his chest and sent him skating toward the tunnel. He stepped onto the mats and moved past the rack of carefully honed hockey sticks. He'd wanted a life without chaos. He didn't know what that felt like or what it meant anymore. He only knew that he wanted a life with Lexie in it.

In the dressing room, he unlaced his skates and shed his gear. Perspiration soaked the armpits of his practice sweats and wet his back where his shoulder pads had rested. He quickly exchanged the sweatshirt for a Nike hoodie and grabbed his running shoes. He headed out of the locker room, hopping on one foot and then the other as he moved down the tunnel toward the exit. He needed to breathe. He needed fresh air. He needed to stop her.

John stuck his head out of the manager's office and called after him, "Where are you going in such a rush?"

Shit. Sean looked back over his shoulder. "To tell your daughter that I love her," he said without stopping. He moved through the twists and turns of the tunnel, picking up the pace until he was jogging when he hit the door and stepped out into the fresh Seattle air.

Lexie was many things to different people. Daughter. Boss. Pet rescuer. *Gettin' Hitched* bride. To him, she was sunshine and chaos. Laughter and lover. She was madness and peace. She was his and he loved her. It hadn't happened in six months or a year. He didn't know when he'd fallen for her. The exact time didn't matter. The minute she'd shoved herself onto the *Sea Hopper*, he'd been a goner.

A cold breeze blew across his cheeks and through his damp hair, and he pulled up the hood of his sweatshirt to cover his head. He'd walked to the arena that morning, and he glanced at his watch. "Shit." She was his, but she was about to leave for her grand opening and announce to the world that the *Gettin' Hitched* bride was back on the market.

He jogged to the parking lot, didn't see any other players leaving, then he took off toward the front of the Key Arena. He figured his best chance of stopping her was to head her off at her apartment. If he ran to his own place to get his car, he wouldn't make it in time to stop her. He glanced around, his gaze searching for a friend or a cab. A steady stream of traffic filled the road, but he didn't recognize any vehicles exiting the arena and didn't see one cab.

His glance moved past tourists studying maps as he ran to the curb, looking up and down First. He stopped next to a cement security bollard, and his gaze landed on a bright red scooter parked on the sidewalk. A big metal cooler was bolted on the back with a local phone number and a big sandwich painted on the side. Sunlight caught on the silver key dangling from the ignition, shooting sparkles into the air like a sign from God. Before he could think it through, Sean hopped on the red seat and fired it up. He'd had a Ducati once upon a time; he could surely manage a Vespa. The thing didn't have a clutch and he looked around for gears.

"Hey! Get off my scooter."

Sean looked up at a guy in a red jumpsuit moving toward him.

"I'm borrowing it," he said, and turned the gas handle. The Vespa shot across the sidewalk and off the curb with more spunk than he expected.

The deliveryman called after him, "Come back or I'm calling the police."

Sean couldn't worry about a little thing like grand theft, and merged into traffic. He gunned the piece-of-shit scooter and shot down Pike. He wove in and out of traffic, but by the time he made it to her apartment building, her parking space was empty.

He'd been to her store once, but he'd relied on his GPS. He wasn't all that certain he even knew how to get to the right shopping center in Bellevue, but he didn't let a little thing like directions keep him from heading toward the 520.

Wind whipped off the hoodie, and a bug hit the same eye Ed Sorenson had hit a few days earlier. The Vespa topped out at fifty. Cars whizzed past and people honked at him for either driving in the fast lane or because they wanted a sandwich. A Good To Go! toll pass had been taped to the inside of the short windshield. On the east side of the bridge, he took a wrong exit and ended up in an old neighborhood. A dog chased him, biting at the Vespa tires before Sean made his way out again. At a stoplight, he asked directions from a guy on a Harley next to him. The man revved his engine and pointed, as if talking to a guy on a Vespa was beneath him. By the time Sean pulled into the right parking lot, he was bug splattered. His good eyeball was dry, his bad eye was watery, both were dusty. He didn't see anyone out front or the "Grand Opening" banner he knew Lexie had ordered. He didn't see her car, either, just the bright red storefront. He figured she'd parked out back, and was so relieved to make it in one piece, he felt like crying like a girl. Whether from exhaustion or delirium, he accidentally hopped the curb in front of the store. The front tire stopped, the bike flipped over, and he landed on his back in the middle of the sidewalk, gasping for air and surrounded by sandwiches.

"What are you doing here?" Lexie's friend Marie appeared over him, her eyes kind of squinty behind her glasses. "And what are you doing with Jimmy's Scooter Sub?"

"Where's Lexie?" He swallowed past the dry patch in his throat and hoped it wasn't a fly.

"Gone."

Chapter 16

• love is a beautiful madness

A PAIR OF KAYAKERS slid through the smooth waters of Lake Union, gliding past the *Sea Hopper* and paddling toward the neighborhood of houseboats moored farther up the eastern shore.

"I just have one more suitcase," Lexie said as she handed a medium-sized wheelie to the pilot inside the small amphibious plane.

"Geez, how long are you planning to be gone? A month?"

"Just a week." She hadn't planned to get away at all, but Geraldine had called with a Buddy emergency. Lexie's grand opening had been a flop due to a misprint in the *Seattle Times*. Only a few people had shown up, and she'd left early, leaving the recently unemployed Marie in charge. She needed time away to heal and relax. Although it would take more than a week to heal her broken heart, and she doubted Geraldine would be very relaxing.

A week was a start, though. One week would turn into another, then another. Then a month would pass, until one day she would wake up without thinking of Sean Knox.

They'd never even been a real couple, but the love she felt for him was very real. So was the pain.

At her feet, Yum Yum barked at the kayakers and wagged her tail. The little dog wore a down parka with a faux-fur trim to shield her bare skin. Lexie picked her up and put her in the plane.

From within the cockpit, Jimmy's cell phone rang and he said loud enough for Lexie to hear, "What? You're kidding. Did you call the police?"

He jumped out of the plane with a frown creasing his brow just beneath his aviator hat. "That was one of my drivers. Someone stole one of my Scooter Subs," he told her, and shoved his phone back inside the pocket of the old leather jacket he'd loaned her a few months ago. "The police are on the lookout for it."

"The police are looking for your sandwich motorcycle?" Had it really been just a few months since he'd mentioned his latest business scheme? So much had happened it seemed like a year.

"It's a scooter. It was parked outside the Key Arena and some guy in blue sweats jumped on it and drove away."

"That's crazy." She pulled out her sunglasses to shield her eyes from the afternoon sun.

"He had a hoodie pulled up over his head and

no one got a good look at him." Jimmy scratched beneath one earflap. "The police are talking to people inside the arena and the surrounding businesses. Maybe someone saw something." He put his hand beneath Lexie's elbow to help her into the plane but dropped it a second later when his phone rang.

"Hello." He paused and turned to Lexie. "Really? You're telling me my scooter's in front of Yum Yum's Closet? Am I hearing you right?" That got her attention. "What the hell?" He shook his head. "How bad? Uh-huh. No shit? Right now?" He looked toward the parking lot. "Let me talk to him."

Lexie's gaze followed but she didn't see anything but a few parked cars.

"That's messed up . . . My driver already called the police . . . Okay. You owe me."

Marie's silver MINI Cooper screeched to a stop. The door opened, and first one long leg, then the other seemed to unfold from the little car. Then a whole man appeared and from within the car, Marie waved. The Cooper sped away, leaving behind Sean Knox in a dark blue sweat suit. He moved toward her, his footsteps a quick, steady thumping on the docks.

"What's going on, Jimmy?" she wanted to know.

"Apparently, Sean is my scooter thief."

Unable to take her eyes off the man walking

toward her as if he was on a mission, she asked, "Why would he steal your Scooter Subs scooter?"

"I have no idea. He not only stole it—he wrecked it, too."

With each step of his feet, her heart pounded a little harder in her chest. With each second, she feared she might pass out and had to remind herself to breathe. Then he stood before her, his hair and cheeks windblown. One of his eyes was glassy, the other black, and a grim line pulled at his mouth. With his gaze fixed on Lexie, he said, "Sorry about your scooter, Jimmy."

"Not cool, man."

"I'll pay for the damages." He swallowed, and Yum Yum stuck her head out the door and barked at him. "Can you give me a few minutes, Jimmy?"

"Is that okay with you, Lex?"

That almost got a smile out of her. What was Jimmy going to do if it wasn't? Sean was taller and outweighed him by at least fifty pounds of pure muscle. "Yeah. It's okay." She glanced at the pilot as he turned to climb into his plane. "Thanks for asking, though."

"I'll be sitting here dealing with the scooter situation if you need me."

"Did you talk to the press yet?" Sean wanted to know.

She turned toward him and shook her head.

"The paper got the date wrong and very few people showed up." A part of her, the part that wanted to throw herself at his chest, had been relieved that she hadn't had to make the breakup announcement. The other part, the one that wanted to throw him in the lake, just wanted an end to the pain. She shook her head. "I'll get ahold of Sylvia and tell her it's over between us. She'll be happy to get the first scoop."

"What if I don't want it to be over?"

Had he chased her down because he wanted to wait the two weeks as they'd planned? Was he that selfish? Mean? "Well, I told you that—"

"What if all I want is to be with you?"

"I can't do—wait . . . Huh?"

He took her sunglasses from her eyes and put them in the pocket of his sweatpants. "What if I want all of you all of the time? Everything, for all the reasons on your made-up lists and some you haven't thought up yet." He paused and said, "I love you, Lexie. Not the fake kind. Not the love that looks good on paper. No sections and subsections and columns of bullet points."

She wanted to believe her ears. With all of her heart. "Did KO threaten to put his stick up your butt again?" She folded her arms under her breasts. "Is that what this is about?"

"No." He placed his hands on her elbows and looked into her eyes. "I'm not afraid of anything but you getting on that plane and Jimmy gunning the engine. I'm afraid that I've already blown my chance." Then he pulled out the big guns and blew her away. "It's only been two months. This sounds crazy. Hell, it *is* crazy. You said you see me. I see *you,* too, Lexie. I see all of you. I want all of you. I feel you so deep in my heart, there's no way I can get you out again." He paused, then added just above a whisper, "I don't want to try."

She bit the corner of her trembling lip. "You're not afraid that it's only been a few months and we haven't spent enough time together?"

He shook his head. "Neither of us is going anywhere. We have all the time in the world." He slid his hands across her shoulders to cup the sides of her neck. "I found a saying."

"A what?"

His cheeks turned a little redder. "A romantic quote."

"All on your own?"

"Yes, and it's not cheesy like yours."

She bit her lip to keep from laughing. "What is it?"

" 'Walk with me. We'll figure out where we're going later.' "

So simple. "I love it." Her smile slid clear down into her heart and she took his hand. "I love you." It might not be the most romantic saying. It wasn't:

1. Shakespeare.
2. Byron.
3. Nicholas Sparks.

No more running. Not from weddings or each other or love. Not from lies or fear or limits.

Sean kissed her lips and smiled. "Ready to walk with me?"

"Yes."

He reached into the *Sea Hopper* and grabbed her dog. With her hand in his, the three of them walked side by side up the dock and into a future full of real love and genuine possibilities.

Center Point Large Print
600 Brooks Road / PO Box 1
Thorndike, ME 04986-0001 USA

(207) 568-3717

US & Canada:
1 800 929-9108
www.centerpointlargeprint.com